Just When I Thought

Jae Loy

Andrea Johnson Books Publishing

Road trips with you were the highlights of my weekends. Driving down the highways, jamming to Marvin Gaye, Sir Charles, Betty White, etc. I remember you telling me, "you should write a book," and now look at me. I miss you granny. I miss your singing, your laugh. You left before this one could be published but I know you're looking down on me smiling because I did it. This one's for you!

Love you always; gone but never forgotten, Debra Hollis: Loving mother, friend, and grandmother.

- Jae Loy

Just When I Thought

Cover art designed by Andrea Johnson Books Publishing.

First published by Andrea Johnson Books Publishing. 09/22/2021

6565 N. MacArthur Blvd, Suite 225 Dallas, TX. 75039
www.Ajbpublishing.com

This book is a work of fiction. Names, characters, places, and incidents are the product of the author's imagination or are used fictitiously. Any resemblance to actual events, locales, or persons, living or dead, is coincidental.

Because of the dynamic nature of the Internet, any web addresses or links contained in this book may have changed since publication and may no longer be valid. The views expressed in this work are solely those of the author and do not necessarily reflect the views of the publisher, and the publisher herby disclaims any responsibility for them.

ISBN: 978-0-578-97818-5

Part I

Prologue

Even after the heartbreaks, Jean fell in love unexpectedly. But Tony thought he could count on his boy.

However, when all things turn, he finds out who his real potna is. Will Tony change Tiffany for the better?

There is nothing like three close friends that are sticking together, who ride for each other through it all.

But sometimes Business can get pushed back when personal lives interfere.

It will all come down to Tiffany, LaLa and Jean...and what they must do...and overcome... to make it happen.

Chapter One

JEAN

LALA: "Girl, I'm so sick of Slim tryna talk to me, knowing ion want his short ass."

JEAN: "Girl, give him a chance, La."

LALA: "Okay, bitch you date him then."

The way I looked at her, because shawty had me messed up, almost broke my neck.

JEAN: "Don't you ever say no shit like that to me again. You know how I feel about Slim anyway. And let Ray find out he got competition."

I took a little pause to register what I said, then repeated it.

"Bitch let Ray find out, but yunno that being his boy, he probably wouldn't even care."

LALA: "See now, that's who you need to be fuckin with..."

I looked over at her, and we made eye contact.

"Yea that's right. Bitch you, and Ray need to be dating." She did this smirk like she was up to something.

JEAN: "La, yunno that's my best..."

But LaLa interrupted me, mockingly.

LALA: "yunno that's my best friend. Blah blah blah. Sick of hearing that best friend crap."

I was speechless at that point.

LALA: "Y'all always together, always talking nshit. Might as well. Y'all probably done fucked."

I sipped my henny on that one.

LALA: "See bitch! I knew it. You done got a piece of that dark chocolate. Spill the tea hoe."

La spun around in my chair, and I completely ignored what she was talking about.

JEAN: "Just because I took a sip, doesn't mean anything."

LALA: "Yea. Yea, spill the tea..." she *gasped,* "and bitch you knew me before him, and ain't tell me shit. Trashy... best friend my ass."

Sis most definitely rolled her eyes at me.

JEAN: "iight bitch!" I rolled my eyes back.

LALA: "J, just tell me what happened."

She did this whine like she always do.

JEAN: "I can't. I don't want you to look at him any differently."

She started jumping around, clapping her hands and shit.

LALA: "Bitch I knew y'all had something going on!"

La started singing, *'J been fucking her best friend. J been fucking her best friend.'* I closed my eyes and took another sip of my henny.

JEAN "La sit yo childish ass down."
She sat down so quickly. I am telling you; it is the fastest I ever saw her move.

LALA: "Man, tell me the tea! Was it good? Was it bad? Is his dick little? Big? COM'ON."

I bucked my eyes at her.

JEAN: "Quit all that damn yelling, might wake up my neighbors."
It was 3 in the morning, and her dumb ass yelling. La took a sip of her drink.

LALA: "Don't be shushing me. Clearly it wasn't good enough you can't tell your best friend."

Let me explain to you who LaLa is. I have known her damn near all my life. We're the same age, she's just older by 2 months, and she wears that shit out. Every time we get into it, *'you need to respect your elders.'* We have had our fights, but what friendship does not? We always come back as one, and if any hoe tries us, we are just a phone call away.

I did not like the last nigga she was with. He was just using her for money, and sex. It took her a while to see that. If she wanted me to, I would have popped off on him. My circle is really small, and I only trust a select few.

La is tall like me, chocolate, and as thick as I am. She is a little more on the BBW side, but my bitch fine.

My other best friend is Tiffany. We've been cool for about 18 years. I met LaLa in kindergarten and Tiffany in the 1st grade, been tight ever since. Tiffany is totally different than La. Tiff is still milk chocolate, and tall, but other than La and I, Tiffs' slim. Baby girl still carrying weight in that ass though. Sometimes Tiffany can be on the quiet side, but LaLa... my girl has no filter.

'Ring Ring'

I looked down at my phone and it was Ray, my male best friend, then looked up at La. This hoe was smirking.

LALA: "You gone answer for *your* man?"

I let the phone ring and ignored La's comment. Ray called again, so I started to think something was wrong. I picked it up.

JEAN: "Hello."

RAY: "Where you at Jean?

JEAN: "Home with La, wassup? You okay?"

RAY: "Yea, I wanted to come through for a minute."

I frowned a bit, and saw LaLa waving in my peripheral, trying to get my attention, while mouthing, 'what's wrong?'

JEAN: "You sure you okay, Ray?"

Sometimes he gets in these shutdown moods, where he didn't want to talk about what's hurting him.

RAY: "I just want to talk to you, J."

JEAN: "Does La need to leave?"

This bitch bucked her big ass at me, and I could not do anything but laugh. La was mouthing off.

LALA: "You're just going to kick me out for some dick?"

I put the phone on mute to respond.

JEAN: "Stop being a baby La. Something's not right with him."

She fanned me off and continued to her drink.

LALA: "I no longer like y'alls relationship. Just kicking my drunk ass out."

La was being dramatic as usual, and started gathering her belongings, while downing the last of her henny.

JEAN: "Stop being dramatic, hoe. You are not even drunk, let alone tipsy. You're about to go home, call up Wade to come drop dick." I took the phone off mute.

LALA: "You know me so well. Aight be safe, love you."

I walked La to the door.

JEAN: "Love you too."

She turned back to me.

LALA: "I'm still waiting on that tea."

La walked off and I put the phone back to my ear.

JEAN: "Hello?"

There was no answer. I looked at the phone and saw he'd hung up. I called back, but he did not answer. After a while, I dialed up La's number, and she answered. She moaned loudly.

LALA: "Yes bitch, what can I do for you?"

I looked at the phone mouthing, 'what the fuck?' All I could hear is pounding and the headboard beating on the wall.

JEAN: "You only left not even 20 minutes ago, and already getting cakes beat? You a fast hoe!"

WADE: "Hang up the damn phone, La, or call whoever you talking to on Facetime so they can see this my pussy."

Moaning...

LALA: "ima call you back, J."

I hung up so quickly. A part of me thought she was gone call me on Facetime, knowing her nasty ass. Not even 2 seconds later, she was Face Timing me. I promptly swiped the *IGNORE* button.

I called Ray one last time, but still no answer.

JEAN: "Now I would be crazy to just do a pop up at his house? What if he is not even home?"

All these questions running through my head.

JEAN: "I just hope he's okay."

Chapter two

The Next Morning

'Knock Knock Knock.'

I jumped, almost falling out of my bed. Checked my phone to see the time, and saw it was 2 in the morning. Who the fuck could be knocking on my door at two in the morning?

JEAN: "Who is it?" I got no answer.

'Knock Knock'

JEAN: "Who is it?!"

Where I live, you do not answer the door for anybody. I still got no answer.

TIFFANY: "Bitch, open the damn door."

I rolled my eyes at the sound of Tiffs' voice. I have not heard from her in about a week, and I was about to go *OFF*. I swung the door open.

JEAN: "Hoe when somebody yell out *who is it,* you respond with a name or something. Yo camel back ass was gone stay out there, playing at my damn door."

She rushed through me and into my house with her night cap bag.

TIFFANY: "You should have looked through the peep hole, saw it was me, and opened the door."

JEAN: "Orrrrrrrrr bitch, just hear me out… you could have just answered me. And what's with the bag?"

She plopped down on my couch.

TIFFANY: "Girl, it's Tony!"

I was confused because the last time I checked, Tiff and Tony were good. Hell, I thought they were just fucking around too, but clearly that's the case.

JEAN: "Okay, what about him?"

She burst out crying, and I ran to comfort her.

JEAN: "Tiff talk to me. What's wrong?"

TIFFANY: "Tony got some bitch pregnant. We had got an apartment together and decided to take our relationship to the next level. So, bitch, my new man got somebody else pregnant. We've talked about having some kids of our own. I mean, since we both at a place where we want them."

She started crying even harder.

JEAN: "Tiff how did you find this out? When did y'all move in together? I do *not* want to make this about me, but *damn*. I feel some type of way. Yo ass been MIA for over a week, not answering phone calls or text. La and I was gone do a pop up."

She wiped her face and made eye contact with me.

TIFFANY: "I'm sorry J. I've been out the zone lately. We moved in about a month ago, and just wanted to keep it between the two of us. I mean we've been fucking each other, for the past 2 years. Why not take it to the next level? Well at least I've been fucking him 2 years. Clearly, I wasn't the only one he was fucking. Like how could you do that to me, after all we've been through? I just wanted to be alone until I was ready to be around others."

I still felt hurt that she could not come, and talk to me sooner, knowing how close and tight our friendship is.

TIFFANY: "Now this nigga won't stop calling and texting my phone. Then keep coming to *MY* house."

I bucked and did a double take to what she said.

JEAN: "*Your* house? Don't y'all live together?"

TIFFANY: "I don't give a fuck. That is *MY* house like I said. I kicked him out."

I could not do nothing but laugh.

JEAN: "Okay so wait. How you find out? Do you know the bitch?"

TIFFANY: "Girl she called my phone with that shit. I was out with Tony when she called. I must have slapped the shit out of him. I had to leave ASAP before they started calling the cops nshit."

She started crying again, making me shed a few tears myself. It killed me to see my friend like this. I brought her in for a hug.

JEAN: "I'm here for you, girl. Stay however long you need."

TIFFANY: "I just need like 2 weeks. I found a CPN to get another apartment." DaBaby, 'Bop' came on. "Look he's calling my phone."

I snatched the phone out her hand to answer it, but then thought, this nigga knows where I stay and could pop up thinking she here.

TIFFANY: "What do you want, Tony? You see I didn't answer your other calls, why you still calling?"

I zoned out for a while and did not even notice she was talking to him.

TONY: "Baby please talk to me. I can explain."

TIFFANY: "Ain't shit to explain. You fucked another bitch and got her pregnant, but had me waiting to get pregnant!"

TONY: "Man it ain't even like that, so chill. Can you just sit and talk with me?"

TIFFANY: "I am good love, enjoy!"

Tiff hung the phone up and blocked Tony's number.

JEAN: "Tiff regardless of how you feel, and wanting to put them paws on him, I think you should hear him out. It might be good for you." She glared at me like she wanted to put the paws on *ME*. "Nun uh do *not* look at me like that. I am just throwing out suggestions."

TIFFANY: "J, I understand how you may feel, but right now; talking to him ain't for me. I'm at the point where I can blow his balls off and feed them to the hoe."

I don't think I've ever seen Tiffany this mad and hurt, and I do not like it.

JEAN: "Ight. Well, you know how I'm rolling behind you and La, so whatever you on, count me in. Until then, you can get the couch or share the bed with me." I got up and walked to the kitchen to fix us a drink. "But look hoe, don't try no freak shit. You probably don't need this drink knowing you."

Tiff got up and ran behind me to the kitchen.

TIFFANY: "Girl fix me that drink... and if I decide to suck on your pussy, later I will."

I stood in shock and yelled.

JEAN: "Rape!"

I fixed us one of my famous strawberry, pineapple and peach margaritas and we walked back over to the couch.

TIFFANY: "Imma sleep on the couch for tonight. Do a little thinking. Eventually I need to talk to him."

JEAN: "That's cool. You want to watch a movie, or I can leave you alone."

TIFFANY: "Nah, don't leave. Can you call La and have her come over?"

I almost spit my drink, because us three together is Cray.

JEAN: "Yes bitch." So I called La up.

LALA: "Yes baby. What can I do for you?"

Tiff snatched the phone out my hand and started yelling.

TIFFANY: "Bitch Tony had a baby with some broad. Bring your ass to J house so we can handle this." then hung up.

JEAN: "Um ma'am what you got up your sleeve?"

TIFFANY: "Nothing yet. I just wanted her to hurry the hell up."

I snatched my phone out her hand.

JEAN: "Now she's going to come over here ready to shoot somebody."

TIFFANY: "So? I can give her the bitch address."

JEAN: "YOU KNOW WHERE SHE STAYS?!"

TIFFANY: "I made Tony tell me before locking him out *MY* house."

There she goes with that "my house" shit.

Suddenly Ray ran through my mind, and how he never called back from yesterday. Now I was beginning to worry. I tried calling him again, but he still did not answer. That is not like him. He always answered my calls or at least sent a text letting me know he was busy, then would call back.

JEAN: "Tiff I'm worried about Ray."

She was just finishing up a sip of her margarita.

TIFFANY: "Why, what happened?"

Tiffany, Ray and I are the only ones who know about us messing around. I could not tell La at the time because I know she is pet-ty! Every joke or sentence she would say to him, would put two and two together that we fucked. And if La found out that Tiff knows and she does not, her dramatic ass probably would not talk to me for a month. I was stuck at that point, and it was a lose, lose for me.

'Knock. Knock. Knock.'

LALA: "Open this damn door and let's go!"

Tiff and I looked at each other and burst out laughing. I swung the door open.

TIFFANY: "This why I love you and you are forever my ride or die."

LALA: "Let's go hoes. You ain't moving fast enough for me."
Tiff and I could not breathe from all the laughing we were doing. La got even more crunk.

LALA: "WHY ARE Y'ALL STILL SITTING DOWN LAUGHING?"

JEAN: "She was just playing La, chill..." still laughing, "yo, this bitch brought a bat and everything. You trying to take her, and the baby to base... batter up!" I took the bat from her and swung it. "Oh, it's a homerun!"

La stood in the doorway with her arms folded, clearly pissed.

LALA: "Why y'all play me like that? I was ready for war." Tiffany got up and walked towards LaLa with open arms.

TIFFANY: "Thank you for coming to my rescue. I love you to the moon and back."

LALA: "You drunk now?"

TIFFANY: "Tipsy yes, drunk no."

La looked back between Tiff and I.

LALA: "You hoes gone be on that freaky shit?"

We all burst out laughing.

TIFFANY: "It only happened one time and you hoes keep bringing it up. J knows she like what that mouth do."

I spit my drink out.

JEAN: "I like that better than you coming over, eating up all of my groceries."

Tiff grabbed one of the couch pillows and threw it at me.
TIFFANY: "Yea, yea, whatever."

Then twirled her tongue at me.

JEAN: "Oh bitch you nasty nasty." We all burst out laughing more.

LALA: "J, did Ray ever call you back, he good?"

Ray never called back, and I called him a few times.

JEAN: "Nah. He must be in one of his shutdown moods. I'll try again tomorrow."

For the next few hours, we just vibed, drank, watched a movie, then turned on some music. 'Girlfriend' by Heavyweight came on, and Tiffany got drunk. She began to sing along.

TIFFANY: "Your girlfriend wants to be my girlfriend. She be calling me telling about you. How you ain't hitting like you suppose to hit it. You slipping I think it's time I slipped in."

LaLa and I looked at each other, then got up and started singing at the top of our lungs and dancing. This was one of our favorite songs, we even had a whole dance for it.

LALA: "Uh huh, run that shit back!" LaLa screamed out.

We all got in position, and started performing once the song came on, putting in a whole sweat.

LALA: "I need to get back in the gym." LaLa damn near could not breathe.

TIFFANY: "Girl I'm right along with you." Tiffany managed to get out.

JEAN: "Let's get back in the gym together. I see we all done gained a few pounds over the years."

    Both Tiffany and LaLa looked at me, like I had stupid on my forehead.

JEAN: "Or not."

Chapter three

RAY

It had been three days since I last talked to Jean. I just could not grasp myself to tell her, I got some girl pregnant. She had been calling me, but I did not have the balls to tell her. It crushed my heart to sit there and ignore her calls. Knowing she was the only one who really cared about me, hurt even more. Nobody knows but us two, talking about working towards a relationship. I have known Jean for seven years and been best friends from the start. Tiffany, and La sometimes get mad jealous because Jean, and I are always talking. It is so easy talking to her about shit, but this time was different.

I remember the first time I saw Jean. We were at the mall. She had on this skintight red dress that showed every beautiful curve she was blessed with. I know some of them curves came from lifting weights and being in the gym. She had her hair up in two puff balls. She was natural, and you could see her curls a mile away. She was walking with Tiffany and LaLa, but they didn't compare to Jean, and I've told them to their face til this day.

I was walking with my girlfriend at the time, shopping for a birthday gift for my moms. I saw Jean, and instantly knew I had to have her. Bethanee and I were trying to recover from a hard time. She had cheated on me with some nigga, that she used to fuck with before me. It was not just a one-time thing either. Like these niggas were meeting up every Thursday, while I was at work, and fucking in the bed Bethanee and I were sharing.

She was staying with me, since her and her moms got in to it, and kicked her out. We had been broken up for two months, and she kept blowing up my phone apologizing and shit.

I ain't gone lie that shit hurt and really fucked me up. So that day I decided to hear what she had to say, plus she mentioned going shopping for her moms birthday and offered to buy me something.

Jean and I made eye contact while Bethanee was not looking. Jean was so beautiful, and I am not even exaggerating, this woman is indeed a gift from God.

Bethanee saw a jacket she could possibly get her moms and I told her to go without me. I walked over to where Jean and her friends were.

RAY: "How're you doing beautiful? My name is Ray, I'm seventeen years old. Technically I still have a girlfriend but we're on a break since she cheated on me… multiple times."

At that point, Jean spit out her drink.

RAY: "I know this may seem like a lot, and I may have come on too strong, or told too much, but I'm just looking for a friend honestly, and would love to get to know you."

I extended my hand out so she could shake it, but she just stared at me like, 'a deer in headlights.'

LALA: "Uh yes, Hi. I'm LaLa, J's best friend. You sure you're not trying to play her? You probably just another nigga wanting to fuck, and let me tell you, she ain't the one to be played with. She got two best friends coming hard behind her. So, if you're running game thinking you can come in fuck her over and break her heart, you got another thing coming for you bud."

Tiffany and LaLa stood tall with their arms crossed. "PeriodT," Tiff joined in.

RAY: "I understand and respect your loyalty to Miss. J, but that's not my intentions. I genuinely want to be friends. I just got out my three-year relationship; I'm not trying to be on no hoe shit."

Jean held out her hand, and I took the honor of shaking it.

JEAN: "You can call me Jean; J is short clearly."

We just locked eyes.

RAY: "Nice to meet you Miss. Jean." She smiled so big and beautiful.

JEAN: "You as well Mr. Ray."

RAY: "You mind if we exchanged numbers?"

She pulled out her phone.

JEAN: "You can give me yours."

I felt a little played.

RAY: "Will you use it?"

She looked off.

JEAN: "Sure."

At that moment, I knew she was playing me. I gave her my number anyway.

RAY: "For real, Jean hit me up."

She turned and walked off with her friends. My phone started to vibrate, and I thought it was Jean, but I frowned up when I saw it was Bethanee.

RAY: "Yea I'm on my way," then hung up.

Two days go by, and I still had not heard from Jean. A nigga was really feeling played. Bethanee just kept calling and texting me. I ignored a couple of them and blamed my shitty cell service for some. Knowing I really hung up. There was no rekindling with us. I wanted Jean to hit me up.

I was in the mood for seafood, and decided to check out this place called, 'Cajun Goodness' I had been hearing all types of reviews, and it's black owned. As soon as I walked in, I saw Jean and her two best friends. My stomach felt so empty, and my heart dropped to my stomach. I was beginning to approach her when she looked up. Those small, kinky eyes got so damn big.

JEAN: "Ray," dragging my name. "What's up how're you?" I just stood there in awe.

RAY: "I could be better if you stuck to your word. What's up, what happened to you texting or calling me?"

JEAN: "I really do apologize. I've been busy with work and school."

RAY: "I see you ain't too busy right now."

LALA: "Hold up nigga. Don't be talking to my friend like that."

RAY: "Bro shut the fuck up. The first time, I let you slide, but now you're doing too much."

Jean stood up and put her whole hand in my face.

JEAN: "Now I'm talking. Don't disrespect my friend like that."

RAY: "I wasn't even trying to be disrespectful she came at me sideways at the mall. She was being a good friend, cool. But you don't know me and can't be talking to people any kind of way. Now I think you are an incredibly beautiful woman, and did want to build a friendship, but I understand I'm not worth your time."

I turned and walked to the counter to order my food.

RAY: "Aye, delete my number too… if it's saved."

As I was waiting for my food, I received a text from an unsaved number… 'Hey Ray. I apologize for not texting sooner. You think we can try this friendship thing?'

I looked over at Jean table and saw her cheesing at me. I smiled back, closed my phone without replying, and put my phone down. I could hear her gasp.

'Order number 23'

looking at my ticket, I saw my food was ready. I took one last look at Jean and left. I was only a good ten minutes from the restaurant, so my food was still hot. *'Fresh Prince of Bel-Air'* was on, so I tuned in, and poured me a glass of milk. Apparently drinking milk with spicy foods, tones it down, and my ass got extra hot. It was indeed finger licking, and I would for sure go back.

I just could not get over the fact that two days went by, and Jean was just now texting me, being petty. I read over her text a few times, and then finally decided to reply.

RAY: "Wassup I'm done eating."

JEAN: "Oh now you want to talk?"

RAY: "I was mad, and hungry. Plus, I felt like you was on some playa shit."

JEAN: "That ain't it whatsoever. I have a full-time job, and school just started for me. I'm trying to be successful as possible."

RAY: I understand and respect that. When are you actually free? Maybe we can link up."

JEAN: "I'm free right now, wassup?"

RAY: "Pull up...?"

    She texted me her address and in 30 minutes, I was outside her house. She did not invite me in, because she still stayed with her parents, and pops did not play that. She came out in some Betty Boop, sleeping pants, a black tank top and some pink fuzzy house shoes. I was surprised she did not have her bonnet on too.

RAY: "Hey, beautiful." I spoke as soon as she opened the door, and stepped in.

JEAN: "Wassup Ray."

RAY: "No bonnet?"

    She glared at me.

JEAN: "You trying to be funny, with yo bald-headed ass."

    I had some waves at the time, so it was kind of funny.

RAY: "Don't do me like that best friend."

    She frowned up so quickly, I saw her nose flare up.

JEAN: "What's this game you playing?"

    I was a bit confused.

JEAN: "Oh, now I'm best friend?" She paused for a second. "Are you bipolar, crazy, schizophrenia, or a mental patient?"

RAY: "Whoa, Whoa, whoa chill out Jean! I'm not crazy."

JEAN: "Okay but about this schizophrenia?"

I just stared at her, but I really wanted to tell her to get out.

RAY: "Didn't I say I wanted to be friends? At this time in my life, a legit friend is what I need."

We looked into each other's eyes, and I started to feel butterflies in my stomach. At least that's what I thought.

JEAN: "You hungry best friend?"

It was just then my stomach started growling. It had been over an hour since the last time I ate. I rested my hand on my stomach.

RAY: "Yes the fuck I am."

JEAN: "It's a McDonalds up the street, you want to go? "

RAY: "Yunno it."

She ran to change pants, grabbed her keys off the TV stand as she walked out of the house. Being the gentleman that I am, I opened the car door for her, walked to the driver side, cranked my car up, put it in drive, and drove off.

RAY: "So what are you going to school for?"

JEAN: "Business."

RAY: "Damn my bad, I'm just trying to get to know you." I mugged her some, because shawty was starting to get rude.

JEAN: "What the hell are you talking about?"

RAY: "You're talking 'business' and shit."

JEAN: "Yea dumb ass, I'm a business major. I want to own my own shop one day. You can get your nails, and hair done while eating, and shop in the same building. It sounds like the mall some but nah. I want to sell original clothes. You know Tiffany is in fashion design, and La can beat the fuck out somebody face with makeup? We're going to be in business together."

RAY: "Damn J, that sounds lit as fuck."

JEAN: "Thank you. I know it takes a lot of work, and I'm ready for it."

To see her smile did something to my spirit. We had ordered our food, and then headed back to her crib. The next few hours, we chilled, ate, vibed, laughed, and had deep conversations. She even told me about her miscarriage with twins, by some toxic nigga, named, Amar.

Seven years later, Jean and I are still best friends, and I still couldn't tell her I had a baby on the way with Bethanee.

Chapter Four

JEAN

It Was All Peachy in the Beginning

It was a week later, and I still have not heard from Ray. I was starting to get worried. He should know me better. I pulled up to his house but did not see his car. I then pulled up to his job, went in asking for him. He had taken the day off. As long as I have known this man, he's never taken a day off from work. Something is not right.

I called up Slim, one of Ray's homies to see if he knew where he was at. I was so worried, that I even called his mama phone, and she did not even know where he was at. This nigga Ray was really playing with me, and I was about to put a police report out on him. I began to drive down Rancho Road thinking of where he could be.

About 10 minutes driving, I saw someone I didn't want to see. I saw Amar. I hit my brakes so hard, the car behind almost hit me. I could not let him see me. I kept driving until I got to the nearest gas station to calm down.

Amar is my crazy ex, and I do mean crazy, and toxic. It was all peachy in the beginning, but after a while he switched up on me. He cheated on me the entire relationship. Now that I look back, I was dumb and in love at the time. At least I thought I was in love. We had taken a break after five months together, and he went off and had a baby on me. Then this nigga came back and got me pregnant. I do not know if it was what he was going through, but then he started putting his hands on me.

He used to be this big-time football player while we were in high school, but he tore his ACL in the last football game and went nowhere with his career. He settled for less, working at McDonalds. It was cool at the time, but he started hanging with drug dealers, even selling that shit.

He had got jumped, and put in the hospital once, because instead of selling the man's products, he smoked it. That was at the time he got me pregnant, with twins. I had found out he was sleeping at his other baby mothers' house, instead of with his boys, or at work like he said. Nigga was lying to me the whole time.

Some girl he was fucking with while I was pregnant called my phone, talking about he was at her house that night, and fucked her raw, in my car. Like this bitch was going on, and on bragging about a nigga with two kids on the way, nuttin in her.

I was heated, and ready to cut that nigga throat open, and slay his head on his mama porch.

That same day the bitch called; I had a miscarriage. The doctor said it was stress, and I believed him. Every time I got around Amar, my head would hurt.

I had pulled up on him to tell him, wassup. He was still trying to be in a relationship with me, even after the miscarriage. Talking about he loves me, he's nothing without me, and he would do whatever to get me back.

Nigga was even crying. I literally sat there, staring, and almost began to laugh. I was Like, 'nigga is you serious right now? I just had a miscarriage, and you talking about a relationship, and confessing to all your bullshit? I'm stressing because of you nigga, and it's not worth it.'

I simply got in my car and cranked it up. This man legit jumps his big ass on my hood, beating on the window.

AMAR: "Don't leave me Jean-pooh. I'm so sorry baby!"

Jean –pooh was the nickname he would call me. I was beyond irritated and turned my wind shield wipers on.

JEAN: "Get your big ass off my damn car!"

AMAR: "Bitch I said I love you and I'm sorry. Get out the fucking car Jean."

JEAN: "If you don't get off of my car Amar, you gone be on this hoe until you fall off."

Next thing, his fat ass mama come running outside. Fastest I've ever seen her run, besides when she going to the kitchen or the bathroom. I kid you not.

MICHELLE: You bet not run over my son! Stop holding him hostage with that baby. He doesn't want you hoe."

I rolled my window down...

JEAN: "Girl your son broke as hell, and ain't shit. You did a great job raising him, be proud, you big, fat, blind, gorilla.

Now tell your broke ass son to get off of my got damn hood, before I run his ass over. PERIODT!"

All the shit I took from this hoe, the lies and cheating.

JEAN: "Bitch you used to call my phone every damn day, trying to be friends. You ain't shit, just like your son. Now again, TELL YO MUTHAFUCKING SON TO GET OFF MY MUTHAFUCKIN HOOD BEFORE I RUN HIS BROKE ASS OVER!"

I took my phone out and started secretly recording. This nigga, and his mama both sneaky, and I must stay ready.

AMAR: "GET OUT THE CAR JEAN, AND TALK TO ME."

I put my car in drive, and pulled off, yes with Amar still on my hood. His mama threw a brick at my car, but totally missed. I only took him four houses down the block. He did not fall off like I had hoped, so I put the car in reverse; and started jerking the car by slightly pressing on the gas.

He finally fell and I went straight *Cleo* from 'Set It Off,' and sped the fuck off while still in reverse, until I reached the end of the street. Thank God there were no cars coming the opposite way. Once I got the end, I put my car in drive, and looked back.

This was the day I knew this nigga was crazy. Here he comes running down the block, screaming.

AMAR: "Talk to me Jean. I said I'm sorry!"

I see his neighbors coming outside, being nosey.

Later that day, nigga was calling me from a Behavior Correction Center. I immediately hung up and blocked the number. Nigga was living off of Wi-Fi, so I blocked his email, and deleted all pictures, and videos. My girls came over to comfort me and helped burn Amar shit.

His cousin Shaunee, was blowing up my phone, trying to blame me for Amar getting hurt. This hoe called me her friend, Sus, 5o, Twin, all that, knowing damn well we did not look alike, and I just went with it because she was Amar's cousin. Bitch was trying to fight me, and everything. I spoke to her briefly.

JEAN: "You are crazy just like your broke ass cousin. You would have had four kids, with no job."

She knew the whole time that Amar was cheating on me. Shaunee, Amar, and his other baby mama Trish, all used to hang out, smoking. I have vented to Shaunee so many times about her hoe ass cousin. Bitch gave me advice and knew the whole time he was doing wrong.

So, I fasho got my round with her, and to beat her ass.

She had about four other bitches with her, all on that jump shit. I already knew wassup. Like Shaunee is related to Amar, Amar came out of Michelle, Michelle fucked up, so I knew they would be sneaky when it comes to fighting.

I had brought my girls La, and Tiff. LaLa has two older sisters that are as bad, and roughish as her, and they were down to have my back. Shaunee friend tried to jump in when I was beating her ass, but my girl La handled that.

Tiffany has an older brother, Jared, who had just got out of prison that same day. He considers me as a little sister, just like Tiff, and La. He pulled up just for Amar, and ended up giving him a black eye, and a busted lip. I just knew Jared was excited to beat Amar ass. Even after all the fighting, Amar was still trying to get back with me. Shit crazy!

Calming my nerves, I finally pulled from out of 7-eleven, and decided to go home. Pulling up to my house, I saw Chris's car. Chris is this tall, skinny, light-skinned brotha who has been trying to talk to me for the past two years. He is cool and all, but being with him in a relationship, just ain't it. He is a pretty boy, and he always talks about himself.

On our first date, we went to dinner, I kid you not he only talked about him, his job, his past and more. I could barely get a sentence in about anything. He was paying for the date, including drinks, and I for sure was throwing them bitches back, trying to keep my ears from bleeding, listening to this man go on and on about him. Just seem too cocky for me. I gave him the benefit of the doubt and went on a second date with him. It was the same thing, and my ass got drunk again. That time I had to call LaLa to come get me. Tiffany was boo'd up with her man Tony.

After a while, I guess Chris noticed the distance, and dry conversations I was giving. He decided to switch it up, seeming like he was interested in my life. That was the third date we went on. The same night he moved up on me. Nigga thought just because he started to be concerned about what I had going on, and continued to pay for dates, I was supposed to give him some pussy.

Think again. He was mad and stopped talking to me for about 2-3 months. I did not really give a fuck. I had started talking to this tall, chocolate man, sent from above, named Trey. Not saying Chris was not attractive to give him some, but I've never really liked light skins. I guess I was trying something new with Chris.

As I was pulling into my assigned parking spot in my apartment complex, Chris was stepping out of his car. I simply rolled my eyes, at his big pearly white smile. What could this man possibly want? He only reaches out every now and again trying to take me out. I always end up turning him down. There is no need in leading him on, if I know I am not interested.

CHRIS: "Hey, Jean." He opened his arms, initiating a hug. I did not want to be too much of an asshole, so I went in for the hug. "I've been missing you."

JEAN: "Awe, Chris you shouldn't have."

He turned to his car, and pulled out a bag from Macy's, and handed it to me.

CHRIS: "Put this on and be ready by 8."

Looking inside the bag, I saw this cute beige dress, and red heels.

JEAN: "This is really cute Chris, but I won't be able to make it. I'm seeing someone else."

His eyes bucked out at me.

CHRIS: "Oh wow. I am guessing I'm late. You can keep the dress, and shoes."

Just as I was about to give Chris a hug, Ray was calling. My fumes started rising. I answered the phone...

JEAN: "Are you fucking serious Ray? I've been calling you for a week now. What the hell is wrong with you? Are you okay?" He wasn't responding, and he knows I hate that. "Hel-lo. Can you hear me? "

RAY: "Jean, I need to talk to you, and not over the phone."

Chris was just standing there, watching me go off on my best friend.

CHRIS: "I'm gonna go, seems like you got a lot on your hands with ya new man."

Did this nigga just throw shade? I mean mugged the shit out of him.

JEAN: "The nerve of you, you mad? Feeling some type of way that I don't want you?"

He bucked his eyes at me, and I did not give one, two, or three fucks.

CHRIS: "Yea. Let me get that dress back so I can give it to my hoe."

I threw the bag at him and walked away.

CHRIS: "You Bitch!"

I did not have the time to even respond, because I was about to get on that nigga ass. Then Ray spoke up.

RAY: "Aye who is that nigga?"

I looked at my phone and saw Ray was still on the line. Chris started walking to the other side of his car.

RAY: "Hellooooo. Who is that nigga calling you a bitch?"

JEAN: "Chris, his frail ass mad I don't want to talk to him."

CHRIS: "Girl fuck you and whoever you on the phone with."

I glared at Chris and gave him the finger.

RAY: "Aye you're popping off at the mouth stay right where you at nigga. I'm on my way."

Ray screaming all through the phone like the nigga can really hear him.

RAY: "Tell that nigga what I said Jean." Then he hung up.

JEAN: "My best friend said stay where you at."

CHRIS: "What she trying to do?"

JEAN: "*HE* trying to beat your ass. You already know how Ray coming behind me. So, you get back in your car, and wait until he gets here, Bitch!"

CHRIS: "Fuck you like I said. I ain't waiting on that nigga. Fuck both ya'll bitches."

JEAN: "Cause your ass scary."

Clearly Ray was close as hell to my house, I see him whipping that 2015 Chrysler. He got out so fast; I did not even see him put his car in park.

RAY: "What was that shit you was talking over the phone?"

Chris started moving his car in reverse. Ray legit walked to this man car and was beating on his window.

RAY: "Get out the car fuck boy. You can talk all that shit to a female, let alone my best friend. Talk that shit to me. Bitch!"

Something else was up with Ray, he was on ten.

CHRIS: "Get the fuck away from my car."

RAY: "You a bitch nigga. Keep her name out your mouth, respect her, and if you start popping off at the mouth again, that's your ass. I don't play about this one right here."

Chris could never be my man. If he could not stand his ground right now with Ray, that shows what type of man he is. He a whole bitch and he cannot protect me.

RAY: "Why you always got to fuck with these weak, tired ass niggas?"

I turned to Ray with a whole frown on my face. I was speechless.

RAY: "You need a real man. Every nigga you have fucked with was not, and ain't shit. You are too good of a woman to be going through that bullshit. I'll beat all them niggas behind your ass, and you know that Jean." He began to walk away, leaving me standing there in shock. "Gone have me in jail and shit." Ray turned to me, "what you just standing there for, looking like 'a deer in headlights.' Bring your ass."

At that point I did not know if I wanted to slap the hell out of him or fuck the shit out of him. I have seen him mad, but not like this. He has never talked to me like that neither. I think I kind of like it.

Once we got inside of my crib, Ray threw his key on the couch and plopped down, while putting his head in his hands.

JEAN: "You want something to drink, or hungry?"

He raised his head, and just glared at me.

JEAN: "I guess not."

I walked to the kitchen and fixed me a cup of Sunny D. When I walked back over to the couch, Ray still had his head in his hands. I sat next to him and thought I heard crickets. It was so quiet it was ridiculous. I rubbed his back while sipping on Sunny D.

RAY: "Jean, I really need to talk to you about something... the reason why you haven't heard from me."

The conversation switch caught me off guard, but I knew we had to talk about it sooner than later. I was trying to keep my fumes down, because at the very moment, I could have knocked fire from this nigga.

JEAN: "You know, I can really throat punch you right now."

RAY: "I know. I know, I fucked up. I really do apologize about ignoring your calls... and I--"

JEAN: "Ooooo, you been ignoring them on purpose?"

RAY: "Chill. Just hear me out because this is serious."

JEAN: "I'm listening Ray."

He took a long pause, and I was beginning to get frustrated. It has been days since I have heard from him, then he comes in my house on some weird shit. His actions just were not sitting right with my spirit.

My phone started vibrating and it was Tiff. I ignored her call and waited for Ray response. She called again, but I ignored. Not even two seconds later, LaLa was calling.

RAY: "You want to answer that? It may be important."

I rolled my eyes at what he said, he was trying to avoid telling me whatever it was. Tiff called again. This time I picked up.

TIFFANY: "GET DOWN TO LALA HOUSE NEOOW."

I did not have time to respond before she hung up. Ray and I made eye contact, and immediately jumped up. He grabbed for his keys, and we headed for the door.

Chapter Five

He Was a Target

As soon as we got to La's house, I knocked once, and Tiff swung the door open. I saw La, Keyvaune, Tony's cousin, and some random nigga with his feet propped up on La's dinner table.

JEAN: "What's going on here?"

Ray and I were still standing in the doorway, so we walked towards the living room where everyone else was sitting. I looked over at the random nigga and he winked at me, something about him just did not sit right with me. No one answered me, so I looked over at La, whose eyes were so red from crying. Everyone's eyes were red from crying, except the random nigga.

JEAN: "Somebody going to tell me what happened, and why the phone call seemed so urgent?"

I still got no answer.

RANDOM NIGGA: "Some nigga named, Tony, got shot and paralyzed from the neck down. We just came back from the hospital."

JEAN: "And who are you?"

RANDOM NIGGA: "Oh my name is Pete, and you are?"

JEAN: "Stephanie... why is you here?"

KEYVAUNE: "We are not going to just speed past the fact that you acknowledge my cousin as 'some nigga.' Do *not* disrespect me like that in my face nigga.

PETE: "My fault kinfolk, ion mean no harm."

I rolled my eyes at the sound of his voice. What he was saying, just did not sit right with me.

JEAN: "So what exactly happened? How did Tony get shot?" I was started to get a bit upset at the fact that no one was answering me. "HELLO..." I looked over at Ray, and saw that he was comforting La, while Keyvaune, and Tiffany comforted each other. I still got no answer.

PETE: "All we know is...'

Keyvaune raised his head up and glared at Pete.

PETE: "Is... *Tony* was with some of his boys, and ended up getting shot in the shoulder, just a few inches from his *neck*."

How ol boy Pete sounded was a little creepy. His whole vibe came off as creepy. I tried to ignore it, but every time I glanced over at him, we made eye contact and he would smirk. Ray saw It the last time and made the 'what the fuck' face. The laugh I tried holding in, just wanted to be heard.

A few moments had passed by, and I started to smell an odor. It had a mixture of vinegar, and cheese. Nobody had cooked, and the trash had just been taken out, so I had no idea what I was smelling.

JEAN: "Sooo nobody else smells the ass in the room?" I was just about tired of being ignored, everyone just looked at me, and frowned up. "I understand Tony got hurt, and everyone is in a mood, but dam'it y'all have got to stop ignoring me. Something doesn't smell right."

KEYVAUNE: "Nigggaaaaaa, is them your feet?"

We all looked over at Pete and saw that he done kicked his size 14's off, and got the house lit up.

LALA: "Boy if you don't get your musty ass feet off my got'damn table, and put your trashy ass shoes back on, ima beat you so bad, *you* gone be paralyzed right next to Tony."

Never saw a man move so fast. I did not know if I should laugh or how to laugh. Either way, I hollered.

JEAN: "Why are you even here? You clearly don't know Tony in any kind of way, wassup with you?"

PETE: "Wassup with me? ... wassup with *you?* You been on my ass since you walked through the door."

JEAN: "You've been a creep since I walked through the door. Now why are you even here?"

He paused for a moment like he was thinking of a lie.

PETE: "I was waiting on Keyvaune when he got the call that his cousin had got shot. He didn't have time to drop me off before coming to the hospital, then we came here."

JEAN: "Why you just didn't ask to be dropped off when y'all left the hospital? You not even comforting anyone, with your funky ass feet. How you walk out the house like that?"

PETE: "I didn't go home last night," then he smirked at me.

LALA: "Both you and the bitch you were with is nasty."

JEAN: "How you figure it's a bitch?" We made our 'yea you right' face and burst out laughing.

PETE: "Nah, don't even play like that," then stood up like he was ready to fight.

I look over to my left and see Ray standing.

RAY: "What you trying to do, I mean you standing up. Did she hit a nerve?"

PETE: "Yo, Keyvaune, can you drop me back off at my spot?"

LALA: "Yeah, take him and them funky ass feet back to his house."

PETE: "Yo, ya'll got to chill on me. Fuck all y'all."

It was like harmony with La, Ray, and I.

JEAN// RAY// LALA: *"Who?"*

PETE: "Fuck all three of ya'll. Vaune take me home!"

Clearly Keyvaune was paying no attention to Pete.

LALA: "Pleeaassee take this bitch home."

PETE: "Bitch?"

LALA: "That's what I said, bitch! Take his ass home."

PETE: "Yo get me out of this house before I smack a hoe."

RAY: "Who are you talking about smacking?"

Ray started walking towards Pete, while pulling up his pants. Any African American knows that means to 'square up.' He got a little steam coming out. I kind of like when Ray gets mad, it is sexy. Nobody else knows that, not even Tiffany. Keyvaune ran up trying to break up the fight before it started. Pete needed his ass beat *fasho*.

KEYVAUNE: "Aye, chill out. Today is *NOT* the day for this shit. Calm y'all childish asses down for real."

Ray glared at Pete while backing up to where he was standing next to LaLa.

PETE: "Get your boy, Vaune."

RAY: "He doesn't need to get me. You just need to watch out who you talk to, and how you talk to them."

KEYVAUNE: "Aight. Aight. Bring your ass Pete."

PETE: "Don't be getting rowdy with me; I'm just defending myself from these three dicks."

RAY: "You talk a lot of shit. Watch yourself."

PETE: "I will. You do the same."

JEAN: "Don't make threats. Tear your ass boy bef..."

Ray completely cut me off before I could finish what I was saying.

RAY: "What I tell you about jumping in a man's fight? Chill. I got us baby."

When he called me baby, my panties got a little wet. Ray is just so fine to me, and I wanted to jump on him right then and there. Both La, and Tiff turned their necks at me so fast, with bucked eyes.

LALA: *"He got you baby,"* trying to mock him. "Don't worry about a thing, girl."

Latonia is one of the most childish women I know. If you are wondering, Latonia is LaLa's government name. She does not really like when people call her *Latonia*. She feels her name is too ghetto, like LaLa is not.

KEYVAUNE: "Pete, let's *GO!*"

Pete's' vibe was off, and he seemed a bit sneaky.

LALA: "Yeah, funky feet. Tear your ass."

PETE: "Girl fuck you, ol lima bean head ass."

KEYVAUNE: "PETE!!!! If you want a ride, you better bring your ass now. I am not for this shit. My cousin just got shot, and this is what ya'll want to do? Bring your muthafucking ass."

PETE: "QUIT TALKING TO ME LIKE THAT." Pete motioned towards Keyvaune, and Keyvaune glared at Pete like he wanted to strangle him by the throat.

KEYVAUNE: "Bring your ass, bitch."

PETE: "Bitch? Yo, you bugging right now."

LALA: "No, you are. This man has told you multiple times, TODAY IS NOT THE DAY, and to bring your ass. Looka here, you're still standing in the same spot you were about to get your ass beat at. Move a little."

   Pete was glaring at everyone in this apartment. Before he started walking towards the door, he flicked his nose, and sucked his teeth.

TIFFANY: "You be safe, Vaune. If you need anything at all, you call us."

   LaLa frowned up, like she still smelled Pete feet.

LALA: "Don't say *us* hoe. Speak for yourself, I'm broke."

   Keyvaune gave LaLa the finger.

TIFFANY: "You don't need money to talk or listen to someone. Stop being so damn stubborn all the time.

LALA: "Who are you to tell someone to stop being stubborn?"

I scowled at LaLa.

JEAN: "I love the hell out of you, La, but you're the most stubborn individual I know of."

LALA: "Okay whatever. Fuck both of y'all and kiss my ass." She folded her arms and pouted.

KEYVAUNE: "I appreciate that Tiff. It means a lot."

TIFFANY: "Don't mind La, I'm here for you."

JEAN: "Yeah, so am I."

KEYVAUNE: "Thank y'all, I really do appreciate that." LaLa sat back, with her arms still folded, and still pouting. "Now I see why they call you stubborn, look at you pouting."

LALA: "Stop it y'all."

TIFFANY: "You're being a big ass baby."

LALA: "Whatever," she simply rolled her eyes.

I did not care one bit. Keyvaune hugged Tiffany, LALA, and I, and both him, and Pete had left. Tiffany closed the door behind them and locked it. Not even thirty seconds after they left, here comes La,

LALA: "Who wants a drink?"

Tiff, and I made eye contact, and burst out laughing.

TIFFANY: "Girl, are you serious right now? Are you really trying to drink at this moment? You know you are an alcoholic, right?

LALA: "How does that make me an alcoholic just because I happen to want a drink right about now?

TIFFANY: "Keyvaune, and Pete Literally just left, and the first thing that comes to mind is a drink? Not, *'I hope Keyvaune is okay,'* but a drink? WOW!" Tiffany walked over to the kitchen, "What you got to drink in here anyway?"

We all burst out laughing.

LALA: "And *I'm* the alcoholic." La had got up, and walked to the kitchen, and opened her liquor cabinet. "I got some Hennyyy, apple whiskey, Ciroc, Grey Goosey Goo, this pink lemonade Amsterdam..." She pulled out this big ass pink bottle and advertised it off.

TIFFANY: "This right here is exactly why you are indeed an alcoholic. How much more liquor do you have, La?"

LALA: "Don't do me like that, we always having Girl's night at my house, so I stock up."

I walked to the liquor cabinet where La, and Tiff stood. Sister girl had all types of liquor since our last girl's nights over. There was Malibu, Bacardi, Captain Morgan,

Bombay, and other Brandy's'. Her cabinet looked like a liquor store. I could understand though. We did always have our girl's nights at her house.

JEAN: "You got ice?"

LALA: "Yes ma'am I do..." She walked towards the freezer and pulled out the bag of ice. "Margarita anyone?"

She was definitely the bartender of our friendship. I could make a mean ass peach, pineapple, and strawberry margarita. As far as the drinks you will find at the club, La got me on that.

TIFFANY: "I'll take one." La took out three wine glasses, three crazy straws, her blender, and a few more supplies.

JEAN: "And you know I want one." Tiff and I walked back over to the living room and sat on the couch. Tiff reached for the Television remote and put on some Netflix. We could barely hear the television from that loud ass blender La was working in the kitchen. I assumed Tiff was getting annoyed and started turning up the television.

LALA: "Daaayyuuummmm, can you turn it down some?"

TIFFANY: "Well can you turn the blender down some? We can't even hear the TV."

LALA: "Bitch do you want a drink or nah?" Tiffany rolled her eyes and turned the television down some. "Thank you."

TIFFANY: "You're not welcome."

LALA: "Just for that, I'm spicing yours up."

TIFFANY: "I bet I'll still drink it, Sus." La went back to making our margaritas.

We had heard about this series called, '*Altered Carbon,*' with Lela Loren, and Anthony Mackie. Anthony is one of our favorite actors. He played in this one film called, '*Crossover*' as Tech. He was this fine brother working with his best friend at a shoe joint. They were a part of a small basketball team, playing to keep their throne as champions. Anthony also played in *Notorious*, as 2 Pac. Notorious happens to be another one of our favorite movies. He also played as Falcone in all of the '*Avengers,*' except the first one. Anthony plays in a lot of other good movies. As far as Lela, she played in a TV series, '*Power,*' as Angela, from season one through five.

I looked over my shoulder, and saw La making her way over towards Tiff, and I with our drinks.

TIFFANY: "Thank you baby," and then handed me mine.

JEAN: "Thanks Sus."

La took a seat next to Tiffany and joined in the TV series. In the back of my mind I noticed Ray had left, but before I could act on it, Tiffany's phone began to vibrate, and it was Keyvaune calling, so she answered.

TIFFANY: "Hey, wassup?"

KEYVAUNE: "I need you."

Tiff put her drink down and sat up on the end of the couch… La, and I made eye contact, and ear hustled, or at least tried to.

TIFFANY: "You okay? What's wrong?"

 KEYVAUNE: "Are you alone, busy? Can you come to me or we can meet up?"

TIFFANY: "Keyvaune what's wrong?"

I nudged Tiffany to see what was up with Keyvaune, and she brushed me off.

JEAN: "You bitch." I mouthed.

Apparently, she was irritated with both La, and I, and got up, and headed to the back room. Our mouths dropped to the floor in awe, and she turned back to us, and grinned.

Chapter Six

TIFFANY

KEYVAUNE: "I really just want some company right about now. I went back up to the hospital, and doctors say he might not make it."

TIFFANY: "Oh my. Where are you now?"

KEYVAUNE: "Outside your door!"

I thought that was weird. Even though Tony had cheated on me, and had a baby, I was scared for him to die.

TIFFANY: "How long have you been there? I'm still at La's house right now."

KEYVAUNE: "Maybe about 20 minutes. I was really going to leave, but a lot of shit is on my mind."

TIFFANY: "Give me about 20 minutes, and I'll be there."

KEYVAUNE: "Okay, thank you Cookie."

Keyvaune liked me even though I was with his cousin. Always told me that I deserve better than what Tony was doing. Sometimes I believed him. Scratch that, a lot of the time I believed him.

Keyvaune is extremely attractive, and I can honestly say that he looks better than Tony. But I never looked at Keyvaune like that until the night Tony first cheated on me.

When I found out about the baby, that was it for me. I knew he had cheated, and we were trying to work past that, since we freshly had moved in together. But now you got a kid by her, nah buddy. When I needed someone to comfort me, Keyvaune was there, and here is my chance to be there for him.

We ended up kissing that night, and it just felt so right. There was no guilt knowing the fact that I was still dating his cousin. If I had told Jean and LaLa about the first time Tony cheated on me, *that* would have been the end of it. La would have tried to beat his ass; Jean probably would have tried to burn him.

Tony was always in some drama, fucking with peoples' money and women. It was just a matter of time before something happened to him. The way I see it, either way it goes, Keyvaune would have been hurt by Tony getting hurt, whether it was by LaLa, Jean, and I or someone else. I ain't gone lie; I was tipsy as hell from them margaritas, so I ran to the bathroom to splash some water on my face. By the time I walked back to the living room where my girls were, they had finished another episode of 'Altered Carbon.'

TIFFANY: "Hey, y'all I'm about to head out." Both La, and Jean turned their heads at me.

JEAN: "What, why?"

TIFFANY: "I'm meeting up with Vaune. He's in need of a friend."

LALA: "Okay, 'friend.'"

TIFFANY: "Don't start that shit. I said what I said, *friend.* Stop playing with me, La for I beat your drunk ass."

LALA: "You ain't bout it nigga."

I walked up on La and bucked at her. I ain't never seen La flinch that damn hard.

TIFFANY: "Yea, *nigga.*"

JEAN: "Aight, calm down ladies. You good though Tiff? Is Vaune good?"

TIFFANY: "His cousin just got shot; he just needs a friend to talk to."

JEAN: "I understand. Just be safe."

TIFFANY: "You know I will."

*** JEAN***

Tiff walked closer to both La, and I and embraced us with a hug. La was still upset about Tiff bucking at her, me on the hand, I did not care. La always got in these moods like she is some big baby. I assumed since La was still mad, she would not want to walk Tiffany to the door, so I did.

JEAN: "Remember, be safe Tiff, and call us if you need us." I heard La 'Tuh,' in the back ground. I simply rolled my eyes, "Call *US* like I said."

TIFFANY: "Thank you Jean." She looked over at LaLa, "Bye La, I love you."

LALA: "Yeah, mhm." I turned to her...

JEAN: "You ain't even got to be like that."

LALA: "I said what I said."

I had closed the door behind Tiff after she left.

JEAN: "Why are you like this?"

LALA: "So I'm wrong being mad?"

JEAN: "No, but you're mad for a dumb ass reason. Get over yourself La. It ain't even that deep. *If* something does happen to her, you're going to be hurt after what you said."

LALA: "I hate it when you're right."

JEAN: "I love you too." I leaned over to embrace La with a hug.

We ended up watching another episode of *'Altered Carbon,'* then switched to bench watching *Friday, Next Friday, and Friday after Next*. LaLa has this exotic crush on Mike Epps. Every now and again, I will look over at her, and she would be licking her lips. Shawty was already feeling the three drinks she's already had: now over here daydreaming about a one night stand with Epps.

LALA: "All I need is one night with him, and I promise he'll be putting a ring on my finger the next. Laawwd that man is fine."

I ain't going to lie, Mike Epps is fine, and I will probably be firsthand watching La, and him. O'Shea Jackson, also known as Ice Cube on the other hand is sexy as hell. He got this mean, 'don't fuck with me' demeanor, and Mike is just funny. Niggas know bitches like to laugh, that is how you get them.

A few hours had passed by when I noticed it was one in the morning. I was still a little tipsy, and tired. There was no way I was about to get up and leave to go home. I would get up alright... and take my ass to La's bed... eventually.

LaLa ass was laid out on the couch, damn near hanging off. I nudged her gently. Girl did not even flinch, so I nudged again, this time harder.

LALA: "Damn bitch, take my shoulder off then."

Y'all already know how dramatic La is. Know damn well I did not push her that hard.

JEAN: "I'm going in your room to lie in the bed."

LALA: "Just make sure you flush," and fanned me away.

She has got to be out of there, talking about flushing. I did not have the energy to even respond, and simply got up and headed to her room. La had one of the most comfortable beds I have ever laid in. I was even jealous about my bed. I checked my phone to see if Tiffany called or texted, and nothing.

Keyvaune had this little secret crush on Tiffany; well at least he thought it was a secret. Every time Tiff walked in a room when Keyvaune was around, he would start smiling from ear to ear, blushing and shit. He is light skinned, so it was always noticeable. He would sometimes even bring her flowers to her job. For a while he was bringing them every Wednesday; lilies, and dandelions the first week, Rhododendron's and sunflower the next.

It was always so cute, I was sometimes a little jealous, like where my flowers? I understand why they would want to keep their relationship or whatever they had going on, on the low, but it was really no secret. Everybody knew Keyvaune liked Tiffany. He just thought nobody else knew. About twenty minutes later, La came strolling in the room.

LALA: "Scoot your shitty ass over."

JEAN: "How the fuck is I shitty?"

LALA: "I just hope you flushed my toilet and sprayed."

JEAN: "Ain't nobody even used your bathroom with your drunk ass. You clearly have had one too many drinks. They were a little stronger than usual."

LALA: "Yeah, yeah, yeah... drunk or not, scoot over shitty."

JEAN: "You got one more time to call me shitty."

LALA: "*Shitty!*"

I grabbed a pillow from her bed and threw it directly at her face, then rolled out of the bed onto the floor. The lights were off, and it was a majority pitch black in there beside the light that was coming from the alarm clock on her nightstand.

LALA: "Don't run now muthafucka."

I quietly moved over towards the closet.

JEAN: "Take your ass to bed La, before I body slam you."

LALA: "You're lucky I'm tired, and don't have the energy for your foolishness."

La got in the bed, and I checked my phone to see if I had missed calls or messages from Tiffany, but nothing. I got in bed next to LaLa and fell fast to sleep.

The next morning, I woke up to three missed calls from Tiff, and a few messages from Ray. I was a little upset with him at this point because he seems to keep dodging me. I was not in the mood to speak with him, so I ended up calling Tiff back, when La walked back in the room with two plates of breakfast food: scrambled eggs, bacon, toast, and grits.

My boy Wade better quit playing with La and put a ring on her finger. My girl was drop dead gorgeous, could cook, clean, a boss lady, and more. If I were into girls, hell I would put a ring on her finger.

JEAN: "Thanks bae."

LALA: "You're welcome. Have you heard from Tiff?"

JEAN: "Oh now you're worried about her?" She rolled her eyes at me. "I was just about to call her back; I had three missed calls from her."

The phone had rung a couple of times but no answer. I am pretty sure she would see the missed call and would call back. I sat my phone down on La's nightstand, and prayed before eating my breakfast.

JEAN: "Mmm, this looks good."

LALA: Yah and you better eat every bit of it. We don't waste food around here."

JEAN: "Girl I'm not worried about you. As hungry as I am, I might want seconds."

LALA: "Look now; don't be coming in here eating all of my groceries. There are plenty of eggs, and grits but the bacon...all gone," then she took a big ass bite of her toast.

JEAN: "With all of this good food, sure would be nice to have something to drink."

LALA: "Dammit, I left the orange juice on the counter. I was not thinking about no liquid, only food. My bad girl."

We burst out laughing, as La was getting up to head to the kitchen. A few seconds later she came strolling back with two cups of orange juice in her hand, and a piece of toast in her mouth. Her plate was already leaning over with eggs and grits.

JEAN: "Damn La, you hungry, huh?" I took a bite of bacon. "Are you pregnant?"

LALA: "Bitch do not play with me. Are you pregnant, talking about you might want seconds?" Her mouth was full of food, but she was still going to get out what she had to say.

'I should run a whole blog at this rate; they using my name for clickbait...' Clout, *Cardi B* ringtone played aloud,

I didn't let the phone continue to ring, since I already knew who was calling, Tiff! I put the phone on speaker before talking, so La could hear. If I did not, nine times out of ten, La would have been bitching on why I didn't put the call on speaker.

LALA: "Was the dick good at least?"

TIFFANY: "Really, La?"

JEAN: "Really?" LaLa could not help from laughing. She always says the wildest things. "Do you ever think before you say what you're about to say, or do you just blurt it out?" She rolled her eyes at me, and just like any other time... I did not care.

LALA: "Apparently it wasn't. What's the Tea?" There was a slight pause before Tiffany spoke.

TIFFANY: "I called to tell y'all about what happened with Vaune and I. I do not need the judging right at this moment so La... Shut the fuck up."

We all burst out laughing because we knew how bad La mouth is.

LALA: *Gasp*... "Have more faith in me, damn."

JEAN: "We have plenty of faith in you, we just know you talk shit."

LALA: "And I know how to back my shit talking up."

TIFFANY: "Annyywaaayyyyy. I went over to Vaune's house to see what was up with him, this nigga opens the door, and I see a candle lit dinner, dandelions, Keith Sweat; Nobody, playing in the background. I am like, what the hell is this nigga trying to do? I came over to talk, and he trying to eat me out of my panties..."

LALA: "Did it work?"

TIFFANY: "La, SHUT UP!"

LALA: "Grrr. Temper, temper," then rolled her eyes.

Chapter Seven

TIFFANY: "If you would just hush for once and let me get the story out. Like I was saying before being interrupted, I was in awe once I walked in. So, I was like, *'Keyvaune what is this? You called me over to talk about Tony, did you not?'* Then he was like, *'Yeah, but I wanted to talk about us too...'*

JEAN: "Pause, do you really have to do his voice like that?"

   Tiffany legit sounded like a whole man, and it kind of freaked me out.

TIFFANY: "Jean, don't be La... you hush too!"

LALA: "Now you wait a damn minute, she done got some new dick, and talking to us all crazy."

TIFFANY: "JUST SHUT UP. Y'all want to know what happened, and I'm eager as shit to tell y'all." She chuckled, paused for a few seconds, and then sighed. "Can I finish now?"

LALA: "Girl tell the damn story."

   I was beginning to get a bit frustrated, and just wanted the story to be over with.

TIFFANY: "As I was saying...he was trying to talk about *us*. I'm like what about us? He starts expressing his love for me, how he been in love with me since he first laid eyes on me the day, Tony cheated. He was saying how he cares for me and wants to see me happy because he could see Tony was giving me hell on earth. He wants to show me different... this next moment took me out. This fine, tall glass of Henny on rocks, muscles beyond me, said he wanted to take me in the room and make sweet, sweet love to me until I screamed out his name or told him to stop." She paused...

LALA: "Giiirrrrll, I bet them panties got wet after that."

TIFFANY: "Indeed they did bitch. I did not even want to eat the main course... Wait y'all, listen here. My eyes got big as day, and I walked closer to the dinner table to see what he had cooked. It was some steak, mash potatoes, asparagus, and Texas toast. This nigga gone say, *'for dessert, I can eat you, or we can just eat the strawberry cheesecake.'* In my head I was thinking, Lord I picked the wrong cousin, but you have shown me Keyvaune is for *ME.*"

   It was starting to get hot in the room from hearing Tiff's story, so I got up and walked to the kitchen for a cold bottle of water.

JEAN: "You want one, La?"

LALA: "Please." She had got up to turn on the AC.

TIFFANY: "Hello, y'all still there?"

LALA: "Yeah, we got hot, shit. Gone and finish the story"

TIFFANY: "So y'all know my little nasty ass was like, '*you can eat me... with ice.*"

JEAN: "Oooo Bitch, we have taught you well."

Before Tiffany got with Tony, she was this sweet, little girl, who only knew the missionary position. She had lost her virginity to this one dude who went to the same school as us, Leon.

Boy did Tiff love her some Leon. After we all graduated from high school, Leon moved to Montana with a full scholarship to play college basketball at University of Montana. It was her first heartbreak because she did not want him to leave, but she knew it was best for him. She thought of applying at that school but, they did not have a fashion design department. She wanted to get out of Texas but not too far from her family, and both La, and I because she thought it was too much at the time. Her having to breakup with her first love, and being far away from her loved ones, so she decided to apply at The Art Institute of Miami, Florida.

It was good for us three. Every spring break was our own tradition to go down to Florida to spend that time with her. Some years our spring break would start or end differently.

One year La's started before mine, so I had to meet them down there a few days later. LaLa graduated from Arts and Sciences Institutes in Atlanta Georgia, with her B.A in cosmetology. We would spend partial of our summers with La before headed back to our home in Texas. As for myself, I graduated from Allen University in

South Carolina, with my Master's in business. I was also a part of the Delta Greek life. My girls La, and Tiffany would come visit me there when I was performing at shows. On Christmas, and Thanksgiving, we all met up at the nearest airport, and flew back home to Texas together.

Tiffany graduated with her Associates in Fashion merchandising, and her Bachelors in Fashion Design. Even though we were in different states, we made sure we kept contact with each other. The first year in college, Tiff, and Leon tried the long-distance relationship but it did not work out. Leon ended up getting a whole different girlfriend in Montana.

At first, Tiff did not even know until the new girlfriend called her phone telling her to stop texting Leon because he had moved on, and she needed to do the same. When La, and I found out, we really wanted to take a flight up to Montana to beat Leon's ass, break an ankle or two so he couldn't play basketball anymore, but we took the first flight to Florida to comfort our girl.

That same year, when we all came back home in Texas, we were fed up with men and was in a little, semi hoe stage. Always screaming, 'Get money; Fuck niggas,' shout out to you Lil Kim.

LaLa could not hoe much because she was in her relationship with Kelvin. She met him up at school, and they were the cutest together. They always got in fights over some broad that went to the same school. He cheated on La a few times, always talking about he was fucked up, and she made him, blah blah. La could handle hers, and she would just beat his ass. One time breaking his nose and blacking the chicks' eye. After a while, La got tired of that mess, and after she graduated college, she dropped Kelvin where she found him. Then met Wade, they are doing great so far.

Tiffany met Tony at the club when we came home for Christmas a few years back. He basically swept her off her feet. They had hit if off strong, but a couple of months later, he cheated on her with Shaunee, Amar's cousin. I assume around this time, that's when Keyvaune started feeling Tiff. Tony was talking about Tiff was not pleasing him in the bedroom, and he was tired of just missionary, that is why he say he fucked that hoe.

Bitch, that does not mean you cheat on her, tell her wassup *at first* so it does not ruin ya'll trust. We started watching Pinky on *Porn hub*, and little Jada Fire to learn a few things. That weekend, she rocked his world.

As for me, y'all remember Amar, the crazy ex. Before him was Isaac; fine, Hispanic ass. I had met him at school too. He was majoring in business to own his own weed dispensary. He got caught up a few times and was in jail for six months. I would still go to visit him, write him letters, and put money on his books when I could. He thought it was over for him since he had missed a whole semester of college. Our relationship was still fresh, so we kind of just fell off after he got out of jail. We were still friends, but I was not with that go to jail for X amount of time, get out and be distant, then months later the same thing.

Do not get me wrong, for a Hispanic dude, he was packing, and I had needs that he could fulfill. We kept our relationship strictly friends with benefits, and that is when I met Amar. I wish I would have kept walking when he shot his shot, because baby nah, that relationship took a toll on me.

A few moments had passed by, and Tiffany's voice brought me back to the present...

TIFFANY: "Okay, so we're eating dinner, the music is playing; he had some sweet red wine... La you need to add that one to your collection."

LALA: "Can you just skip to the fucking?"

I looked over at her as my mouth dropped. I was feeling the same way, I wanted to know about the fucking part too, but I did not want to rush anything.

JEAN: "I'm like La; can you skip to the fucking?"

TIFFANY: "Damn, he could actually be the one for me and y'all only care about the sex."

LALA: "And your point? Now get to it."

TIFFANY: "Y'all rude as hell... I don't even want to talk anymore, bye."

Next thing I know, she hangs up. I tried calling back, but she sent us straight to voicemail.

LALA: "She's *mad*, mad."

La and I had a few drinks and watched a couple of episodes of '*Wild n Out*' with Nick Cannon as the host. Tiffany ended up calling us back after she '*cooled off,*' talking about how we had her fucked up. La ignorant ass just laughed.

TIFFANY: "Okay so, after we were done eating, he looked me in my eyes and said, 'I'm ready for dessert.' When I tell y'all my panties got so wet, I just wanted to sit on his face backwards. So, we get up and head to the bedroom. He had oil, rose petals and candle lit. It was so romantic and beautiful. He tells me to lie down on the bed and by the time he comes back I better be butt ass naked."

There it goes getting hot again.

JEAN: "La, is your air on, it's hot as fuck."

LALA: "Nah don't blame my air, that lil monkey between your legs getting *hot*. When was the last time you got your walls beat?"

I rolled my eyes.

JEAN: "Whatever. Where is your fan?"

TIFFANY: "You might need some water, because clearly your pussy draining it all."

JEAN: "Just finish the damn story."

I sat the phone down on the living room table and ran to the bedroom to grab the fan. It *had* been a minute since I had sex. Nobody does me the way Ray does, and he was all I craved.

TIFFANY: "...I just wanted to freshen up a little. My little twat was *hot*. I ran to the bathroom like I had to pee. I come out and head back to the bedroom, this nigga had whip cream and ice. When I tell you, I got weak in the knees, I ain't lying. He motioned for me to come sit on his lap, so I did. We start kissing while he is working his fingers down my back, trying to unclip my bra. He took a piece of ice and started sucking on my neck, and then flipped me over to where I was laying on my back. Tony has never done no shit like that."

LALA: "Now I'm getting hot."

JEAN: "Nah, that's that lil puss between them thick ass thighs of yours."

LALA: "And your point? Wade cools it off. Who cools down yours? Ray?" then took a sip of her Stella Rose.

TIFFANY: "YOU TOLD HER ABOUT YOU AND RAY?"

I wanted to throw the phone against the wall. LaLa sat her glass down on the table. I thought she had damn near broke the glass.

LALA: "So you tell Tiff and not me? What kind of shit is that?"

She got up from the couch and folded her arms, almost knocking over her glass of wine. I am fairly sure she didn't care. All I was thinking was, 'damn, why did I have to say anything to anybody?' It was just Ray, God, and I who knew, and I should have left it like that. I was just to a point feeling guilty, like I had done something wrong, but it felt so right, it felt so good to have him between my legs. Every thrust he gave me, every inch filling my body with greatness. It felt like it was meant to be, and I wanted more.

JEAN: "You talk entirely too much shit and can never hold water."

LALA: "I'm over this friendship at this point." She grabbed her glass of wine, finished it off, and then walked to the kitchen to get something stronger... that Hennessey. She gulped the first glass down, and then fixed an Incredible Hulk, which is Hennessy and Hypnotic.

TIFFANY: "That's exactly why she didn't tell you. Stop being so dramatic all the time. All of that pussy cooling Wade doing is throwing you off."

   We all burst out laughing to where we were crying. La walked back over to the couch and sat down, while offering me a sip of her drink. The Incredible Hulk is one of my favorite drinks, so of course I took a big ass sip.

LALA: "Dayum!" I handed her back the drink as it was dripping down my chin.

TIFFANY: "Okay y'all, so he pulls my pants off. I had just gotten a wax a couple days ago, so that pussy was bare."

LALA: Did it stank?"

TIFFANY: "Bitch don't play with me."

This is why I love my girls, no matter what situation we were in, we always laughed together. Tiff talked about how his tongue felt on her clit, how he was bigger than Tony, even how his strokes were better. She talked about how his dick game was so good; he made her cum six times that night, and twice with his mouth. She was screaming *daddy* and *Key* all night. The neighbors started beating on the wall because they were so loud. I was jealous and in need of some TLC. A couple of licks from La did not sound so bad after all. I wanted to call Ray but decided to call Trey. He was no Ray, but he got the job done... at least he would have to because my pride just wouldn't allow me to call Ray.

JEAN: "Where you at?"

TREY: "Home, wassup?"

JEAN: "Pull up, I'm horny."

TREY: "Damn, just like that?"

JEAN: "Is that a no?"

I was not trying to be rude or anything but all I wanted from him were his jewels. My hormones were acting up, and I was tired of using my vibrator.

TREY: "...I'm on my way..."

Thirty minutes later, I hear him knocking...

Chapter Eight

I Miss You Pooh

I was still waiting on Ray to tell me why he had gone M.I.A on me, and looks like he did it again. I have not heard from him since he left La's house after Keyvaune left with Pete. I was not about to stress myself out behind him. If he did not want to talk about it, cool, I see where our friendship is going.

Trey was trash. He started doing too much, like he was trying to tease me, and I was in no mood to be teased. I ended up kicking him out in the middle of us fucking; he did not even get the chance to stick it in, playing too much. After he had left, I changed my batteries for my butterfly vibrator since the other ones stopped working. That is how I know I masturbated too much; I had damn near used all of the batteries... I had fallen fast asleep after pleasing myself, making me cum three times.

The next morning, I was just finishing up some work on my business layout, when I received a call from an unknown number. Looking at the phone, I just let it ring, and got back to work. My stomach began to growl, and I felt my head starting to hurt. La had made some fried fish, salad, and corn, and I still had a plate left over, so that is how I fueled myself up, as well as a tall glass of wine.

The unknown number had called me back, and I let it ring again. As you can see, I got it bad not answering the phone. 'Whoever it is can leave a message,' I said aloud.

That is exactly what they did, left a message. Unlocking my phone, I checked my voicemail.

UNKNOWN NUMBER: *"Hey Jean, this Amar. I got your number from a friend and was calling to check up on you. Is there any way we can meet up? I miss you Pooh."*

My appetite had officially been lost. I did not know what to do. All these questions ran through my head, why is he calling me, who gave him my number, what could he possibly want? When I saw him a few weeks back, I had hoped I never saw him again. This man needs to leave me the hell alone. I blocked the number, deleted the contact from my call log, and deleted the voice mail. Not even ten minutes later, another unknown number was calling. I assumed it was Amar calling from somebody else phone. He had it bad doing that.

Later that day, I popped up at La house to see if she was okay, even though the hoe said she was fake crying about Tony getting shot. Tony is not my business, La is. Before knocking, I had heard a loud bang, and a scream from La's next-door neighbor. It startled me a bit, so I decided to knock on his door. Next thing I know...

NEIGHBOR: "Who is it?"

JEAN: "My name is Jean. I heard someone screaming.

A few moments later, he opens the door, and my mouth dropped to the ground. I just could not believe my eyes. It was Amar's cousin Benny.

BENNY: "Jeeeeaaaaaannnnn." He had open arms. I had no beef with Benny, so why not hug him.

JEAN: "Beeennnyyyy." There was absolutely no enthusiasm in my voice whatsoever. His facial expression showed how upset he was in my response. We had separated from the hug, and he just smiled at me. "So how have you been? You're okay; I mean the loud bang I heard."

BENNY: "Oh yea, I accidentally tripped over the coffee table. I am watching one of my favorite movies, '*Love and Basketball.*' I had got a little distracted when I saw Sanaa Lathan fine ass when she was losing her virginity." He was rubbing his hands together like Bird Man, while licking his lips.

JEAN: "Oh cool. That scream sounded a little high pitched. Your pinky corn alright?"

BENNY: "Do you really want to go there? I was just on the phone with Amar, how about I invite him over for you. Maybe you guys can rekindle the love."

JEAN: "I will beat your ass AND Amar's. Do *not* play with me, Benny. You already know how I feel about him, and for you to be funny like that. I should beat your ass for the hell of it."

BENNY: "Chill out. You know I don't mean no harm."

JEAN: "Yeah, okay. You already know wassup, don't play." He had reached to give me a hug, but I backed away. "Nah, you good Lil fella."

BENNY: "You ain't even got to be like that. I thought we were better than that." Benny folded his arms and pouted like a kid. I did not care whatsoever. "What are you doing this away?"

JEAN: "Business" and rolled my eyes.

BENNY: "Your man live over here?"

JEAN: "I said what I said, *business*."

BENNY: "iight."

He Made this grin like he was up to something, and knowing him, he just might. Lord only knows I do not want Amar to know where I am at, where I have been, or none of that. The whole family sneaky. I had a gut feeling, and it was not a good one. I brushed it off though.

BENNY: "What you have planned for today? I am hooking up with some friends later for some drinks. You're more than welcomed to come." I glared at him.

JEAN: "Will Amar be there?"

BENNY: "Now why I invite you if he was coming through?"

JEAN: "Cause you trifling just like him."

BENNY: "Awe that hurts my feelings." His fake ass pouting, and my eyes rolled.

JEAN: "You full of it just like him."

BENNY: "Damn, that's how you feel? After all we have been through, this how you do me?"

JEAN: "Stop being dramatic boy. Just like your cousin, Amar.

BENNY: "Nah, that's where you got me fucked up."

JEAN: "I said what I said." –

BENNY: "Oh I see you *roughish* since you and Amar broken up."

JEAN: "I've been this way; your cousin just may have brought it out more."

BENNY: "Well excuse me, madam," and held his hands up for surrender.

JEAN: "Yeah, quit playing with me, for I send somebody over here to beat your ass. Remember that I know where you live."

He moved closer to my face...

BENNY: "And you remember I know; somebody you know lives next door."

I was tired of talking to him at that point.

JEAN: "I'm going to let you go about your day. You bet not tell your cousin you saw me, or that is your ass. I promise!"

BENNY: "Don't you threaten me."

JEAN: "It's not a threat if I said I promise. Remember that."

BENNY: "I'm sick of your shit."

I waved him off, and waited until he closed, and locked his door before knocking on La's door. I cannot lie; I was starting to freak out a little. Why this bitch had to stay right next door to my ex, cousin. I knocked on La but she didn't answer the first time, so I decided to knock again. There was still no answer from her. I stared to get worried. She knew I was coming over, so I decided to call her...

LALA: "Hello..." In her sleep voice.

JEAN: "Bitch, get your ass up, and open the door, I'm outside."

LALA: "Oh shit, I didn't hear my alarm."

JEAN: "Bet your mouth was open, drooling nshit. Hurry up before Benny see me again."

LALA: "Benny, Amar cousin?"

JEAN: "YESSS!!! OPEN THE DOOR!" And just as when I hung up, Benny opened his front door.

BENNY: "What you still standing outside for? Awe, your little boyfriend not answering the door for you?"

JEAN: "Go fuck yourself."

BENNY: "Temper. Temper."

I was really hoping La took a little longer to open the door so Benny would not see her, and what I was doing. He just stood there, watching me.

JEAN: "Bruh, tear your ass." He smiled and winked at me.

BENNY: "I got something for you." He finally closed the door, and just when he did, La opened hers. Thank God. I wasted no time walking in her apartment and headed straight for the kitchen to fix me a drink.

LALA: "Are you okay?"

JEAN: "No. I'm pissed. Benny saw me, and you took forever to open the door."

LALA: "Damn, excuse the fuck out of me. I apologize for being sleep."

JEAN: "Ugh, it's cool... I'm worried though."

LALA: "About what?"

JEAN: "Benny being childish and telling Amar that he saw me."

LALA: "You really think Benny would tell him?"

JEAN: "That's his cousin, and they all are messy, so why not?"

LALA: "So what you trying to do?"

JEAN: "I just need to stay low for right now."

I took a sip of my drink, and just hoped that Benny did not tell Amar. There was a knot in my stomach, so I had a feeling that Benny would.

-Next Door at Benny's

BENNY: "Ayo, guess who I just seen."

AMAR: "Who? And you bet not say Trish hoe ass."

BENNY: "Nahh baby boy…. Jean."

AMAR: "I just called her the other day, from two different numbers. I think she blocked me. Where you see her at?"

Benny: "By my crib."

AMAR: "Say no more. I'm on my way." Click.

-Back at LaLa

When Amar and I were together, Benny was always around us when we fought. I am quite sure he heard about the last fight Amar and I had with his cousin.

LALA: "Have you heard from Ray? Why he went M.I.A?"

JEAN: "Nope. He was in the midst of telling me, but then you and Tiffany was calling me about Tony."

LALA: "Damn, it must be that bad." I was taking a sip of my drink, and just glared at her. "What, damn. I'm just saying."

JEAN: "Words of encouragement would be great right now, La."

LALA: "Your hair looks nice like that."

 I wanted to punch the shit out of her. My phone rang, and it was the unknown number again... Amar. I started to panic. How did this nigga get my number?

LALA: "You good?"

JEAN: "Some unknown number keeps calling me. The first time it was Amar, and I'm pretty sure it's him still calling."

LALA: "This nigga tripping big time. How did he even get your number?"

JEAN: "*THAT'S THE THING*... I do not know. Couldn't be Benny; Amar was texting and calling before I saw him."

LALA: "Who else do you know that might give him your number?" I tried to think but nobody was coming to mind.

JEAN: "I don't know, La."

 We sat for a few minutes, while she was next to me, getting drunk. The number called again and La snatched the phone out of my hand and answered it...

LALA: "Who the fuck is this and why the fuck you keep calling?"

AMAR: "Bitch you see..."

LALA: "*Bitch?* Bitch I will send some niggas to come jump your monkey, countertop head ass. Do not play with me because you know how I'm coming, hoe. I'll come beat your ass myself."

AMAR: "Bitch fuck you. Put Jean on the phone."

LALA: "She aint here hoe, and the next time you call her phone again, I'm going to pull up on yo ass, and shoot you. You fucking lunatic. *THIS GIRL DOES NOT WANT YOU NO MORE!* Move the fuck on and stop being a bug-a-boo before shit gets crazy."

AMAR: "I'll get my cou…"

Click! Just like that, she hung up in his face, and blocked his number.

Chapter Nine

LALA: "If that calls you again, you better tell me."

JEAN: "What you trying to do, La?"

LALA: "I said what I said, if he calls again, you better let me know." I was not about to argue with her, whatever was for Amar, was coming. We sat and talked for a while, and I thought to call up Tiff to have her come through, but then I remembered she was meeting a 'friend.'

JEAN: "Did Tiffany ever tell you about some chick named, Monika?"

LALA: "No. Who is that?"

JEAN: "I want her to tell you."

LALA: "Why you even mention it then?"

JEAN: "Because I wanted to, dammit."

LALA: "Just tell me."

I got up from the couch and headed to the kitchen to fix me a plate of the nachos La made, and a cup of ice tea.

JEAN: "No!"

LALA: "First you tell Tiffany about you and Ray, and not me; now you don't tell me wassup with this Monika chick."

JEAN: "Can you just understand, maybe sometimes people don't want to tell you anything because you can't hold water." She turned to me; mouth dropped.

LALA: "I can't believe this. Y'all really are holding back from me. We are supposed to be friends, more like sisters, and y'all just keeping shit from me. What's the point?"

JEAN: "You really about to determine our friendship based off from two things both Tiff and I decided to keep between us? Get over yourself La." There was a knock at the door that startled us both. "Are you expecting someone?" She shook her head no, and I just stood mouth full in the kitchen. "This is your house, you get it."

Whoever was at the door knocked again...

LALA: "Who is it?" No answer, but another knock. La stood up and walked to the door and looked through the peep hole.

LALA: "Get my gun!"

JEAN: "The fuck, for what?"

LALA: "It's Amar..."

JEAN: "Are you serious?" I sat my plate on the kitchen counter and walked towards the front door. I motioned for La to scoot over so I could look through the peep hole. With my own eyes, I saw Amar and Benny. He knocked again, and I just looked at them. I wanted to strangle Benny; why would he bring him here? La had turned and walked away toward her bedroom. "Where are you going?"

BENNY: "I know you in there; open the door Jean, let's talk."

AMAR: "Yeah, open up Pooh."

LALA: "I'm getting what I told you to get… my gun." She turned back and kept walking.

JEAN: "So you're going to shoot them both; in the daylight?" They knocked again…

LALA: "I want them Motherfuckas away from my door… NOW!"

I turned between La and the door.

JEAN: "What you going to do? Shoot them?" She turned back to me just before going in her bedroom…

LALA: "I might!"

La waved me away and walked into her bedroom. *Knock. Knock. Knock.*

AMAR: "Come on, Pooh, open up. I know you miss me; I miss you too. Let us talk."

I looked through the peep hole and saw both Benny and Amar laughing at each other. Then here comes La with this 9mm and a 22.

LALA: "I got one for one bitch, and another for the other bitch." She held both guns in her hand like she was advertising which she was going to use on Benny and Amar. She walked close to the door, and I moved to the side. "If you motherfuckas don't move away from my door, I'm going to bust a cap in *both* of y'all asses."

La had put emphasis on both, so they would know she was serious.

BENNY: "Awe, La we're neighbors. What a coincidence."

She opened the door and both Benny and Amar's mouth drop, while motioning to holding their hands up. LaLa pointed one gun directly at Benny's head, and the other at Amar's head. Benny began to step back towards his apartment; the door was wide open. Amar dropped his hands and just stood there. The gun La had held up to Benny's head was now alongside of the gun she had for Amar. This nigga started smirking.

AMAR: "You're going to shoot me La?" His smile got bigger... arrogant ass.

LALA: "If you don't step your ass back into your cousin's apartment and leave my girl the fuck alone... yes I will. The first time I might go easy on you by shooting your foot. After that, and you still fucking with her or myself, it is up in the air for you buddy. Now step the fuck back from my house or lose a few toes." She shrugged... "Makes me no difference." Then she smirked right back at him. Benny was already inside of his house.

BENNY: "Aye man, it's not worth it. She does not want you no more. Let it go and come on." Amar sucked his teeth and shrugged.

AMAR: "I'll let you have it this time." He started to step back into Benny's apartment. He saw me and we made eye contact, and then blew me a kiss. I wanted to grab the pistol and shoot his ass myself. He winked at La... "aight. Ima fuck with you La." La dropped one gun, but still held the 22 to Amar's head as he backed away.

LALA: "Don't purchase any more shoes then." She blew him a kiss back then started backing into her crib. Once Benny closed his door and locked it, La did the same. Oh, she was heated... "The *NERVE* of this nigga to approach my mothafucking door."

She slammed both guns on the kitchen table. My ass jumped; I thought the hoe went off. She started pacing, and when she does that, it scares me. Like what is she really thinking, what does she have planned and up her sleeve? You can never really doubt La, and that is a fact. I sat on the couch trying to find the words to say thank you to La while she is still pacing in the kitchen.

JEAN: "You good, La?" She stopped pacing and made this face I do not think I have ever seen her make.

LALA: "I need a drink. I am alright, are you alright? Them niggas got me a little off and I just want to go next door and shoot Amar just for the hell of it."

JEAN: "Thank you for real La. You don't know how much I appreciate what you just did for me."

LALA: "This is why we're friends; you're like a little big sister to me. Trina and Jewels would have gone to war behind you. Jewels probably would have just shot him without warning. I spared him some when I should have pulled the trigger."

Trina and Jewels is La's older sisters, and I can vouch that if either one of them were here, Amar's toes would be detached from his foot. We both paused and then burst out laughing because she is right. Trina is a little more hardcore than La and Jewels but regardless of the situation, Amar would have been missing a few toes if they were here.

Next Door at Benny's – AMAR's SIDE

AMAR: "I can't believe that shit happened. You think La would have really shot me?"

He looked at me like, 'nigga really?'

BENNY: "No doubt about it she would have shot you. Did you forget who her sisters are? They all with the shits."

AMAR: "Ima get her back; I got to. She was the best thing that ever happened to me and I threw it all away for some hoe that can't keep her legs closed." Benny walked over to the living room table and grabbed the remote to turn on the television.

BENNY: "Ain't that the same thing you did to Jean? You could not keep your dick in your pants and on top of that, you had a baby on her. You know damn well that girl over you and she's not coming back."

I gave this nigga the finger, but a part of me knew he was right. I did a lot of fucked up shit to Jean while she was being faithful to me the entire time. Even after she found out I got Trish pregnant.

I regret so many times for hurting Jean. When a nigga was down and out, she was there for me. I just had to go off and fucked it up with Trish. Like Jamie Foxx say, *'blame in on the Vodka, blame it on the Henny.'* That night I met Trish, Jean and I had gotten in an argument over a post she saw on Facebook. I ain't gone lie, I probably should not have said the girl was looking sexy in her picture she posted. That was a bit disrespectful. Shit, I did not think she would see it; she was not supposed to see it. The girls' page was private; I did not know La was a mutual friend with the bitch. I was all up on that girl page, liking, loving, and commenting. It was just a social media thing to me, I love Jean. Then here comes La sending Jean all these screenshots of me commenting on pictures and shit. I know if it was Jean loving, and commenting on a post, I would get fed up with the shit too. A 'sorry' just did not fix it for me; she kept saying she was done with me.

That night I went out with the boys to get my mind off the whole fiasco. That is where I met Trish. She was looking bad too. I was out with a bunch of single niggas, so that made me feel even more single. Trish kept looking at me, dancing all sexual on the dance floor. Mind you I was throwing back shots of vodka and henny; shots were 2 for $1 that night, *AND* it was payday. My homie Big boy was all in my ear, 'go fuck with her bro, you single.' I knew Jean and I would make it right, but a part of me felt like that was it for us.

Trish walked over to where we were sitting at the bar and offered to buy me a drink, I took up the offer. We were feeling each other, and the physical attraction was there; the vibes she was giving me was, 'I'm DTF.' We took our chemistry to the dance floor; she is grinding all up on me, then *BOOM*; "Do you got a girlfriend?" Why the hell I tell her no? I did not care what happened between Jean and me, she would forever be my girlfriend in my head.

Trish and I still dancing on each other, she is dropping it low, picking it back up, all that good shit. In my head I am like, 'oh yeah, we got to smash tonight.' At that point I was ready to go and drop dick off in shawty. So, I asked her was she trying to get a room, she like, 'awe I came with my girls.' Bitch stop playing and let me dick you down.
I should have just said some understanding shit, left it alone and went home to my baby Jean. But nah, I had to convince her to let me fuck. That is all what it was to me, a little fuck. I was not trying to be in no relationship with her, I just wanted to fuck. She ended up telling her girls she was riding with me, and I told Big boy that I was about to head out with shawty. That is where I know I fucked up at, he dapped me up, handed me a condom and gave me this grin. Trish and I walked out together and found the closest hotel to the club. You most definitely got what you paid for. The room smelled like nut and cigarettes.

She lit up a blunt, took a couple puffs and handed it to me. While I had the blunt to my lips, she starts unbuckling my pants and pulled out my dick. My shit was semi hard because I was ready to push that size 10 up in her stomach. She starts giving me head, it was alright but Jean's way better. She was doing twist and turns, could not deep throat it all, barely could fit half in her mouth. That was starting to piss me off. I spent money on this room, and you cannot even give proper head. I told her to just stop, and she moved to the bed and slipped her panties off. She had on this skirt, and just slid those bitches off. She started opening her legs and playing with her pussy; that was kind of sexy.

This is the part that threw me off a little, 'come eat it daddy.' Huh? Eat what? She had me fucked up.

TRISH: "So I give you head, and you can't return the favor?"

AMAR: "Go wash your pussy girl." She gets up and heads to the bathroom to take a shower. I finished off the blunt by the time she was done. I told her to come lie on the bed but before she did, she lit another blunt. I start eating her pussy... I just breathe on it and she starts moaning, girl calm down. I have dreads and I love when Jean play in them while I am eating her pussy, so Trish starts playing in my dreads, moaning loud and shit. I ain't gone lie, she moans sexy as hell and it was making my dick hard.

I was ready to throw dick at that point. I stopped eating her pussy and got my dick wet by spitting on it. I first put the head in, and she does the Love and Basketball gasps that Sanaa Lathan did when Omar Epps was putting it down. She had some pussy, but it was not Jean pussy. At that point, I just started fucking to get a nut. It was good, but not I need to moan loud good. She nutted about four times before I finally got one. Trish walked to the bathroom to clean up, while I sat on the bed smoking a blunt. I checked my phone to see if Jean had texted or called me, and nothing. Trish walked out and I walked in the bathroom to freshen up.

She wanted more; I had the energy to give it to her, so we ended up fucking again. This time it was a little better. She got on top and was riding dick like a champ, trying to take every inch in. I was not knocking her game, take that dick baby. Yeah, she was baby then because she was riding my dick like it was hers and the shit felt good. Trish got a fat ass, and it was shaking like Jell-O in my face. A couple more bounces and I nutted. She gets up, walks to the bathroom to pee and freshen up. I am still lying down on the bed, and looked at my dick covered in cum; but I saw no condom...

AMAR: "Aye, where the condom?"

TRISH: "It's Trish, not aye and I don't know, you the one who put it on."

Damn shame I just fucked the bitch and did not even know her name.

AMAR: "I ain't put no condom on..." She snapped her neck at me.

TRISH: "So you mean to tell me we just fucked raw and you nutted in me? Are you fucking serious?" She starts to panic, and that shit gets me going. I got a whole girlfriend at home and just fucked some random hoe raw... "Are you clean?"

AMAR: "...am I clean? Bitch are you clean? My girl gone be pissed." I put my head in my hands and started praying.

TRISH: "Your *girl?* You told me you were single, and you got one more time to call me a bitch or that's your ass." I am just fucking this all up. A one-night stand is about to turn into a lifetime with this hoe. "HELLO! You told me you didn't have a girlfriend." I looked up at her with regret in my eyes.

AMAR: "I lied dammit." I picked my pants up off the floor, check my pants pocket, and pulled out the condom Big boy gave me. How the fuck did I let this happen? So that means I fucked her raw the first time too. Luckily, I pulled out then, but she was taking charge this time and it was on her to get the fuck up when I said 'I'm finna nut.' In the back of my mind, I did not care too much because I thought she slipped on the condom.

TRISH: "Take me home my nigga, ain't shit ass bitch. Let me get pregnant, that's it for you hoe." I knew she was right, let her get pregnant, Jean and I would be over with for real.

AMAR: "Listen, I don't want no beef with you, we can just keep this between us. If you happen to get pregnant, we can figure out options to take."

TRISH: "I hope you're not talking about abortion..."

AMAR: "So you plan to keep a baby by a nigga you don't even know?" I wanted to slap the shit out of her at that point. This bitch has got to be crazy.

TRISH: "By a nigga I *thought* was single. So, I have to abort my baby because you chose to lie?"

AMAR: "We're not in a relationship; what the fuck are you talking about? We are two random ass people who were trying to get a nut in." She has to be crazy to want to keep a baby by someone who clearly does not want a child by her.

TRISH: "Nah bitch, *you* were tr..."

AMAR: "You got one more time to call me a bitch."

TRISH: "What you going to do? I was raised around three older brothers, I used to fight almost every day, nigga I will beat your ass."

Shit made my dick jump...

AMAR: "Look, I apologize. Let us exchange numbers, if anything happens, and I do mean if you end up being pregnant..." I took a pause and said a little prayer. "...hit me up." She stood by the TV, arms folded, clearly pissed.

Chapter Ten

TRISH: "You just don't want your girlfriend to find out that you cheated on her."

AMAR: "That too... can you just keep me posted if something happens?" She started getting dressed.

TRISH: "Can you take me home?" She was already at the door before I could answer.

AMAR: "So we're not going to exchange numbers?"

TRISH: "Can you take me home?"

I ain't going to lie, I felt a little bad. I just did not know this would happen. I began getting dressed, reached for my car keys on the table; Trish had already walked outside and was heading to the car before I could get to the room door. It was silencing the whole drive to her house, I tried talking to her, but she kept ignoring me.

AMAR: "Are we going to exchange numbers?" She gave me this evil eye and started reading off her number. I probably just ruined this girl's life, and I know I for a fact fucked up with Jean... got damn me. Jean never found out, and we were back trying to work things out the next day. Two weeks later, Trish hit me up, telling me that she had missed her period, and was scared to take the pregnancy test by herself. Just when I thought everything between Jean and I was going well and we were going to actually make things work, Trish hit me with this. I had to make something up quick to get me away from Jean, so I could see what Trish was on. Once I get to her, she is crying, and I do mean balling out crying; shit almost made me cry. I tried calming her down, and have her take the test... two minutes later; I am a daddy... I was not going to make her get an abortion, but I did not want Jean to find out until I was ready to tell her, which didn't last long.

Trish and I got into it because she wanted a relationship, and I did not. I was still with Jean, trying to work things out with her. I was in love with Jean, and just wanted to be with her. Trish was not trying to understand that whatsoever. She ended up popping up at Jean's job with a pregnancy test in hand, telling her the baby is mine. That same night was the first night that me and Jean had a physical fight. I ain't gone lie, she lowkey beat my ass. I had no intentions of hurting Jean, and really did want us to last forever. I wanted to put a ring on this girl finger and give her all the kids that she wanted. Trish thought that just because Jean and I did not work out after she found out about the baby, I would automatically be with her. Aht, aht, aht.

The night after Trish and I smashed, I went back home to Jean and we had made love. That is when Jean had found out that she was pregnant with my child too. I was about to be a daddy... twice. Even though Jean and I were not together when she found out that she was pregnant, I was still going to every doctor's appointment, as well as with Trish. Trish started dating some other nigga, while I was trying to work things out with Jean. It took about a month or two for us to finally get things back on track. Jean hated me even though I had done everything in the book to get back right with her. When Jean found out I smashed both her and Trish in the same night, she immediately made an appointment at the clinic. Luckily, she did not have anything. Till this day, I regret fucking with Trish. If I had kept my dick in my pants, Jean and I would still be together, with our twins.

BENNY: "You good bro?"

I had blacked out thinking about Jean.

AMAR: "Yeah."

BENNY: "You trying to play 2K?"

AMAR: "Yeah." Sad as shit, I walked over to the couch and grabbed the other remote. Damn, I miss Jean.

Oooweeeeee

Tiffany, LaLa, and I had scheduled a girl's days out at Elite Nails, and I was delighted. I have not seen La since the last time I was at her apartment when Amar and Benny showed up. Ever since Tiffany and Keyvaune hit it off, she had been M.I.A herself. So, this day was well needed. We all met up at the nail salon at the same time, damn near all dressed the same; muscle shirt and jeans, La had on jean shorts though. This was our regular spot, as soon as we walked in...

LING: "Awee La, Jean, and Tiffany. Long time no see. Where you three been?"

TIFFANY: "Busy." Ling looked at Tiff blushing.

LING: "You got man now?"

TIFFANY: "Not too much Ling, and I got something."

LING: "Oooo. So, you need long nail, glow in the dark. Pick a color." We all burst out laughing. "You want Pedicure too?"

TIFFANY: "I want the whole works!" Ling motioned for her to sit at her station while La and I walked over to pick our color. "I need a cut down too Ling, you know wassup."

   We had got at the nail shop pretty early and it was only a few other ladies in there. Bo walked over to where La and I was sitting.

BO: "What can I do for you ladies today?"

LA: "I want a medi and pedi, and I need these brows done." She rubbed across her eyebrows and Bo covered his mouth in awe.

BO: "You need done now." La's mouth dropped to the floor. It has been a minute since we have been to the nail shop with all of this drama going on. Ling and Bo were never the ones to sugar coat with us, and that is one of the reasons why we loved going to Elite Nails. They had good nail techs, but we preferred Ling and Bo. Shin walked over and motioned for me to come to the pedi section. My toenails had grown so long it was ridiculous. La was so damn ghetto, yelling from across the room.

LALA: "So Tiff, did Jean tell you what happened at my house the other day?" Tiff raised her head up and looked over at me. I ducked down so she could not see me.

TIFFANY: "What happened?" Then here comes Ling putting her two cents in...

LING: "What happened girl?" We all burst out laughing.

BO: "Ling, get out they business." We all loved coming here! Besides them doing A1 nails, they always had us cracking up.

LING: "You worry about yourself and mind your business." Bo rolled his eyes at Ling and started back doing La's nail. He was clearly talking shit under his breath and said something to La to make her burst out laughing. "What's funny? I know he said some shit." Ling started talking in her language so we could not understand them two going at it.

TIFFANY: "La, what happened?"

JEAN: "Nothing!" I know it was the nail shop, but I was not about to blurt out my business way across the room so the other two ladies could hear. Who knows, they could probably help with some advice.

LALA: "Amar came to my house with Benny."

TIFFANY: "Shut the fuck up!" Tiff had jumped a little and Ling slapped her hand.

LING: "You stay still ma'am."

TIFFANY: "Excuse me." Ling got back to doing Tiff's nails, and then looked over at me.

LING: "Who is Amar?"

LALA: "Jean's ex." The whole nail shop gasped, especially Tiff and Ling. By my surprise Bo even chimed in with a gasp.

JEAN: "Can you shut the fuck up?" Ling had turned to Jean with her eyes wide as day.

BO: "Did you let him in?" We all turned to Bo and burst out laughing.

LING: "Get out they business."

BO: "Hush up." Both Ling and Bo started going back and forth, speaking their language, while Tiff, La and I were laughing. Their little arguments were so cute. They would be mad at each other for a few minutes then back to loving and caring for another.

Shin had finished on my feet and walked me to Ling so she could start my nails. Between us three, LaLa is about the only one who can sit through a nail session with Bo. He was a little rough with Tiff and me. Every now and again, you would hear La, 'Aight now, Bo.' Tiffany and I would make eye contact and start laughing. Bo was a little rough, but he got the job done.

While Tiffany was washing her hands off from the excess acrylic, Bo was finishing up La's set so she could wash her hands. Shin was starting on Tiff's toes and Ling was doing her thing with my nails. There was a new nail technician who was walking around offering drinks to the ladies. Some were alcoholic and some not. Tiffany loves her some wine, so she took her a glass and a bottled water. La is hardcore, she was trying to get something a little stronger than wine. Elite nails have a whole bar inside as well as a kid's section for them to play while mothers get pampered. With the hard liquor, they limit it to three shots or margaritas, as far as wine; you can get up to seven glasses. I usually get wine but decided on a margarita. Once we all were served with a drink, the nail techs were doing their thing.

TIFFANY: "Jean, have you heard from Ray?"

JEAN: "Nope, not all."

LALA: "Speaking of which, I feel like I deserve to know what happened between you and him after what happened at my house the other day."

TIFFANY: "I'm still trying to figure out what happened at your house."

BO: "Me too." The whole nail shop started laughing.

It was a whole rotation going on in the nail salon. Bo was finishing up on La's nails, Shin was finishing up on Tiff's feet, while Ling was finishing the first part for my nails. I was getting up to wash my hands of the excess acrylic, wobbling like a penguin with the slides that Shin provided. My toes were about dry, so I was able to put my own sandals on. Shin had started doing La's feet, while Ari was starting on Tiffany's eyebrows. As I was walking back to Ling's section, Bo called me over to him; Ling just glared at him. I leaned down to him...

BO: "What happened with your ex?"

JEAN: "Really?" I started walking away when he called for me to come back. "He just popped up at La's house trying to get back with me." The other lady that Bo was working on for a new set looked up at me.

LADY: "Are you going to take him back?" Bo was looking at me; the lady was looking at me, like damn.

JEAN: "If you knew all of the things he had done to me while we were together, you would think I'm stupid as hell to take him back. So, to answer your question, N-O-P-E... No!" I simply walked away, and sat back in front of Ling.

LADY: "That's a good girl. Know your worth honey. I can go on and on about what I went through with my last husband. All the fights, arguments, cheating, and so much more with him. Get out of it before it is too late. There is someone out there for you, just wait on it. Now look at me, happily engaged to my future wife."

In my head, I am thinking, 'wife, huh?' I don't know her, but if that woman makes her happy, go for it. Tiffany started acting a bit strange after the lady said something about her future wife, but I didn't pay much attention to it.

After we were done getting our nails done and brows, we paid and even tipped Shin, Ling, Ari and Bo. Us three had been coming to Elite Nails for years and felt like we were a part of their family. Before leaving the building, La pissy ass ran to the bathroom. Tiffany and I were sitting at the front waiting for her to come back. Ling and Bo hugged us all and we headed out. Everyone had drove their own cars, but Tiffany had this bright idea to drop both La and my car off at her house and we ride with her. I was all down for saving gas, so I was willing to ride. Trailing us both to her house was interesting. Someone always got stopped at a light or another car jumped in front. Tiffany wanted to splurge off her new Chevy Cruz, had it smelling brand new. I sat in the front while La was in the back.

LALA: "I'm still waiting on Jean to tell me about her freak show with Ray." We were at a stop light, so I turned the radio up on her. "Bitch you are rude." I surely did not give one or two fucks.

TIFFANY: "You? Shit, I'm still waiting to hear what happened when Amar pulled up on y'all."

LALA: "Bitch I was ready to shoot his monkey ass for sure." We all burst out laughing and Tiff vouched for me that if LaLa sister Trina or Jewels were there, Amar would have got shot. I am dealing with some rough riders, and it was cool with me because I knew they would always have my back. While driving to our favorite restaurant spot, La kept asking about Ray and me; Tiffany kept asking what happened when Amar pulled up. At that point, I just wanted food in my belly and a drink; maybe a few.

When we finally made it to the restaurant, *Peco*, I saw Trey with some chick. He had looked directly at me and I simply smiled. I could tell the girl he was with did not like me smiling at him whatsoever.

She immediately started going at his throat. I could hear her from afar; "Why you smiling and waving at bitches? That is what you want? Go get her." Nah baby, you keep your man on a leash because I sure as hell do not want him. The waiter brought us to our table, sitting directly behind Trey and his chick. La asked for us to be moved and the waiter did just that. The female Trey was with looked a bit familiar, but I did not care enough to figure out who she is. All I know is shawty rolled her big ass eyes at me and I simply smiled at her and blew Trey a kiss. She did not like that, started another argument.

Once we got to our new table, the waiter provided us with menus, and asked if we wanted to start with an appetizer and drinks. We all tried speaking at once, ready for some liquor. Peco was one of the top hot Mexican spots in the city. They were best known for their food and drinks, and the prices were very reasonable.

You can come in with only 30$, get you a meal, dessert and a few drinks. I ordered enchiladas, La got a taco meal and Tiff had quesadillas. Our drinks came out before our meals, right along with the chips and salsa. Tiff and I enjoy us some guacamole, so we ordered a side of that. Their margaritas are our favorite; you could actually taste the alcohol in them instead of just juice or water like most restaurants. Then here come La...

LALA: "These margaritas ain't got *nothing* on mine." She was right. Her Pineapple, strawberry margarita be hitting. "So, Jean, are you finally going to tell me about you and

Ray?" I took a big ass gulp of my drink, ready for another. I was not trying to talk about Ray. I have not heard from him, and he was back dodging me. Just when I thought after that night we made love, that our relationship would be stronger. Boy did I play myself.

TIFFANY: "Can somebody tell me about when Amar pulled up?"

LALA: "That's nothing compared to her and Ray," with a whole chip and salsa in her mouth.

TIFFANY: "How it's not? You were talking about shooting his damn foot off."

LALA: "You tell me what happened with her and Ray, I'll tell you what happened with Amar."

TIFFANY: "Bet, you first though." I glared Tiffany down like a hawk in the sky. "Why are you looking at me like that?"

JEAN: "So both you bitches just gone spread my business around like that?"

LALA: "At least we're doing it in your face and not behind your back."

JEAN: *"THERE'S NO DIFFERENCE."*

TIFFANY: "Whoa, okay you need to calm down Sus. We are in a public setting, don't loud talk."

JEAN: "Don't tell me how to speak. You're not my damn mother." Both La and Tiff's mouth drop.

LALA: "What is up with you, girl? Like seriously, you have been off the edge lately. Spill the tea, wassup?" The drink was not helping, only making matters worse. I just kept thinking about Ray and why he diss me again. I took a deep breath, sighed and the tears started flowing. I was sitting next to Tiffany and she immediately started to comfort me. La reached her hand across from the table to move my drink from in front of me and caressed my arms.

TIFFANY: "Girl what's wrong? Talk to us, Jae."

JEAN: "I'm just so emotional right now. Ray has been M.I.A again, then the whole Amar thing, popping up at La's. This is too much for me right now. I am trying to focus on my business and get that up off the floor. That is hard to do when you keep thinking about why this man that says he loves you keeps dissing and going M.I.A on you, or how my job did not give my raise like they were supposed to. We made promises that night, promises that he clearly cannot keep. I feel like a fool." I put my head in my hands and started crying more.

LALA: "No, no, no. This makes me want to beat his ass now. You have not heard from him since everyone was at my house about Tony. That is weird though, have you tried calling him?" I looked up at La and Tiff.

JEAN: "Damn near every day. I am tired of calling him and he keeps ignoring me. Not a *'hey, I'm busy, I'll call you later,'* nothing. I am over him and that friendship. Seven years I've known him, and seven years thrown away... and I can't get back."

Chapter Eleven

I just wanted to rewind back in time the night we had sex and stopped it. I wanted to rewind back in time the day I first met him; the day we first looked in each other's eyes like, 'damn, this my best friend for life.' Just when I thought I gained a best friend who would never betray me, never leave me out and dry. What a big mistake to fall in love with him. We made promises to always be there for each other in need, even with one another's' pride wouldn't let them say, '*I need you*,' we would be there. Ray always had my back, and he knew I always had his. We were both coming hard behind each other. Just like Tiffany and Latonia did for me. Our friendship was unbreakable, or at least I thought it was unbreakable.

The waiter came back with our food and my appetite was gone. I was in no mood to eat anymore. La looked at me curiously.

LALA: "So you mean to tell me this nigga got you so gone you can't even eat this 5-star ass plate?" She took a chip, dipped in salsa then took a big ass bit of her taco. "If you do not eat it, I will. Ray is no..."

TIFFANY: "I bet you would."

La's mouth full and she still talking. I could not help but laugh at Tiff's comment.

LALA: "Not too much hoe." Mouth still full… "Like I was saying…"

JEAN: "Can you *say* when you don't have a mouth full of food?" She had her hand gripping my plate like she was really determined to eat my food. "And unhand this grip you have on my plate."

TIFFANY: "I'm trying to tell you; she was ready to eat your shit." We all burst out laughing. I was not hurt anymore. I was still a bit curious about Ray but not going to put myself down behind him.

LALA: "Can I say what I was trying to say?"

TIFFANY: "Before your mouth was full of shit? Go ahead." LaLa rolled her eyes at Tiff.

LALA: "Like I was saying, there is no need for you to be feeling all down. Fuck Ray at this point and I will shoot him in the foot just like Amar behind you. Now eat up." She took a spoonful of rice and gulped it down right along with some beans. I do not even think she chewed, just put it in her mouth and swallowed. "So yeah, don't be worrying about that nigga. People make time for who and what they want."

And she was right. If Ray cared about me as much as he says he does, he would make all the time in the world for me, instead he's been ducking and dodging my phone calls.

TIFFANY: "Do you want to talk about it? It seems a bit more than what you're making it if you are sitting out at girls day crying, bitch."

JEAN: "I just fell in love with my best friend. We made a bond that night to never hurt each other. If one of us started fucking with somebody else, we would tell another..." I took a pause while about to take a sip of my margarita. "Maybe that is what it is, he found somebody else and giving them his attention."

The waiter had come back around to see if we were okay or needed anything else to eat or drink. Everybody said no except La. She was ordering more chips and salsa and another peach margarita.

TIFFANY: "You steady asking if we're okay and what not, are *you* okay? You are eating like a wild donkey at this point. Slow down La."

LALA: "Jean been talking about her and Ray, I haven't heard from Wade. And he knows I'll beat his ass for doing this." Tiffany and I burst out laughing.

TIFFANY: "Maybe that's why he went M.I.A; your ass is beating on him."

LALA: "He likes that shit. He tells me all the time how he likes when I am mad; he thinks that shit is sexy. Then when I start putting those paws on him, he is screaming how crazy I am." She balled up both of her fist and advertised them off. "Yeah, don't play with me nigga."

TIFFANY: "You just need some dick is all. I bet if you texted him on some, '*I'm done, and moving on to the next nigga,*' he'll be knocking on your door."

LALA: "Nah, then he might try to beat my ass." We all burst out laughing. "Look, as much as I want to know what happened the night you and Ray fucked, I see you're not in the mood to talk about it and I don't need you being mad at me. Honey when you're mad at me, makes me feel like shit. You can get so mean; make a motherfucker regret making you mad." Tiff chuckled some and I glared at her.

JEAN: "You agree with this nonsense she's speaking?" She took a sip of her drink and a bit of her quesadilla; mouth full...

TIFFANY: "It's not lady like to talk with a mouth full."

LALA: "The hell is you trying to say?" Food started falling out of Tiff's mouth as she started laughing.

JEAN: "You bitches are nasty." We were the loudest ones in the restaurant, laughing loud as ever, drawing so much attention to our table. Those people must have thought we were crazy and drunk as hell.

TIFFANY: "Can we at least talk about Amar then?" La and I locked eyes, back and forth between us two and Tiffany. "I guess that's a no."

JEAN: "Okay look, Amar came over to Benny house, I don't even know how he knew I was there..."

LALA: "Now you know damn well the only way he found out was from Benny."

JEAN: "Okay maybe, anyway… He knocks on…"

TIFFANY: "Can you start from the beginning? Like how does Benny even know La lives next door to him?"

LALA: "Aht, hold the fuck up… you tell her about Amar, can you suck that shit up and tell about Ray? This ain't fair. Tiffany knows every damn thing, and I'm missing out." She pouted and folded her arms together.

TIFFANY: "Stop being a big ass baby." Tiffany grabbed one of her titties as though she was about to pull it out. "You want a titty to suck on, baby?" La gave Tiffany the finger as she mocked her.

LALA: "You want a titty to suck on baby, kiss my ass." LaLa got up and started to walk away.

JEAN: "You that mad that you're leaving?"

LALA: "I'm going to the bathroom; not like you hoes care why I'm mad." She took another sip of her margarita and a bit of her taco. "I'll be back. Hopefully, you're done telling her about what the fuck happened so we can move on to something else." She rolled her eyes and turned away. LaLa got us both beat when it comes to acting like a big ass, spoiled baby.

JEAN: "Girl get out of your feelings. I'll tell you what happened with me and Ray." She started smiling from ear to ear, doing the cabbage patch.

LALA: "I'll be right back."

TIFFANY: "Make sure you wash your hands and don't drop piss on the toilet seat." I could not do nothing but burst out laughing. Tiffany said that shit so loud that people started looking our way. I was surprised LaLa had no come back to that.

LaLa walked away to the bathroom and Tiffany immediately turned to me.

TIFFANY: "Spill the tea." I finished off the rest of my margarita just as the waiter walked up to take empty plates and glasses. I ordered one last margarita since we were just about done eating.

JEAN: "I went over to La's house and heard a long ass bang as well as a loud ass scream. My extra considerate ass just happened to knock on the door to see if whoever it is, was okay. They open the door, *boom* its Benny." In my head I am like, '*awe damn, I done fucked up.*' I rolled my eyes a bit and continued with the story. "We start talking, but nothing major, and then he mentions Amar. I had a feeling already that he might end up calling Amar and telling him where I was at. You know the whole family just messy as can be." Tiffany bucked her eyes open and nodded, agreeing with what I had just said.

TIFFANY: "Remember that one time, Amar cousin Shaunee saw you talking to some dude, then ran back to tell Amar."

JEAN: "Girl yes, just messy. Know damn well I wasn't doing any wrong." The waiter had come back with our drinks and

I took a sip before I finished the story. "So, Benny and I going back and forth, then he is asking who I am coming to see, you know damn well I wasn't telling him. He finally goes back inside his house; I am beating on La's door for her to open up. I am hoping this nigga does not come back out to see what I'm doing. Next thing I know, both him and Amar knocking at La's door. This is the part that tripped me out. She looks through the peep hole, and then starts walking back to her room. I'm like, *'where you are going?'* This bitch goes to get her gun." We both started cracking up as La was walking back up to the table.

LALA: "What's funny?" She sat down and took a sip of her water. "I feel so relieved."

TIFFANY: "How you were running to get your Glock."

LALA: "I sure the fuck was. Amar and Benny had me fucked up. Do not come knocking on my damn door like we fuck with you. I had my 9mm for Amar and my 22 for Benny." We all burst out laughing, Tiff ass shed a tear.

TIFFANY: "So you were going to shoot them?"

LALA: "I sure in the fuck was. Knocking on my damn door, he well deserved it." The waiter had come by to give our tickets so we could pay.

TIFFANY: "How much y'all tipping?"

LALA: "N-O-T-H-I-N-G. I don't even know her name."

JEAN: "You can at least give 1$ or 2."

LALA: "2$ towards my next drink." Every time we all went out, LaLa was the only one who never tipped the waitress.

TIFFANY: "We're going to stop going out with you."

LALA: "I don't give a damn. I'll go out by myself, or with Wade... still might not tip the waitress."

JEAN: "Go out with Wade, once you find him." I mumbled under my breath. I heard Tiff '*Ooop*,' while LaLa just stared at me like she wanted to beat my ass.

LALA: "I ain't even going to say that about you."

JEAN: "Say what, something about Ray going M.I.A? Go ahead La, you know damn well you want to." Tiffany raised both of her hands up to separate us two.

TIFFANY: "Both of y'all need to calm down. We are out in public, don't start a scene."

LALA: "Says the one telling me not to piss on the seat."

JEAN: "You've had one too many drinks today and need to chill out."

LALA: "Both of y'all can kiss my ass." She pulled out some cash to pay for her food and drinks, and got up from the table, heading to the front entrance.

TIFFANY: "Did you forget you rode with me?" Tiff yelled out.

LALA: "Bring your ass, unlock the door." Tiff and I burst out laughing and waited for the waitress to come back since we both were paying with a card. Once she came to pick up the tabs, and then back with our cards, we both got up from the table and left a 3$ tip a piece.

LaLa was sitting in the back seat of Tiffany's car on the phone with someone. Once Tiffany and I got in the car, we overheard La talking. Trying not to be *so* nosey but still wanting to make out who she was on the phone with. She looked at us both and gave us the finger. Tiffany was looking at her through the visor mirror and gave the finger back. She cranked up her car, put it in reverse and drove to our next destination, the waxing spa. It had been a while since my last wax and was well needed.

LALA: "Alright baby, I'll talk to you later." La hung up the phone and stared at us both. "Don't even start, yes that was Wade and I was getting on his ass. He told me he dropped his phone in the toilet and had to wait a few days to get a new one." She puckered her lips and flipped her hair. "My baby knows not to go M.I.A, or ima beat his ass."

TIFFANY: "You're so abusive."

LALA: "And your point. We about to go get these cats waxed, right? I'm trying to get mine licked on tonight."

Cardi B *'Be Careful,'* came on the radio and Tiffany turned it up. "I wanna get married, like the Currys, Steph and Ayesha shit But we more like Belly, Tommy and Keisha shit Gave you TLC, you wanna creep and shit Poured out my whole heart to a piece of shit..."

Once the song went off, Tiffany turned the radio down...

LALA: "Don't think you're slick. I still want to know about you and Ray." I really thought she had forgot, and I was not going to budge to help her remember. As we pulled up to the stop light on Curl street, we saw a black BMW with a few good-looking fellas in there. The driver had his eye on me, and he sure was looking scrumptious enough to eat. I nudged for Tiffany to roll her window down since he already had his down. LaLa in the back clearing her throat like she about to run some game, know damn well Wade gone beat her ass if he finds out she is flirting with some other dudes. Knowing her, she did not give a damn.

DRIVER: "How you are doing beautiful?"

  Tiffany cleared her throat.

TIFFANY: "I'm doing well, how about you handsome?"

DRIVER: "No offence love, but I was talking to baby in the passenger seat." LaLa in the back seat burst out laughing, while I almost spit out my drink. Tiffany looked through her rearview mirror and gave LaLa the finger.

JEAN: "I'm alright, hun." The light had just turned green and there were a few cars behind both Tiffany's car and ol boy trying to holler. Someone had already started beeping their horn at us and here comes La, *'Aight lil bitch. Chill with the horn*.' Them *Peco* drinks were getting to her.

JEAN: "Pull over to this gas station on Curl so we can exchange numbers."

DRIVER: "Bet." He turned on his blinkers to notify the cars behind him, that he was trying to get over and Tiffany let him over. She pulled up behind him to the corner store on Curl Street. I unbuckled my seatbelt, about to get out when I noticed he was already heading my way.

LALA: "Well damn, get it girl."

TIFFANY: "Right!" He walked up to the passenger side window and I hit the button for the window to come down. Tiffany decided to be childish and lock the window. I glanced over at her and she just laughed. Just as he was walking up to my side, Tiffany unlocked the window.

DRIVER: "I'm Steven, and you are?" He extended his arm out to shake hands. I am pro germophobic and was a bit skeptical on shaking his hand. I ended up giving him the fist pump.

JEAN: "I'm Amber." Both Tiffany and LaLa in the background laughing; '*Who*?' I am ninety-nine percent sure almost every woman in the world has a fake name they give out when they're not trying to tell their real name. Mine just so happens to be Amber. Tiffany and La need to shut the hell up with all that extra coughing they are doing.

STEVEN: "Nice to meet you Amber. Can we exchange numbers?" I reached for my phone out of my purse.

AMBER: "You can give me yours." He reached for my phone and began to enter his phone number. He even called himself to make sure he got mine.

STEVEN: "Make use of that number Amber. I would like to take you out on a date fairly soon if that's cool with you."

AMBER: "Tomorrow?"

STEVEN: "It's a date." He smiled at me and I got chills. Those pearly white and straight teeth beamed at me. You could tell he once had braces and I wondered what his teeth looked like before them. I had got one last waft of his Polo cologne.

LALA: "Hey Steven, your friend in the passenger seat single?"

STEVEN: "Actually he is but I'm telling you right now, my boys a hoe and not looking any time soon to settle down or be in a relationship."

LALA: "That's quite alright, neither am I. Tell him to come over so I can talk to him." He chuckled some.

STEVEN: "Y'all just might be made for each other. That is some shit he would say, and you sound like you about to run some game."

LALA: "Don't be a hater. Just have him come here, please and thank you." He raised his hands up as a surrender and began to walk back to his car.

STEVEN: "Say no more. I'll have him come over." Both Tiff and I turned and looked back at LaLa.

TIFFANY: "Are you crazy? Are you trying to get hurt or something? Wade will kill your black ass if he finds out you talking to some other nigga."

LALA: "Wade been doing him for a while and it's time to start doing me."

JEAN: "You were just talking to him on the phone when we left the restaurant, and now y'all not good?"

LALA: "That was not even Wade." She rolled her eyes at us and ol boy Steven sent for was on his way to Tiffany's car. LaLa rolled down her window as he stepped up to the car. "Do you need for me to get out or is this cool for you?"

PASSENGER: "Nah this cool shawty." He looked to Tiffany and I and pointed back to Steven's car. "Aye, my potna in the back seat wants to holler at you." He then pointed to Tiffany in the front seat as she was trying to get a look at him. As soon as she took a glance at him, he was cheesing from ear to ear.

Chapter Twelve

TIFFANY: "Oh he kind of cute. Is he a hoe too?"

We all had confused looks on our faces.

PASSENGER: "A hoe too? What are you talking about?"

She hurried and tried to change the subject. I saw La rolling her eyes in the back seat like she did not already know ol dude was a hoe.

TIFFANY: "Nothing. Don't even worry about it." I didn't even know Tiffany had it in her, but she sure did shoot her shot. My girl has been around LaLa too long. "Are you going to come to talk to me or just sit in the car smiling?" He had rolled up the window and hopped out of the backseat. I looked back at LaLa and see her and her dude cheesing from ear to ear know they just being hoes with each other. Who knows, they might end up falling for each other.

LALA: "What was your name again?"

SAMMY: "Sammy! You can't forget that and if you do, we're going to have some problems LaLa."

Sammy boy sounded like he meant business with them having problems if she forgot his name again. I am fairly sure La did not give a damn. She likes them type of men; the ones who are able to put her ass in check. I was sitting

125

in the passenger seat looking at both of my girls run game and it was the funniest thing. LaLa was promising this nigga to have his baby, while Tiffany got her nigga blushing. I am just going back and forth between them two until they finally exchanged numbers. Tiffany had the idea that we should all go on a date together tomorrow. I actually wanted to go out with Steven alone, not a triple date... just yet at least.

LaLa stepped out of the back seat to give Sammy a hug and got back in as he walked to Steven's car. Tiffany still in the front seat running game on ol boy, whose name she still does not even know. That is exactly how you can tell they're really not into these men, you didn't even ask his name. It amazed me how both of them either has a man or leading someone on, but still find the need to add an extra player to their team. I was not hating on their game though, just don't get caught up.

BACK SEAT RIDER: "Aight, I'm gone and let you beautiful ladies go. We will see y'all tomorrow." I cleared my throat some to see if she would finally ask his name and it was a no. She just smiled and waved at him as he hopped right back in the back seat. I yelled out to him...

JEAN: "Uhh sir, what's your name?" Tiffany snapped her neck at me, eyes wide as day. She knew she was wrong for not asking his name. If you are going to run game on someone at least get their name to make them think you actually care and want to get to know them. My girl was doing it all wrong. I cannot put all the blame on her though, because he sure as hell didn't ask for her name.

BACK SEAT RIDER: "Oh damn, it's Trevor. I was distracted by her beauty." I rolled my eyes at his comment.

JEAN: "Awe, good one." Tiffany turned back to me.

TIFFANY: "Don't be a hater." I rolled my eyes at her and waved bye to Steven.

JEAN: "See y'all tomorrow."

STEVEN: "It's a date beautiful." He winked at me and blew a kiss. I began blushing and smiled back at him. Tiffany cranked up her car, put it in drive and drove off to the waxing parlor. Steven, Trevor, and Sammy were still parked at the gas station when we pulled up to the light. They were probably making a bet to see who would smash first.

LALA: "Who y'all think going to give the cat up first?" And clearly so was LaLa.

JEAN: "That's all your little nasty ass thinks about. One day you're going to catch something or get knocked up.

LALA: "I wrap up every time I have sex, even with Wade. I'm telling y'all, he has been acting funny lately, like he's been fucking around on me or something." The car was silent as we looked at La through the rear-view mirror. You could tell on her face she was feeling some type of way about the whole Wade situation.

JEAN: "Don't even trip over that, La. You just got a fine ass brother number who wants to take you out tomorrow."

TIFFANY: "Fix your face before I punch you in it. You're too pretty for that shit." We all burst out laughing.

LALA: "We're about to get these kitties waxed and I just might give up the box to Sammy tomorrow." Tiffany spit out her drink on that one and La popped her gum. "Oh, and Jean, don't think I forgot about you and Ray." I rolled my eyes at the sound of his name coming out of her mouth.

JEAN: "We had made love, *Boom*, that's it." She made a straight face at me with her mouth almost touching her chin.

LALA: "I know you fucking lying. If you do not give me the sugar, honey, ice and *TEA* bitch. Stop playing with me."

There was silence in the car, so I took initiative to turn the radio up. Evans, Faith *"Soon as I Get Home"*

> *"So baby, soon as I get home, I'll make it up to you*
> *Baby, I'll do what I gotta do..."*

I immediately turn the station. I love me some Faith Evans and that song, but it reminded me of Ray. That song was playing when we were making love. It is like my pussy wanted more of him, but she has got to detain herself. He does not want you Fat Mama; move on.

TIFFANY: "What's up with you, that was my song."

JEAN: "Get over it." I turned the station until I found something that matched my mood. Do not get me wrong,

I'm a classy type of chick, but Trina really raised me. Trina, *"Fuck Boy"*

"You's a fuck boy, fuck boy
My bitch been said it
That's why I should've let your best friend get it
We went on trips you bought Chanel
But money ain't shit when you soft as hell

Cause you's a fuck boy, fuck boy
My momma even said it
Got a new nigga I ain't even gotta sweat it
You still gone talk and that's a got damn shame
But a hoe gone be a hoe and a lame gone be a lame FUCK
BOY..."

I turned the radio up on blast. We had pulled up to this white couple at the light next to us. The wife was looking at me very peculiar, but I did not give a fuck. LaLa in the back seat laughing at me, but I still did not give a fuck. I am screaming at the top of my lungs...

JEAN: *"BUT A HOE GONE BE A HOE AND A LAME GONE BE A LAME, FUCK BOY."*

The lady starts looking at me like she was scared. I rolled down my window a little more so she could really hear Trina and me. Tiffany wanted to be childish and rolled the window up, as well as locked it so I could not let the window back down.

JEAN: "You're childish for that." I rolled my eyes at Tiffany and turned the radio back down just as we pulled up to the waxing bar. Tiffany pulled up in the parking lot and put the car in park. She then turned the car off and made eye contact with me.

TIFFANY: "You sure you're okay Jean?"

I did not want to lie to my girl, but I did not want to talk or even think about Ray. I knew I had to get it off my chest at some point. Let each wax strip pulled off this kitty be the pain pulled out of my heart for Ray.

JEAN: "It's Ray. I'm just so upset about him going M.I.A again."

LALA: "Maybe it's for a good cause. He has to have a legitimate reason." I snapped my neck and turned to La in the back seat.

JEAN: "Whose side are you on? Mine or the nigga who took your best friend cookie then turned on her?"

LALA: "I would be a hoe if I said his because you still have not told me what happened. But now y'all see how I am feeling about Wade. I do not mean to make this about me, but girl we're in the same predicament..." She took a pause and reality hit me. She was right. "Today is our girls' day and we need to stop thinking about these niggas. Get these kitties right for our date tomorrow and let it be."

While LaLa was being funny about which one of us was giving up the box first, it just might be me. I needed some new dick and I needed it now.

We were regulars at the Waxing bar, so Kim greeted us with wine. We were just about drunk for the day. We had liquor at the restaurant, liquor at the nail salon and now more liquor. In order to bear the pain from these waxes, we would need something stronger than wine. We were not too picky on who we would get the wax from because everyone in here was good and just as gentle as the next. It was just who was getting their wax and walk of shame first. After every wax, we all were walking a little funny, but not too much. LaLa is always the extra dramatic one, holding her legs open like she is riding a horse. Business was not booming like it usually is at the wax parlor, so we were able to all get a room together and get waxed at the same time.

LALA: "Who ready to make a bet?"

JEAN: "On what?"

LALA: "Who screams first?" LaLa knew damn well she was the one always screaming so loud I bet the building next door could hear her.

TIFFANY: "But it's... always you." Tiffany and I burst out laughing while LaLa gave us the finger.

Three different ladies walked in with all white, a mask, and gloves on. They each made sure the wax was hot enough and it was show time. We come here so much that we were already in our robes, naked from the waist down, legs gapped open, in butterfly positions ready for the work.

LALA: "Ahh *shit*!"

TIFFANY: "And you were trying to make a bet; girl already screaming."

We all burst out laughing. My phone started ringing but it was on the other side of the room. A part of me had hoped it was Ray, but I was not trying to get my hopes up too much.

LALA: "Jean this would be a good time to talk about what happened." Tiffany and LaLa turned to me, and I looked away towards Sarah, who was doing the damn thing between these thick thighs of mine. She is one of my favorites.

They had us turned different directions, so no one was able to see the other's kitty. Not like we have not seen each other naked before. The music was playing, and the drinks were consistently coming. I was starting to feel the wine and the waxing became numb to me. LaLa is still across the room doing all that extra screaming, while Tiff and I taking it like a G. We were both laughing at her because she was actually trying to make a bet and is the main one screaming. Sarah did get me one good time and I let out a little grr. My kitty was a little bit hairier than usual, and I wanted Steven to get a good view of this pink paradise I was working with. I kept looking at his lips. They were big, fine and juicy. I just knew he could eat the shit out of some pussy and I was trying to find out tomorrow night.

We were just about done with the front side and were getting ready for them to wax that ass.

TIFFANY: "You want to make that bet La?" Tiffany burst out laughing and I could not resist the laughter, and joined in.

LALA: "Fuck both of y'all." Tiffany even had Sarah and them laughing.

The ladies were just about finished with our wax. LaLa and Tiffany finished off the rest of their drink, while LaLa requesting for another. I left them in the back and headed to the front to pay for my services. I had remembered that my phone rung and checked to see who had called. Still hoping it was Ray, I saw I had a missed call from Steven as well as a text.

STEVEN: "Can't wait to see you tomorrow, beautiful."

JEAN: "Same." That was so dry of me, but I wanted it to be Ray texting. Do not get me wrong, I was excited to see him tomorrow but… Ray. I closed my phone as Tiffany and LaLa walked up on me to pay for their services.

TIFFANY: "You good Jean?" I turned to LaLa and her big ass grin on her face turned into a curious look.

JEAN: "You still want to know about Ray and me?"

LALA: "Only if you want to talk about it. I see you are not in the best mood, and I do not want to pressure you Sus. Do you even want to tell me? Do not do it to make me happy either. I care about you and this friendship too much to see you like this." I checked my phone one last time and saw no new messages or calls from Ray. I had to get this off my chest.

JEAN: "We can talk about it."

We said our goodbyes to Sarah and them and headed out of the door. Once we got to the car Tiffany cranked it up and I had asked for her to turn it off, and she did. They both had curious looks on their face.

JEAN: "So here it goes..." I took a deep breath and began to talk. "Ray had come over to my crib one day to talk and to chill with me since I hadn't seen him in a while. We are laughing it up, drinking some margaritas that I had made, while watching TV. A lot of the time the TV was watching us. His phone kept going off and I was getting a little bothered by that. He had told me about some chick he was entertaining, but he would say it is nothing major; that is who he was texting. He could see that I was getting upset and turned his phone off." I had paused for a moment to gain myself.

I remember the way he'd been looking at me gave me chills. I wanted to jump on this man throat. Nobody knew about this before that night but me. I have been having some feelings for Ray for a while but never put action to it for the simple fact that I did not want to ruin our friendship... This is the part that got me. He starts to say how none of the females he be fooling with matter to him, and how he honestly just wants to be with me. I turned my whole body toward both LaLa and Tiffany.

JEAN: "Do y'all know he has been wanting to talk to me since the first day we met, eight years ago? He just mentioned a friendship because that is what he was looking for at the time, to build a strong bond. Ray has been in love with me for years and never said anything. He was just as scared as I was to confess his love."

Both Tiffany and LaLa placed their hands on their heart and gave puppy dog eyes like.

JEAN: "He mentioned how he would get mad and sometimes jealous when he sees me with other men or how they would treat me. Said he would never do me in that way, and I believed him... Fat mama started jumping for him." We all had burst out laughing. "It all started with a kiss and it felt so magical. His lips are so soft and *LAWD* he is a great kisser. Then he touched my thigh, started massaging it, and that made fat mama jump even more. I did not want to stop kissing him whatsoever. It just felt so right, and I didn't want it to end."

I had a little flash back to the first time we made love. Tiffany gave the same reaction she was giving the first time I had told her the story.

LALA: "This story is more exciting and juicier than you and Keyvaune, Tiff."

TIFFANY: "I know... keep going."

I chucked some.

JEAN: "So he picks me up from the couch and carried me to the bedroom, still kissing along the way..."

LALA: "Yeah, Sammy getting some tomorrow."

TIFFANY: "And so is Trevor." We all burst out laughing. With these freshly waxed kitties, all three of them just might be getting some tomorrow.

LALA: "Okay, okay. Keep going with the story." LaLa all in tuned with it, sitting at the edge of the seat while gripping on the head of the passenger seat.

JEAN: "Okay, so we make it to the bedroom, and he lays me on the bed... still kissing. I told y'all I did not want to stop. He then pulls down my pants; I was not wearing any panties, so he had easy access to fat mama.

LALA: *Cough* "hoe."

TIFFANY: "I know you ain't talking, just met this man not even 3 hours ago, already talking about fucking him the first date... tomorrow."

LALA: "Like you weren't doing the same; any who... keep going."

JEAN: "So he spread my legs open and just the heat from his breath had my shit on 10. He gently starts kissing my pussy lips, my inner thighs, then opens my pussy lips with his tongue. I wanted to cum right then and there, I promise. I already felt how soft his lips were against mine, now feeling them on my pussy lips." I had to take a moment because I started having another flash back. I fanned myself but that was not helping. "Can you turn the air on?" We all burst out laughing. La has sweat glistening on her forehead, Tiffany upper lip forming sweat. We are just some sweaty bitches up in this Chevy Cruz.

TIFFANY: "Here comes the good part." I think Tiffany was more excited to hear this story again than La was for the first time.

JEAN: "He is eating my pussy, then starts fingering me. I immediately started to cum. He sure as shit didn't stop eating either... and I was loving every lick. It was just so soft and gentle. You know how niggas think they are eating pussy but really not? Oh, baby he was, sucking the clit ever so smooth. I'm moaning loud, he still eating, then this nigga looks up at me; I passed out. I snap back and look back down at him, he still looking at me. That shit drives me crazy, he looks at me while eating my pussy. I told him to stop because at that point I was ready to go down to George Brown Court house and get married. We can get a ring later."

At that point we were all cracking up, dying laughing. Eyes were filling up with tears of laughter. This is exactly what I needed to get over Ray and it was helping.

JEAN: "Okay so then I tell him to stop, and he is asking me why, and if I didn't like it. Like nigga you just made me cum in your mouth less than 2 minutes, the fuck; I love it!"

LALA: "Oh bitch, you got me cracking up."

TIFFANY: "I'm laughing as hard as I was the first time, she told me."

We had to take a moment because we could not stop laughing. Now they see why I was upset, going crazy on why Ray ain't texted or called me. After it had quiet down some, I went ahead and continued the story.

JEAN: "He comes up from eating my pussy and starts kissing me. Yes, I like to taste my pussy juices on his lips, shit sexy to me. He takes off his shirt and those muscles, my Lawd. He was starting to unbuckle his pants and that is when I started to get nervous. So, I pushed his hands to the side and unbuckled them for him. The pants fell to the ground and my mouth almost went with them."

LALA: "You're nervous but still helping him take off his pants?" I looked over at La and burst out laughing.

JEAN: "Just hush. This has got to be the biggest dick I have ever seen in my life. I just knew that shit was going to feel good. He's my best friend and all but I didn't too much trust where he had been sticking his dick, so I reached in my nightstand to get a condom.

I placed it on his dick, really trying to get a feel for it before he rammed it in fat mama. My pussy was just so wet and ready for him, and then he starts kissing me. Y'all he was just so gentle with me and eased that eggplant right up in fat mama and she accepted every inch. I love him..."

I had turned facing front in the passenger seat and turned on the radio. LaLa reached through us two and turned it off.

LALA: "No ma'am you won't. The story ends like that?"

JEAN: "I'm starting to miss him."

TIFFANY: "Girl fuck him. You got you a new piece of meat to try and by the way the bulge was sitting in those jeans,

Steven is working with something." I gasped and snapped my neck her way.

JEAN: "Why are you looking at his dick?"

TIFFANY: "Because I have a 20/20 vision that the man above has blessed me with, and I will use them whenever I please. He walked in my view so boo. I saw a bulge."

JEAN: "I wanted Ray to nut in me and get me pregnant. His dick felt so good up in my stomach. He wasn't pounding my shit, he was gently stroking me, looking me dead in my eyes... making love to me." I had sunk down in the seat. "He started moaning, making facial expressions telling me fat mama was feeling good to him. This is the part that took me; he said I love you, Jean." LaLa was in the back seat screaming and shit. "I wanted to give him babies and be the best wife I can be. You know what I said back?" I turned away from them, did a dramatic wail, '*I love you too Ray.*" I threw my hands up in the air and slammed them on my thighs. "He kept kissing me, licking and sucking on my neck and ears. I am scratching his back, screaming '*oh my, oh my, I'm about to cum.*' His voice then gets weak when he said, '*cum for daddy baby.*' I paused for a moment and put my face directly in front of the vent where the air was coming from. "I was ready for my version of *My Wife and Kids*. I was ready to have a joint account and give him the second key to my apartment. I probably should have so he would not go M.I.A."

I sat back and thought of that night with Ray. It all just felt so right, like it was meant to be. I was just so confused on why he would go M.I.A after we had made love and said those things to each other. At this point, I thought our friendship was done for. I was entirely too upset to even speak with him if he tried to talk. I assumed I was silent a little too long. Both La and Tiffany started caressing my shoulders to comfort me and I leaned my head up against their hands. Glad I finally got that off of my chest and was ready to move on to what God had in store for me.

JEAN: "I fell in love with my best friend and trying to get back right. I've never in my life felt this way about anybody, not even when Amar and I first got together, and y'all remember how I was about him. Ray is different, I feel like we connect on a different level that no other man can compare to." I thought of Steven at that point and did not want to categorize him because of what Ray had done to me.

TIFFANY: "You know we got your back as always girl. Don't even trip over him..." She turned to La. "...and you too. Do not trip over Wade. I got both of y'alls back and coming hard." We all smiled at each other. These are moments I lived for.

To have friends you never have to worry about betraying you, or going behind your back to the next bitch to gossip about you. My circle is small and as long as I have Tiffany and LaLa there, I don't need no other 'friend' in my life. These are my forever girls, and I would do anything for them because I know they would do the same. No matter how many disagreements we have, at the end of the day, I knew they had my back. I love you Latonia and Tiffany forever and always...

Chapter Thirteen

RAY

After I dipped out on La, and them, I went M.I.A on Jean, again. I know she must be pissed off at me. The way that I looked at it, I am making it harder for me tell her, about the baby. I may even be ruining our friendship. I knew I had to pull up on her; a phone call just would not do it. Our friendship meant everything to me, and I did not want it to end. I tried calling her to see if she was available to talk but I got no answer. I deserved it though. This just was not the right time to go M.I.A on her after we had made love.

I had no intentions whatsoever to hurt Jean. I love this woman with all my heart and am willing to do whatever it takes to make things right. This is the woman I want to spend the rest of my life with, and my ignorance was about to throw it all away. I thought about calling Tiffany or LaLa to see if they had heard from Jean, but I am pretty sure she had told them about me and I'm on their shit list. I had to make things right with Jean and I had to do it fast; before she finds out from someone else. I tried calling her cell again and nothing. The way the calls going to voicemail after the first ring, I think she may have blocked me. I just had to try my luck and pull up on her.

My phone had rung, and it was my boy Slim. I was not too much in the mood to talk to him, but I answered anyway to see what was up...

SLIM: "Aye wassup with you?" He sounded a bit questionable in his tone and I was a bit curious.

RAY: "Nun much, why wassup?"

SLIM: "You and Jean not talking or something? After you told me what happened I would assume y'all was getting married." Something had to be up, and I had to find out.

RAY: "I haven't talked to her in a few weeks. What are you getting at?"

SLIM: "I saw her leaving some restaurant with Tiffany and LaLa, all boo'ed up with some niggas." My heart sank to my stomach.

RAY: "You sure it was Jean?"

SLIM: "Bruh, I know Jean when I see Jean, and I sure as hell know LaLa when I see her little thick ass."

Oh yeah, my boy slim been feeling LaLa for a while now but every time he tries to make a move, she back with her nigga Wade. I think he just gave up on trying to holler at her and started doing his own thing. I did not even have the words to speak; I was in shock at this point. I could not blame Jean or even get mad. It was my fault that I had gone M.I.A after she got on my ass the first time. I fucked up big time with this one.

SLIM: "You there?"

RAY: I snapped back to reality, "Yeah, just had a little moment."

SLIM: "What are you going to do? I know how you feel about her and shit. She fucked up for going behind your back with some other nigga."

RAY: "Nah chill. This is my fault. I was the one who dipped out on her after the night. I just could not face the fact that I got my ex girlfriend pregnant. I've been trying to gain my thoughts to tell Jean, but shit been hard."

SLIM: "Your ex, as in Bethanee?"

RAY: "Yeah man." Just hearing her name made my skin crawl. How did I get caught up in this shit? I honestly thought I wrapped up, but I guess I did not. I should not have been fucking her in the first place, like Jean said. I was just tired of beating my dick and wanted a little pussy. I ain't the type to just fuck anything, so Bethanee was it. I should have just waited. Two more weeks of dick beating, I would not be in this predicament. Two weeks too soon. I would have been booed up with my girl Jean.

I know I fucked her raw about a month or two ago and now she is all of a sudden pregnant since the last time we smashed two weeks ago. She never mentioned anything until now, when she sees that she is not getting much of my attention. Bethanee kept texting me the other day, saying how she wanted to meet up and talk about something important. I finally went to go see what she wanted, and she shows me a positive pregnancy test. I did not believe the test was hers since she had taken it just before I got there. We went to the nearest corner store to get her another one and damn, that one said positive too. I even sat in the bathroom with her while she took the test. Shit fucked me up.

I did not know how conniving she is until I had broken up with her awhile back. She just kept blowing up my phone to talk and see if we could work things out. I was not trying to hear it, nor did I want to be with her anymore. I should have just listened to Jean when she told me to stop fucking with her, but nah. Me being the type of person that I am, I was willing to give her another chance. People make mistakes and deserve second chances, so I put my pride to the side and tried to work things out again. Should have kept my distance. I honestly do not think that is my child because Bethanee ended up cheating on me again with some random ass nigga. She claims the time with him does not add up, but I still do not think that's my baby.

SLIM: "Damn, man. What are you going to do?"

RAY: "That I don't know. If that is my child, I am going to step up and do what I must do to provide for what's mine. Either way it goes... I have to let Jean know about it and that's the hard part. Me telling the woman I love oh so dearly, that I might be having a baby by the same female that cheated on me and broke my heart once. The same female Jean schooled me on, but I just did not listen. I fucked up Slim... big time.

SLIM: "I can't say I can relate to what you got going on because I can't but at the end of the day, if Jean is who you really want to be with and you care about y'alls friendship like you say you do, you need to man up and tell her wassup. And I would advise as soon as possible, seeing that she is already linking up with some other nigga. You don't want to lose her right?" There was a pause... *"Right?"*

RAY: "Right. I just do not know how. She's not even returning my calls and I think she blocked me."

SLIM: "Damn, you got to make things right before it's too late. You are going to be stuck being a baby daddy by some hoe that just cannot stop cheating on you and lose the woman you love. It's time to man up Ray, and you need to do it fast."

   As hard as it was for me to admit it, he was right. I do not know what I would do with myself if I lost the love of my life, my best friend, my baby Jean.

SLIM: "Aye, ima hit you back up later, my girl calling me."

RAY: "Your *girl?*" Last time I checked this nigga was single like a dollar bill, and now he got a whole girlfriend.

SLIM: "Yeah man." He chuckled some. "I've been seeing this chick for a few weeks now and shit getting kind of serious between us two. I'm going to have to let you meet her one day."

RAY: "Oh for sure!"

SLIM: "But until then, you need to get your shit together and fix things with Jean."

RAY: "I'm going to make things right. I can promise you that." I ended the phone call and tried calling Jean again... nothing. It is time to make a move and pull up on her. I had put on a t-shirt, my slides, and grabbed my keys of off the kitchen table. I was not about to let my fuck up, or some new nigga, ruin what both Jean and I had.

I had pulled up to her crib and saw her car parked outside in her reserved parking spot. Wondered why she still has not answered my calls. I walked up her apartment door and heard some laughing. I assumed it was LaLa or Tiffany. I knocked on the door and waited for an answer. It had taken a moment, but she finally opened the door.

JEAN: "What do you want?" I did not expect that but deserved it.

RAY: "You."

JEAN: "Look Ray, right now isn't the right time..."

RAY: "I'm not leaving until I get the chance to talk to you. I've been bugging, going through some shit and didn't know how to tell you."

JEAN: "So you think it's okay to abandon our friendship, just after we made love and promises that you wouldn't hurt me? Right? That is okay for you to do, huh?" She whispered the last part like she was hiding something.

RAY: "I know I fucked up but let me..."

JEAN: "Let you do what Ray? Let you do the same shit you did the first time you were going through some things and decided to go M.I.A on me? What is the use of being friends, huh? Best friends at that. Does that not mean anything to you? ... You hurt me *right* after you fucking said you wouldn't."

I was speechless at this point. She was right, and that shit hurt. I had no intentions of hurting her. I adore Jean just as much as I do our friendship.

RAY: "Please just let me explain."

JEAN: "For what? So, you can tell me all this bullshit and make me think we are going to be together for you to leave me hanging, wondering what the fuck I did wrong? Nah, I am good. You need to leave." She began to close the door and I stopped her by putting my foot in the doorway.

RAY: "I'm *not* leaving until I can talk to you. You don't even have to respond, just listen." I may have gotten a little aggressive with her.

JEAN: "You need to watch your tone and move your foot. I'm not to be fucked with right about now and I'm warning you." I did not budge a bit. Jean knew wassup.

RAY: "I said what I said. What are you going to do?" I looked her dead in her eyes, waiting for her to respond.

JEAN: "Move your fucking foot out of my doorway, *now!*" I could see the hurt in her eyes and that shit was tearing me up inside. Some nigga that looked familiar walked up behind her.

147

STEVEN: "Everything okay baby?"

RAY: "*Baby*? Oh, this your nigga now? Two weeks go by and you already fucking somebody else?"

Smack.

JEAN: "Watch yourself playa. *You* left me. Not the other way around. I kept calling and texting your fucking phone. What was I supposed to do? Sit around, sulking, wondering why you left me after that night? You aren't the only one that wants me." The words cut me. She was speaking out of anger. She could not have meant that. "So again, I think it's best that you leave. My man and I don't need this kind of drama."

I chuckled some and looked away to keep from tearing up.

RAY: "I'm not leaving. So, you can let me in willingly, or unwillingly." Ol dude brushed Jean to the side and was standing not even a foot away from me.

STEVEN: "*My* woman asked for you to leave *one* too many times. Now if you do not, we're going to have a few problems."

I stepped closer to him to let him know I was not scared, and he had me all the way fucked up. Jean is worth this ass whopping this nigga was about to get.

RAY: "You should ask Jean herself. I don't do too well with threats. So, if you are not trying to stick with that, step the hell up out of my face."

He threw a punch, but I dodged it and threw one that actually landed. We tussled for a while, and Jean attempted to split us up. I blacked out for a moment and did not notice her and ended up accidently pushing her across the hall. Ol dude was lying on the ground as her next-door neighbors started coming outside to be nosey. I walked over to Jean to see if she was okay.

JEAN: "Get the fuck away from me." She pushed me away.

RAY: "Stop fighting me and talk to me... just listen!" I saw her eyes started to fill up with tears and that shit hurt my soul. I have done it this time.

 JEAN: "Get away *FROM ME!*" What the fuck was I supposed to do now? I was stuck and did not know how to get out of it. I could no longer hold the tears back myself. They just started falling.

RAY: "Please just talk to me, Jean." A few seconds later, nigga tackled me like some football player. I was blocking every hit he was throwing and tossed him off of me. He threw one last punch and it landed. I am not going to lie, the shit kind of hurt.

I heard one of her neighbors yell out how they were going to call the police. I was not trying to get no case with all of this shit that I was going through. I came over to talk to Jean about the baby and to see about working things out with her. Instead, I am in the hallway, tussling with her so called new nigga and about to end up in some hand cuffs. I had to get away, but not before I could get a word in with Jean. I knew if we did not talk today, I would not get a chance any other day. LaLa and Tiffany walked up the hallway and ran straight to Jean to comfort her. Ol dude was over there with them, and I was sitting... all alone a few doors down. Now I see how Jean felt.

LALA: "What the fuck happened?" LaLa looked up at me and we made eye contact. I got my ass up and walked over to where they were. Both Tiffany and LaLa helped Jean up and headed to her apartment. Ol dude was right behind her like a little puppy. I was already by her apartment door and was heading inside.

STEVEN: "Aye, you need to leave."

RAY: "I've said one too many times that I'm not leaving until I get a chance to speak with Jean and that's that. You trying to get your ass beat again; over there holding your eye and shit. Need an ice pack?" LaLa chuckled some and Jean looked at me like she wanted to beat my ass.

JEAN: "I don't want to talk to you.

RAY: "You don't have to... just listen."

STEVEN: "She said leave."

RAY: "Aye, somebody get him a pack of peas. That eye look like it's starting to swell pretty boy."

TIFFANY: "Just hear him out."

The way Jean looked at Tiffany, she wanted to beat her ass too. Then she looked at me and moved towards her apartment. Everyone walked in behind her, even ol boy. She stood in the doorway with the door open... waiting for me to come in. So I did.

JEAN: "You wanted to talk?" I looked around the room and all eyes were on me.

RAY: "Alone."

LALA: "You're lucky she even trying to let you talk." I looked over at her and remembered the first day I met Jean. LaLa was doing all that talking, popping off at the mouth. I wanted to smack her then and for sure want to smack her now.

RAY: "Can you chill much?"

LALA: "Can you go to hell much?"

JEAN: "Aight chill y'all." LaLa rolled her eyes at me and gave me the finger.

RAY: "What's your beef with me? Since day one when I met Jean in the mall, you been tripping." She rolled her eyes and sat on the edge of the couch.

LALA: "Are you going to explain why you're a hoe ass nigga or continue to figure out why I don't like you?" She rested her chin on her hand and looked me dead in my eyes.

RAY: "You're going to get yours." She stood up and started walking towards me.

LALA: "And what's that supposed to mean?"

RAY: "Aye, you need to get your girl. I got too much on my mind right about now and don't need this shit from this ignorant ass girl."

LALA: "Ignorant?" She threw her fist towards me, but I dodged it and grabbed her hand.

RAY: "I don't hit women; your best bet is to sit your little ass down before I get somebody that can handle you."

LALA: "Do it *bitch*."

JEAN: "LALA, YOU NEED TO CHILL THE FUCK OUT!" LaLa turned towards Jean.

LALA: "So you're going to take this nigga side and not mine? I have known you 18 years and he has known you 7, and you take up for this nigga?" She turned and pointed directly at me. "That is exactly why I do not like you now. Since day one you have been for this nigga that keeps doing you dirty. And who is always there for you with a shoulder to cry on? Huh, Jean? *ME* and Tiff." She pointed back and forth between her and Tiffany. "Oh, is it because he gave you a little piece of dick?" LaLa started tearing up. "I've been your girl since day one, fighting your battles right alongside of you, not ever leaving you alone."

RAY: "Stop being dramatic..."

LALA: "Dramatic? Boy..."

RAY: "Let me talk dammit..." LaLa paused and looked at me like a deer in headlights. "You're talking about *I do her dirty* like I'm just out here fucking all types of bitches. I went M.I.A twice and for major reasons. If it were not something serious, I would have never gone ghost... LaLa you got to understand I have absolutely no beef with you and I love this woman like I never loved before. I want to spend the rest of my life with her. I was never trying to *steal* your friend or break things up between y'all. You and Tiffany are like sisters to Jean, and I could never take that away. Yeah, I have went M.I.A and that was wrong on my end, but I would never intentionally hurt Jean. Just like you and Tiffany come hard behind her, you best believe I do the same. Can no nigga or bitch ever step to her or that is it for them. Stop talking like I just dog her out."

I bet her ass listened then. LaLa always popping off at the mouth, not letting other folks get what they have to say out. I looked over at Jean and she looked even more beautiful than ever. I walked towards her and gripped her face to kiss her soft lips.

RAY: "If I ever made you cry, please forgive me." The wells of her eyes started to form tears, and I wiped her face. "You mean more to me than you think. I've never in my life felt this way about any woman." I looked over to ol boy and he was staring at us both, mouth almost touching the floor. "I don't give a fuck what you and that nigga got going on. I am not about to just let him take you away from me and that is simple. If I have to pull up on every date y'all have to beat his ass... I promise I will." I looked back over at him to make sure he knew I meant business.

153

TIFFANY: "Okay so what's the reason you went M.I.A... *again*?" All eyes were on me... again. I walked over to the couch and took a seat. I put my head in my hands. I looked up at Jean and she was looking right at me.

RAY: "Can we talk in private?"

LALA: "You said all the lovey dovey shit in front of everybody, why not this?"

RAY: "That's different. Expressing my love for Jean, I can shout that out to the whole world, but telling what exactly I'm going through, nah... so again, Jean can I talk to you private?"

Chapter Fourteen

Jean looked back over at me and began to walk to her bedroom. I got up from the couch and walked right behind her. Once we got to the room, I closed the door behind me and locked it. I had a feeling that LaLa and Tiffany would try to come and put their ear to the door so I advised if we could go in her personal bathroom. I knew LaLa especially would try to ear hustle. Jean sat on the toilet seat and I sat on the tub.

JEAN: "So what is it? Why did we have to come and talk private... in my bathroom?"

RAY: "I wanted to talk private because this is something serious. I wanted to come talk in the bathroom because I knew your girl LaLa would be trying to listen at the door." She chuckled some.

JEAN: "Yeah, you're right about that." She paused and just looked at me. Those eyes and those luscious lips. This is one beautiful ass woman, and I was not trying to lose her. "Okay, you just staring at me is starting to freak me out. Wassup Ray?"

RAY: "This isn't easy for me. I just want you to know that I love you more than anything and I don't want you to hate me or speak out of anger once I tell you."

JEAN: "You're making me worry... what is it?" Her personal bathroom was not all that big, but I got up from the tub and began to pace the bathroom. I did not even know where to start but knew I had to get it out. It felt like the walls started closing up on me and I was beginning to freak out.

RAY: "I love you Jean."

JEAN: "I love you too... Is that it?" I sat back down on the edge of the tub and grabbed Jean's thigh.

RAY: "No."

JEAN: "Ray what is it? You know you can tell me anything."

RAY: "But this right here is different. It may even ruin our friendship some and I would hate for that to happen." I looked her in her eyes, and I could see the worry. "I got someone pregnant..."

JEAN: "*What*?" She got up from the toilet seat and stood over me like she wanted to knock my ass out. "Are you fucking serious?" I stood up and grabbed her shoulders to calm her down some and she just pulled away from me. "You got someone else pregnant, and you expect for me to be okay with that?"

RAY: "It's not what you think!"

JEAN: "Oh so you come express your love to me, make oh so sweet love to me then end up getting some bitch pregnant?"

RAY: "It's not like that at all Jean."

JEAN: "Then what is it? *Who* is it? One of them stank pussy hoes that you always texting? Maybe LaLa was right. I need to just leave you alone because you keep doing me dirty."

RAY: "It's not like that like I said."

JEAN: "Well get to explaining because right about now it looks like *that*. You are always going M.I.A when shit gets tough for you. What the fuck is the use of us calling each other best friends? If you care for me and this friendship like you say, it would not be *that* hard to tell me things like *this*. We have been friends for seven years, almost eight and you still cannot tell me what is going on with you. I think I'm more upset that you call me best friend, this woman you love oh so much, and you can't even be honest with me *or* the fact that you got someone pregnant, and I feel like I know who it is. If it were some random chick, you wouldn't have taken this long to tell me but if it was someone serious... like your *ex*..." She paused and looked at me and I had absolutely nothing to say. "So, I'm right? It's your ex Bethanee?"

I could not even answer her. I knew she was hurt. She nudged the side of my head.

JEAN: "Man, the fuck up Ray. Tell me what it is... Is it your ex Bethanee?"

RAY: "Yes..." She threw a punch to the wall and created a hole in it. I knew she wanted the wall to be me. "Don't be mad..."

JEAN: "Don't be mad? Do you know how stupid you sound? *'Don't be mad.'* Kiss my ass, Ray."

RAY: "You're speaking out of anger right now, just calm down."

JEAN: *'You're speaking out of anger,* blah blah blah. Kiss my ass like I said. I told you to stop fucking with her months ago but clearly you did not listen. Now she is carrying your baby. How am I supposed to feel? *Oh, jolly, let us all be friends and one big happy family!* Get the fuck out of here."

RAY: "We can work through this."

JEAN: "*We?* You could not even tell me when you first found out. Where did this *'we'* come from?"

RAY: "So that's it, we are done? I got to handle this by myself?"

JEAN: "You should have thought about that before you went M.I.A on me." She started pacing the bathroom and then opened the door to walk in her room. I was still sitting on the edge of the tub wondering what the fuck was I going to do. I just lost the woman of my dreams and stuck with the baby mama from hell.

RAY: "Look, I understand how you may feel, and I want to make things right. I know you may not forgive me at this moment, but I am not giving up on us. You can stay mad all you want but that nigga that is sitting in your living room… he cannot have you. I have seen you go through entirely too much and not just going to walk away because you're pissed at me... before you say *anything*... I know I was wrong for still fucking with Bethanee knowing all the shit she's done to me, and honestly, I feel stupid for not listening to you but after that night we made love, I promise I stopped. That was just the time she decided to tell me she is pregnant because I wasn't responding to her. You and I both know she means nothing to me. I don't even think that baby is mine." She rolled her eyes at me.

JEAN: "And why do you think that? You're the one who fucked her raw and didn't think to pull out."

RAY: "So is this what you're going to do? Say shit out of anger to make me feel worse than I already do?"

JEAN: "Make you feel the way I do? Oh no, not at all."

RAY: "Fuck you and your sarcasm."

JEAN: "Fuck *me*? Oh, that's how you feel? *You* go off and get a bitch that continuously hurt you and I've told you more than once to leave alone, pregnant, leaving me hurt, wondering what I did wrong, and I'm the bad guy?"

RAY: "It was hard enough to tell you and you over here being an ass hole."

JEAN: "*I am hurt Ray*! The man that I love oh so dearly and thought was the one went off..."

RAY: "So because of this, I'm no longer the one for you?" I chuckled some and turned away from her. "You know what... I am over this. Yeah, I messed up big time and I've been trying to sort out my problems alone but what I refuse to do is sit around and let you bash me like I'm just some hoe ass nigga. I never intentionally meant to hurt you and that is what you are trying to make it seem like. Just sit around and let the woman I love hurt and tear me down more than my ex already has, because I wasn't ready to tell her I have a baby on the way." I started pacing the room and saw her eyes starting to tear up. This is not how I wanted things to go. I never wanted our friendship to end let alone lose Jean, but I cannot set myself up for her to hurt me like Bethanee did. "Look, I love you Jean and always will, and when you feel like you can forgive and talk to me, I'm here. Until then, I think its best we just stop talking for a while." The tears started falling down her face and that hurt my soul.

JEAN: "Oh so that's it? That is how you solve your problems, by running away from them?" After she just talked like she was through with me.

RAY: "What DO YOU EXPECT ME TO DO?"

JEAN: "Make SHIT RIGHT!" She stood up from the bed. "You went right back to that bitch, *knowing* she wouldn't do shit but cheat and hurt you again. Only this time, she destroyed you. You are not the same Ray I met almost eight years ago. You let her get to you and you just run and stop fighting your problems. I did absolutely nothing wrong here, but I still get punished because you want to give up on the person who has been there for you every time Bethanee cheated. You get up and dip off on me for weeks at a time because you are not man enough to tell me wassup. *I AM YOUR BEST FRIEND*, your *WOMAN*. You do not do me like that because I would never and could never do you that way. Do not hurt me and make me suffer because your ex fucked up a good thing. I want this... this what we have but I do not want it if I can't get the one hundred percent Ray. I have been through too much with you and for you, to only get seventy- nine percent."

To hear her say all of this... to say she *is* my woman made me weak in the knees. I got butterflies in my stomach and I wanted to make love to her right then and there. She was right in so many ways. I did let Bethanee destroy me. I was always taught to forgive and how people deserved second chances.

Bethanee has gotten one too many second chances and broke me to where I could not even man up to tell my woman what was going on. It was the pride in me to not put my worries and my issues on my woman, so she did not have to worry with her own problems going on. Every King needs a Queen and today, I was about to throw away mine. I walked towards her and wiped the tears from her face. We looked each other deeply in the eyes and I grabbed her face.

RAY: "Let me make things right. Let me love you like there is no tomorrow. Let me give you the one hundred percent Ray. I promise not to let you down... only if you let me."

LALA: "Girl say yes."

RAY: "Get away from the door!"

JEAN: "Get the fuck away from the door." We both burst out laughing and I turned back to Jean.

RAY: "Will you let me?"

JEAN: "Only if you let me beat her ass when she drops."

RAY: "Go right ahead. Only six more months."

JEAN: "Wait, she's already three months? When was the last time you both had sex?"

RAY: "About a month ago. I mean it could be mine, but I don't know, she did cheat on me."

JEAN: "I advise you get a paternity test because she could just be doing that because the real daddy doesn't want anything to do with her. She is using you because she knows no matter how many times, she has cheated on you; you always end up taking her back. Now that she is *'carrying your child...'* you both can be this big happy family."

RAY: "I see you got jokes." I grabbed her waist and pulled her to me. As I was about to go in for a kiss, she moved away from me.

JEAN: "You need to get tested for diseases before we do anything else, honey."

RAY: "Wow. I will not even get mad at that. So, did you smash ol boy?"

JEAN: "This is a new beginning." She walked towards to door and was about to unlock it.

RAY: "Okay you need to get tested for diseases... *Honey*."
She turned back to me and she looked at me like she
wanted to beat my ass.

JEAN: "I haven't had sex with anyone since you, but to
make you happy, I will get tested." I rolled my eyes at her
and walked up to her as she was opening her bedroom
door. And the first person we see... LaLa. She is one nosey
individual. She walked back over to the couch and took a
seat. Tiffany was already sitting down on her phone while
ol boy was in the kitchen.

RAY: "Do you ever get tired of being nosey?" I walked
towards the living room and took a seat on the recliner.

LALA: "Do you ever get tired of running back to your ex?" I
did not even have time to respond, let alone knew what to
say.

JEAN: "You know what La, I think its best that you head
home." LaLa turned to Jean, mouth wide open.

LALA: "Excuse me?"

JEAN: "*Excuse me*? Yeah, I did not stutter. I'll hit you up
later." Jean walked towards the front door and unlocked
it.

LALA: "So you put your dick buddy before your girlfriend?"
She opened the door and motioned for LaLa to leave.

JEAN: "Yeah you need to chill. Not everything is about you.
So, before things get out of hand, I want you to leave my
house." Tiffany tried to jump in and de-escalate the

situation. "You back up and don't put yourself in something that has nothing to do with you."

TIFFANY: "This is your best friend, Jean."

JEAN: "Yeah? And so is Ray. You can leave right along with her. *Everybody* can leave. Since day one LaLa has never liked him and it was because she is jealous. Enough is enough. We are too grown to be acting childish because you think someone is taking your spot. It has been secure for over a decade and you still tripping. I am sick of you always talking down and bad about him when he has never done shit to you. That is exactly why I did not want to tell you about the night we first had sex. I knew you would overreact. Now look at you, popping off at the mouth about a sensitive subject that you do not know shit about. You don't see him talking about you and how many niggas you sleep with throughout the week."

LaLa eyes became wide as day, and I even heard Tiffany gasp.

TIFFANY: "Okay, chill out Jean."

JEAN: "I'll chill once she learns to chill and to control her mouth." Jean pointed to me. "This right here is my man, and I'm done allowing you to disrespect him. He has a forgiving heart that has gotten him in some fucked up situations. He cannot help but to love and give second chances. Am I wrong for giving him another?"

LaLa got up from the couch and grabbed her purse. She headed towards the door and took one last look at Jean.

LALA: "Don't come calling me when Amar finds your ass."

RAY: "She got me!"

JEAN: "You're a fucked-up friend for even saying something like that."

LALA: "Just like you were fucked up to say those things to me. Oh dang, it's Wednesday... let me find a new nigga to fuck." Jean shrugged.

JEAN: "That's you boo. Be careful."

LALA: "Fuck you."

She walked out of the front door.

TIFFANY: "LaLa chill out." Tiffany yelled and ran behind LaLa. Jean turned towards ol boy who was still standing in the kitchen.

JEAN: "Sorry things had to end this way, but you have to bounce too." He gulps down his glass of what looked like Henny and walked towards the front door to head out.

STEVEN: "All is well, but if things don't work out between you two... hit me up."

RAY: "She's in good hands baby boy. Holla!" He turned back to me, gave me a smirk then turned back to head out the door.

Chapter Fifteen

RAY x 2

After ol boy walked out, Jean closed the door behind and looked right at me.

RAY: "You good baby?" I could see tears beginning to form in the wells of her eyes.

JEAN: "This is too much for me today. I potentially have lost my best friend of eighteen years because she just doesn't know how to hush her mouth sometimes."

I walked towards her to comfort her and wiped the tears that were trying to roll down her face.

RAY: "Don't even stress yourself out about that. You already know how LaLa can be. Give her some time to cool down and if you feel like it... hit her up. If not, I understand and I'm here for you." I brought her in for a hug and kissed her soft lips, then her forehead. "I love you, Jean." She looked up at me.

JEAN: "I love you too." We walked over to the couch and sat down.

RAY: "Where and how you meet this nigga anyway?" That probably was not the best time to talk about this based on how she was looking at me.

JEAN: "Really?"

RAY: "Too soon?" He did look a little familiar. "What's this nigga name?"

JEAN: "You're just going to keep asking questions? Can you let it go?"

RAY: "I could but I really want to know." She turned to me with a smirk on her face.

JEAN: "Are you jealous?"

RAY: "Girl quit playing with me. You know damn well I am not jealous." I lied a little, but I was not going to admit that to her.

JEAN: "You keep on asking questions about him, you must be."

RAY: "He just looks really familiar to me." She folded her arms and rolled her eyes.

JEAN: "So you say. It's kind of cute to see that you are jealous, baby."

RAY: "I'm not jealous." She moved towards where I was sitting and got on top of me, straddling my legs. She then started kissing all over my face, working her way to my lips. I could kiss Jean all day long if I could. "Don't start something you can't finish." Jean got up and walked towards her bedroom.

JEAN: "Get checked baby!"

While she was in her room, I pulled my phone out to see if I could find anything on ol boy she was with. I may be a little jealous, but she would never find out. I scrolled through her Face Book friends to see if he was on the friend list. Trying not to be too noticeable of my jealousy, I kept peeping back towards Jean room to make sure she was not coming out anytime soon. The last thing I wanted was her thinking I am trying to be sneaky, hiding my phone when she comes out. I was beginning to get a little frustrated when finally; I came across a picture of what looked like to be him... Steven Coleman.

I selected his profile page and began to go through his photos.

RAY: "Yeah, that's him." I said aloud to myself.

JEAN: "That's who?" She scared the shit out of me. I stopped looking out for her when I finally found his Face Book page. Here she comes, all dressed up like she about to go on a date or some shit. She was not really paying attention to me, too busy trying to put her bracelet on. This was my chance to put my phone away.

RAY: "And where are you going, dressed like that?" She had on this skintight, hot pink dress, some beige sandals, with her beige and pink chain strap purse. Her hair was pulled up in a messy but not so messy bun, titties just out, trying to say hello to whoever, and the fragrance she had on made my dick jump. If I find out she is cheating on me, or trying to go see that Steven nigga, it is going to be World War five up in her crib.

I was not trying to be the controlling boyfriend, who would not allow his girl to go out, or try to dictate what she wears, but damn. She was and always looks good. I was never this jealous before I met Jean. Even when we were just best friends, and she would come out looking like a whole meal, the appetizer, with the side dish, dessert and a couple drinks, I was jealous. Jealous of all the dumb basic niggas she was giving a chance and is blind by my love for her.

When I say I have been loving this girl since the first day we had a deep conversation, she is telling me about all her dreams and what she has been through, I mean that shit. She deserves nothing but to be loved the right way, like the way I want to love her. I had gazed out for a while, but she had not answered me.

RAY: "Hello?" She looked up from putting her bracelet on and seem to be having some difficulties with them long ass nails. They glow in the dark so I know they would look good wrapped around my dick.

JEAN: "Can you put this on?" She extended her wrist out with her bottom lip poked out. "Please?" I just sat there and stared at her. I wanted answers.

RAY: "Where are you going?" She just stood there. Both of us were staring each other in the eyes waiting for an answer. My black ass gave in and grabbed her wrist to put her bracelet on. It kind of made my heart smile to see she was wearing the one I had bought for her last birthday, and I see now up close that's the purse I bought her *'just because.'* "Jean... where are you going?"

JEAN: "Out!" I gave her a straight face, letting her know *'out'* was not good enough.

RAY: "Out where?"

JEAN: "With a friend." Yeah, that did it for me. I did not want to start our new relationship with trust issues, but she was making it hard for me.

RAY: "Don't do this to me." I put my head in my hands.

JEAN: "Do what?"

RAY: "I'm sitting here asking who you're going out with and you say a *'friend.'* How do you think that would make me feel? Let me go out and only tell you it is a 'friend.' You would be just as curious as I am." I knew I was right, and she knew it too. Jean would be ready to fight them.

JEAN: "Steven!" She mumbled under her breath. I jumped up from her couch mad as hell.

RAY: "WHO?" I just know she did not tell me she was going out with the nigga she was trying to get with. Could she be more disrespectful? "I know you didn't just say Steven. The same nigga you were fucking with?"

JEAN: "It's not even like that." She stood there and I walked towards her.

RAY: "We just made this shit official and you're already disrespecting me. Are you crazy to legit go behind my fucking back and go out with a nigga I am pretty sure you thought about fucking? You're a hoe." She slapped the taste out of my mouth.

JEAN: "Watch it. Just because you're used to them doesn't make me one." I grabbed my keys from the coffee table and headed to the door.

RAY: "I'm over this. Have fun on your little date."

JEAN: "You are a bitch like LaLa said." Just as I was about to unlock the door, I turned back to her.

RAY: "I'm a bitch because I refuse to be with somebody that decides to go behind my back?"

JEAN: "It's not what you think..."

RAY: "*THEN WHAT IS IT*? I can't do this no trust shit with you Jean." I was really heading out the door because I knew my fumes were rising and I wanted to leave before it got too crazy.

JEAN: "I understand you're mad but watch your tone."

RAY: "Me or him?"

JEAN: "What?"

RAY: "You heard me... Me *or* him?" She frowned up at me.

JEAN: "You... duh. That is no compatible question. You're being insecure right now."

RAY: "How? Look at how you are dressed. Tight ass dress got on the dick stand up perfume, toes hanging out with the fresh polish. Look at your titties, just waiting for someone to pop one out to suck." She folded her arms across her chest trying to hide her breast.

JEAN: "I've always dressed like this, and you know it. Stop being so dramatic."

RAY: "And you were single back then but now is different. You were just dating this nigga and now you're about to go out with him."

JEAN: "Do you want to come with me? Will that make you feel better?"

RAY: "Yup." I reached for the front doorknob and unlocked it. "And don't try to call or text him to let him know I'm coming either... Little sneaky ass."

JEAN: "Ray shut the hell up and get out of my way." She pushed by me and shut the front door to lock it.

Once we got to the parking lot, Jean walked towards her car. I was staring at her ass the whole time. She must have been doing some squats or something because it looked a little fatter. I did not notice it in the house, I did not notice the glow she had going on either. Jean is one beautiful ass woman and I am ever so glad she is mine... officially. I had offered to drive but she declined. Once we got in the car, she cranked it up, put the car in reverse and we were on our way.

My phone had vibrated and noticed it was Bethanee calling me. I looked over at Jean and she could tell something was wrong.

JEAN: "What's wrong with you? Who was that?" She was looking back and forward between me and the road. My phone rang again, and it was Bethanee calling once more. I still did not answer. "Who keeps calling you?"

RAY: "You don't want to know." I rolled my eyes.

JEAN: "Who's calling you?"

RAY: "My baby mama." She looked over at me and gave me the eyes like she wanted to beat my ass.

JEAN: "I'll fight both of y'all."

RAY: "What's with the animosity? I did not do anything wrong here."

JEAN: "Don't call that bitch your baby mama. Call her hoe or something. Better yet call her Trick, or skank." This was the moment I knew dealing with Bethanee as a baby mama and Jean as my woman, it would be fights consistently. I looked at Jean with a straight face and turned back to the road.

One reason why I offered to drive is because my baby has road rage out of this world. Cut her off on the freeway if you want to. You are going to be called every name in the book; horn beeped at and might even get a ravioli can thrown at your car. I do not blame her one bit because people drive all types of crazy. It mostly be them big ass

Ford trucks or the old people getting over with no blinkers on. Jean is one of the most courteous folks you can encounter with on the road. That is *if,* you are driving at least close by the book. I mean by that put some blinkers on when you are trying to get over. If not, your ass going to be stuck fooling with Jean. And Lawd *please* do not ride her ass. She will become petty and ride her brakes. Let you come too close, she'll brake your ass in a quick second and if you wreck her, that's your fault because you shouldn't have been riding her tail in the first place.

Jean does not give a damn what car you are driving. If she thinks you are being petty with her, she will be petty right back with you. Do not get me wrong, she is a damn good driver, she just got road rage. Kind of made her even more sexy to me. She lowkey drives like a nigga. Be leaning all to the side, arm rested on the center consol. She will have her stunner shades on, skin just glowing, leaning like a nigga. She looked over at me when I grabbed her hand and held it. I do not ever want to lose Jean as my woman, and I will make sure it does not happen. We finally pulled up to some restaurant that I have never been to, let alone ever heard of.

RAY: "What is this?"

JEAN: "Bring your ass or sit in the car." She had a lot of nerve if she really thought I was going to sit in the car while she on a date with this nigga.

RAY: "Yeah aight." We both stepped out of the car and headed inside. I was a couple feet behind Jean, so she walked in first. This nigga was cheesing from ear to ear when he first saw her. Then he saw me. HA. That smiled changed so damn quick I could not do nothing but laugh.

STEVEN: "What is he doing here?"

RAY: "This is a public environment sir."

STEVEN: "Okay, go publicly sit your ass at your own table... sir."

RAY: "If that's the case, my woman coming with me." He looked towards Jean, and she looked at me. I looked at her like bitch you better agree with me. Not trying to call her a bitch but she better agree with me.

JEAN: "He's right. If he cannot sit at the table with us, then we'll get our own."

STEVEN: "What the fuck was the use of you coming anyway if you were going to bring this nigga."

RAY: "Her man."

STEVEN: "Nigga... nobody cares." There were not many people in the restaurant but someone did look over at us.

RAY: "I'm pretty sure you do since we all know you cannot have her."

JEAN: "Y'all two fighting like bitches. Chill out." She looked back between this nigga and me, and I had a smile on my face the entire time. I am the one winning here, getting to wrap my arms around Jean every night. I was starting to feel a little played like why she even came out on this date with him, knowing I would have a problem with it.

RAY: "Now I'm getting curious. Why did you agree to meet with him knowing you got a man?"

JEAN: "We had already made plans before you and I became official."

RAY: "And your point?"

STEVEN: "And?" She looked back between us both like she wanted to beat our ass. She could not be mad though. "Why did you continue to come on this date?"

Jean still did not answer us, making her look sneaky. Just as I was about to ask her again, my phone rang. It was Bethanee and Jean saw she was calling. Before I could even ignore the call, Jean grabbed my phone and answered it.

JEAN: "Hello?" There was no use in trying to grab the phone from her because eventually she would be talking to Bethanee. Whether it was over the phone or face to face. Lawd knows all hell would break lose if it was face to face. My volume on my phone was turned all the way up, so you could pretty much hear the entire conversation.

BETHANEE: "Who is this?"

JEAN: "You called my phone, who is this?"

BETHANEE: "I called for my boyfriend... Ray. Where is he?"

JEAN: *"Boyfriend* huh?" Jean looked at me and sucked her teeth.

BETHANEE: "Bitch you heard what I said."

JEAN: "Bitch? Do not get your head knocked off. Pregnant and all hoe."

BETHANEE: "Where is my boyfriend?"

Steven looked over at me and bugged his eyes. I did the same agreeing with the shenanigans going on between Jean and Bethanee.

JEAN: "Go check the trashcan, where you got them dusty ass bundles. *My* man is occupied. Is there anything else I can assist you with before I end this call?"

BETHANEE: "This must be Jean."

JEAN: "Ding. Glad you know honey. What can I do you for?"

BETHANEE: "You know he's just playing you right? Ray is in love with me and will forever be."

JEAN: "Then why he keeps dodging your phone calls?"

BETHANEE: "That's because he around you sweetie."

JEAN: "I'm not your sweetie."

BETHANEE: "Okay Ms. Sour. Tell my boyfriend to call me so I can update him about his child."

JEAN: "Everybody and they mama knows that is not his baby. Go play in traffic hoe and stop calling this phone before I give your ass a miscarriage by beating your ass." Jean hung up the phone and blocked Bethanee number. She then handed me my phone and gave both me and Steven the biggest, fakest smile.

RAY: "You good?" Jean turned towards me.

JEAN: "Great! Shall we sit?"

STEVEN: "Hold up." He put his hands in front of Jean prevented her to move forward. "We need answers. Why did you agree to still meet with me when you two are together?" I did not like this nigga at first, still kind of do not, but he is right. The fuck she still meeting with him for. She rolled her eyes and I knew she was getting irritated.

JEAN: "Look, the way things played out earlier was kind of hectic. I did not mean for it to go down that way and really feel like I should apologize. You a cool dude and I could see us still being friends *if*..."

RAY: "Oop..."

JEAN: "That's okay with Ray."

RAY: "Now you know damn well..." I could never actually put my hands-on Jean, but she could say some dumb ass shit.

JEAN: "You're acting like I'm going to cheat or lie to you about him."

RAY: "You wasn't even trying to tell me about meeting with him today so..."

JEAN: "Because I didn't need you overreacting like you are right now. You should trust me by now and know I only have good intentions for and with you. I know about your past relationships. You think I'm really trifling like that to put you through the same shit Bethanee did?" I hate that Bethanee ruined my trust. I knew in my heart that Jean would never do me wrong; it's just the thought of it. "This relationship would never work if you don't learn to trust me."

   I knew she was right. I felt a little shame coming to this little get together with her and Steven now. I wanted a healthy relationship with Jean. She looked me in my eyes...

JEAN: "Ray I could never hurt you. Not even if I wanted to. I came here today to really just apologize to Steven and that's it... honestly." Steven was staring at us both while sitting in the booth. I looked over at him and this nigga really do look familiar to me and I am trying to figure out where I know him from.

RAY: "Are you from here?"

STEVEN: "Born and raised. I lived with my pops until I was about 15 then moved in with my aunt. Pops was starting to do too much. Had a different woman over to the crib every day and I did not want to be around that type of environment. Why?"

RAY: "You look familiar to me. I just can't remember where I've seen you."

JEAN: "Oh just my luck that my boyfriend knows the nigga I was beginning to know." The waiter came over to see if we wanted anything to drink or to start with some appetizers. Steven ordered a beer then looked at Jean and me.

STEVEN: "Y'all getting something?" I and Jean both sat down in the booth. Jean was a little harsh when she sat down. As though she was about to panic. She ordered a mango margarita, frozen and I got myself a beer as well.

JEAN: "You know what; let me get some chips and salsa too." The waiter wrote down our orders then walked away to complete them.

STEVEN: "Did you grow up here?"

RAY: "Yeah. Did not really know my pops like that. After I was born, he kind of just dipped out on my mother and me. She tried to stay in contact with some of his family, but you know how that can go. But there was this one lady that she did stay in contact with for years after my pops left." And that is when it came to me. "Is your aunt name Golinda?" The face he made assured me that I was right.

STEVEN: "Yeah, that's my pops sister. The aunt I stayed with for a few years. How do you know her?"

RAY: "That's my mother's friend. She calls her sister in law but never really talked about her and my pops. She came over to the house a few times. Then my mother and I moved a little too far."

STEVEN: "Oh shit. I think I did come to your mother's house one day. Over on Zeisz road, about two blocks from that Gen's corner store." The waiter had just come back with all our drinks, and Jean immediately grabbed for hers. "Your mother's name is Ms. Lucy... right?"

RAY: "Yeah!"

JEAN: "Hold the fuck up... If your mother called your mother sister in law, does that make y'all... bro...thers...?" She damn near gulp half of her drink by now. I don't see how she didn't have a brain freeze.

STEVEN: "... Do you remember your pops name?"

RAY: "I know my mother got my name from his. I think it's Ragenal... Raymond..."

STEVEN: "Raymond!"

RAY: "Raymond Beamer..."

STEVEN: "That's my pops."

RAY: "You're still in contact with him?"

STEVEN: "I talk to him every now and again."

I just found my long-lost stepbrother. I looked over at Jean who was now finished with her drink while Steven and I have not even touched ours. Clearly this is too much for her.

JEAN: "I need another drink. I cannot believe I was about to smash my best friend... now boyfriends' brother." She slumped down in her seat and waited for the waiter to come by.

Part 2

Chapter Sixteen

A Dipp from the Past but I Love Him- LaLa

It had been at least two weeks since I last talked to Jean. I miss my friend like crazy, but she was wrong in so many ways, or maybe that is just me being dramatic again. I mean I was wrong for disrespecting her man but damn, she was my friend first and she knows how I can get when it comes to our friendship. I will not lie; I have gotten worse since that night we got too drunk and shit went down. I do not regret it happening one bit though. Tiffany and I have been talking less since Jean kicked me out too. I guess I really was in the wrong since both of my girls were being distant. I could understand why Jean was being distant, but Tiffany threw me off.

Since that day Wade and I have not really been talking either. Something telling me this nigga cheating on with some stank pussy ass hoe. Sammy and I have been hitting it off heavy. Like texting and talking almost all day, every day. I think I am really starting to like him. We have been on a few dates since our little group date with all three couples and surprisingly we have not had sex... yet! He was just supposed to be some hookup to get and keep my mind off Wade, but our feelings are getting stronger. In no time he will indeed get the box and I was going to make sure he would not get enough of me. Porn hub has been teaching me some new moves that I was ready to try on

Sammy. At this point I am just *'fuck Wade'* it is time to move on.

    Sammy and I had planned a little outing date at the park. After I found out what the true meaning for *'picnic,'* I stopped using it. Tonight, just might be the night Sammy and I take it to the bedroom. Do not get me wrong, we have been close to having sex almost every time we link up but each time, one of us stop it. We are both grown but we also both know what sex can do to a relationship. It is funny how we both started talking to each other as fuck buddies but have yet to fuck. Boy did I want to... and bad. I find myself looking at the bulge in his pants every damn time I see him. I even had him send me some dick picks and this young man is working with something that I wanted to get my hands on. I just do not want to get so worked up and be disappointed with his dick game. Boy got all that meat and do not even know how to use it. Regardless of the situation, I missed my girls Jean and Tiffany bad and must get things back right. I just have to let go of my pride and apologize.

    I know Jean was being a smart ass when she told me to be safe, but she probably meant that. Just at that moment made it seem like she was being sarcastic. She did not have to kick me out like that though. My phone rang and look who finally decided to call me... Wade. I started to ignore his call but a part of me wanted to see what the fuck he wanted.

LALA: "What?"

WADE: "Is that how you answer the phone for your man?" I took the phone from my ear while rolling my eyes to put it in on speaker phone.

LALA: "I am single. Now what do you want?"

WADE: "Single my ass. Quit playing with me LaLa before I pull up on your ass." Picking up the fingernail file from my coffee table, I placed my phone on the couch to tend to my nails.

LALA: "And do what? Get shot?"

WADE: "Get shot?"

LALA: "Yeah by me. Now what do you want? I got a date I need to get ready for."

WADE: "I see you got jokes today. Come open the door." Bucking my eyes, I stopped filing my nails and turned to the front door.

LALA: "I'm not home." I lied.

WADE: "I saw your car parked in the parking lot."

LALA: "That doesn't mean anything. I could have ridden with someone else."

WADE: "I can hear you through the door."

I rolled my eyes, got up from the couch and walked closer to my room.

LALA: "I don't know what you're talking about. I'm not home." I lied again. I just was not feeling him or wanted to see him whatsoever.

WADE: "When you plan on coming back and where you at? Nah wait, who this little hot date?"

LALA: "Business." I sat on my bed and crossed my legs while flipping through the television channels... low volume.

WADE: "I know you're in your apartment La. I can hear a television." Clearly not low enough.

LALA: "And your point? I said I am not home and that is that. What else can I do for you?"

WADE: "Let me find out you out with another nigga..." I put the television on mute.

LALA: "I am. Next?"

WADE: "You all hard now. Wait until I see you."

LALA: "Wade, go back to your little one-night stand ass hoe house and leave me the hell alone."

I hung up the phone, got up and started walking to the front door. I looked through the peep hole and saw he was still standing there looking dumb as hell. That will teach him not to dip off on me. As I was about to go back to getting ready, I actually did have a date with Sammy, I saw Benny and Amar. My eyes got big as a deer in head lights.

They all were dapping it up, handshakes and what not, manly shit.

LALA: "Friendly ass."

Wade knew Jean and Amar but only briefly and knew to cut all ties with him and I thought he did. I could not hear that much but tried to make out what they were saying.

Something on how he is mad that he driven over to my house and I was not home, and they should link up sometime for drinks when the next game comes on. Amar mentioned what had happened a few weeks ago when Jean was over here. I even heard Wade mention how he could bring over some chicks, but then nigga was just knocking on my door and on my phone trying to make shit right. Next thing I know, Sammy walks up... with flowers. I did not know if I should be mad or excited. No one has ever brought me flowers but, why did he have to show up now?

LALA: "Shit. Shit. Shit. What is he doing here?" Then it hit me... our date.

He knocked on my door while Wade and they just looked at him. I could not just turn him around. I had already told him I was home, getting ready not even ten minutes ago. I paced back and forth in my living room, contemplating if I should open the door or not. I mean Sammy does know about Wade but only briefly. The only problem is, Wade was just knocking on my door, and I did not answer. Sammy knocked again... and I opened my door. I just could not find myself to ignore him.

SAMMY: "Hey baby girl." He came in for a kiss as Wade and I made eye contact.

WADE: "What is this? I just knocked on your door a few minutes ago and you were talking about how you were not home and shit. My nigga you really cheating on me?" Sammy turned to Wade. Amar and Benny mouths wide open in shock.

SAMMY: "Oh *you* must be Wade?"

WADE: "You've been discussing me with this nigga La?"

LALA: "You were just talking about how you wanted to bring over some bitches to your little get together with your boys. Boys that you were supposed to lose contact with after Amar and Jean broke up. I'm single and will do as I please." I folded my arms across my chest, while standing in my doorway.

WADE: "You really do have me fucked up if you think I'm just going to let this fly." Wade started walking towards my apartment.

SAMMY: "You want to just skip our date and chill in the house?" I looked over at Sammy worried like why he would want to do that. Sammy whispered 'let us go in the house so I can make love to you' in my ear and had me smiling from ear to ear. At that point I was cool missing out on the outing. Wade was still standing there looking crazy, but I did not care. He made his own bed, now he has to lay in it. I turned towards my apartment, grabbed Sammy's hand and headed inside. Wade came storming in behind us and stopped me from closing the door all the way by putting his foot in the doorway.

LALA: "If you don't move your motherfucking foot, I'm going to shoot it." I smirked at him. "You of all people should know who raised me." He sucked his teeth and looked over at Sammy who had taken off his shirt and pants. Damn I was turned on and ready to jump on him. Wade does not have shit on Sammy body wise. Do not get me wrong, Wade has a nice body with the muscles, but Sammy... you can see every crease, every cut. You know that little feeling where it feels like your period just started out of nowhere and blood is just overflowing your pussy? But in all reality, your pussy just wet as fuck? This was happening staring at Sammy. I may have drooled a bit.

WADE: "So you're about to fuck this nigga?"

SAMMY: "You want to watch?"

WADE: "Bitch..." He pushed through the door trying to get in, and almost did, right along with breaking my foot. Sammy ran over to push him completely outside of my door and locked it. "THIS AIN'T OVER LALA."

LALA: "Kiss my ass and go to hell." He beat on my door one good time and growled like an angry dog. I did not give a damn though. Wade got exactly what he deserved. A slap in the face for how he has been treating me. He goes M.I.A then I overhear him talking about some bimbos. Even before that he has been sneaky. Always having some random ass late calls that required him to leave the room we are in or coming home late, even leaving late. Seems like every time he left, he could never tell me where he is going, why he is leaving or say bye. After a while, I just assumed he was cheating on me. That is when I started really doing my own thing.

SAMMY: "You're just going to stand over by the doorway or bring your sexy ass over here?" I had zoned out for a moment. He licked his lips and my pussy got even more wet from just by looking at him. As I started walking towards him, he came closer to me. For the first time in my life, I felt butterflies in my stomach. I was nervous to have sex with Sammy and this has never happened to me. He touched my arm and I got chills.

They always say you have three loves in life. The one who's your play love; you do not take him that serious. The one who is your hard love; this one may determine how strong you really are. You all will go through so much drama, pain and more. The pro about it is that it builds your character. Then the last one is *'the one'* for you. Could Sammy be the one for me? I was not trying to over think the situation for the simple fact I did not really know Sammy's intentions with me. I bet it was only to fuck since that is how we met and what we both planned on doing. It was too soon to say but I think I was now starting to fall for Sammy. I know I have done my share of wrong but why should that keep me from being happy? I deserved my happiness just like anyone else and I was about to have it with Sammy.

SAMMY: "You're so beautiful La." He looked me in my eyes and those butterflies were back. It has only been weeks since we started talking but it felt like years.

LALA: "I love you..." I bucked my eyes wide open like what in the fuck did I just say? I was trying to switch up the mood but ended up nervously laughing. "I was just ki..." Sammy grabbed my face and kissed me. This was no regular ass kiss either. This was an *'if you don't let me make love to you to show how much I love you; I'm going to get mad'* kiss. Do not ask me how I would know that. Shit just felt right. Oh yeah, we are still kissing. Could this be my moment like Jean and Ray or Tiffany and Keyvaune? Was I about to be screaming out *'yes daddy,'* disturbing my neighbors? If this nigga cannot make me cum at least seven times, he is not the one. Okay five... no no, three. Sammy just make me cum baby.

He straddled me around his waist, and I could feel his dick pulsing up against my pussy. Those dick pictures he sent better match his dick game or I will have to leave him alone. Maybe it was my emotions because I felt like I had already cum, and his dick had not even made it inside me. I had on this little orange dress that came about two inches from my knees... no panties, no bra. He sat me on the couch, but I pushed him off of me just before he was about to start eating my pussy.

SAMMY: "Where you are going?" I got up and ran to my bedroom and came back with some blue raspberry flavored lube. He was sitting on the couch with his arm over his eyes like he had fucked up or something.

Sammy did not notice I had come back until I had started pulling down his briefs just enough to whip his dick out. Damn that thing was massive. My whole hand could not even fit around it. He looked me directly in my eyes. I kissed the head of his penis then made my way down to the shaft. You can never forget the balls. He started moaning softly, and that was turning me on. I put his penis in my mouth just to see how far it could go. I have never had a dick this big or wide, but I was going to make sure he would never want to give his dick to anyone else.

I grabbed my flavored lube and smeared it on the shaft of his dick. It was sitting in my nightstand but was kind of cold. Made both Sammy and his dick jump. I teased him a bit by gently, and slowly licking the shaft of his dick. Mind you, he is a little bigger than I am used to, so I definitely wasn't trying to choke trying to give him head. I eventually licked every drop of the lube off and ended up putting more. I enjoy sucking dick and blue raspberry is my all-time favorite flavor. Those two combined made a happy ending for my man. I could see his toes started to curl; he was clenching his ass cheeks and moaning a lot louder than before. I began to speed up the licks and slurps I was giving him and did some hand motions as well.

Some men like when the woman spit on his dick. That is a bit messy for me but when I am in the moment; I don't be giving a damn. There is a little technique you can do to make you not gag when you are sticking the dick a little further than you usually do. And there I was... every inch was in the back of my throat. I did it. I knew he had to be about nine or even ten inches, and I was able to take every inch. At this point he was screaming.

SAMMY: "Damn girl. Take that dick." And that is what I did. I started moaning myself because I had started playing with my pussy. "Ain't nobody ever took that dick like you are right now baby. Oooo don't stop."

I sped up the motions and even deep throat a few times but not too many. His dick was too long but that is something I can become accustomed to. I looked him in his eyes, and he frowned up at me. This was a good frown though. One that was pleasurable. He bit his bottom lip and I continued to look in his eyes while I took every inch of that long dick in my mouth.

SAMMY: "Fuck, you about to make me nut." All I could say with a mouth full of dick was *'Mmm huh.'*

LALA: "You gone cum for me baby?"

SAMMY: "Yes… Ooo shit don't stop." He started rising from the couch, but I pushed him down. At this point I did not know if he was being dramatic, or I was really taking his soul. A few seconds later, he exploded in my mouth.

SAMMY: "I love you too, what the fuck." I could not do nothing but laugh. Some of the nut fell from the creases of my lips as I was walking to spit in the toilet. "BRING YOUR ASS HERE GIRL." I brushed my teeth and headed back to the living room. He was standing over the couch as he motioned for me to sit down. He ran to the bathroom, and I heard water running.

LALA: "Is this nigga taking a shower?" That is so sweet. Wipe off the sticky lube before you stick my vagina. Yeah, I love him. He came back from the bathroom, body just glistening.

SAMMY: "Get up." I had a confused look on my face. He turned me around and bent me over. Next thing I know, his tongue was in my ass. Yeah, I love him. Made my pussy so wet. He went from licking my ass to sucking my clit. Good thing I did a deep cleaning before he had come over. Then boom... every inch was making its way in my pussy, and just like that, I came. A few more strokes in, I came again. Yeah, I love him. He flipped me over...

SAMMY: "I said I wanted to make love to you girl."

LALA: "You're trying to make me crazy..." He stuck his dick in my pussy, giving me slow strokes. Yeah, I love him. He looked me deeply in my eyes with every stroke. It is like my pussy was craving more of him and did not want him to stop. He gave me one good long stroke...

SAMMY: "You like that baby?" I frowned up but in a good way. It felt so good, nothing like I am used to. "Tell me you like the way daddy giving you these strokes." At this point, I am convinced that he is trying to make me crazy. Giving me all of these slow strokes and asking if I like it. Sammy, I love you baby, I just could not find myself to respond to him. Hell, I did not even know if I should. He stopped fucking me and just looked me dead in my eyes.

LALA: "What is it? Why did you stop?" He started putting on his clothes, and I was confused as to why. While I am just sitting, ass naked on the couch, he's still getting dressed. One thing I hate is being ignored. "Hello?" He glared at me.

SAMMY: "Imma hit you up." I tried running after him and grabbed his arm, but he snatched away from me. I had to remind myself that I am still naked and too fine to be chasing this nigga. He unlocked the door and left. I stood in my doorway in awe. He legit stopped fucking me and left.

Chapter Seventeen

I plopped down on my couch... still naked then searched through my contacts for Jean number. I clicked on it but could not gain the urge to call her. I knew she was probably still mad at me but at some point, I am going to have to get it together to fix our friendship. I ended up calling Tiffany since it had been a minute since I last talked to her too, but there was no answer. So, I was just sitting on my couch ass naked still wondering why Sammy dipped out the way he did. As I was about to get up, my phone rang from some random number. I don't answer unknown numbers, so I forward them to voicemail, but they ended up calling again.

LALA: "Hello."

KELVIN: "I miss you La." I recognize that voice anywhere. Kelvin, my ex before Wade, was calling me. He knew not to hit me up ever again after the way we ended, and he got a lot of nerve. That boy put me through hell for five years and I was not trying to go back.

LALA: "What do you want?"

KELVIN: "I'm glad you know it's me. How you been baby? I miss you." Every few years this nigga hit me up out of nowhere from all types of numbers or even social media on how he misses me. He needs to find him someone else to play with because my patience running low... been running low.

LALA: "Again... what do you want?" I got up from the couch and headed to the kitchen to fix me a drink... still naked. It is not like this is the first time I walked around my house naked.

KELVIN: "Damn, like that?"

LALA: "You're full of shit Kelvin. Why are you calling me? You always do this shit." I slammed my hand on my kitchen counter in frustration.

KELVIN: "I miss you like I said. Let me take you out or something. Make things right between us."

LALA: "Nah I'm good... you..."

KELVIN: "Come on La. I know I've fucked up in the past but I'm different now." Okay, *2 Chainz*. He has said this to me before. "I promise I've changed. There is no other woman out here like you. I miss you smile, your touch, your hugs, being around you. Come on baby, let me make things right."

Was I about to be dumb again and give him another chance? Plopping down on the couch, I took a sip of my rum and coke.

LALA: "Nah."

KELVIN: "Dammit La. You must have a new nigga?"

LALA: "Nah. I'm just not about to fall for your lying ass again. You haven't changed a bit."

KELVIN: "I can prove it..."

Do not get me wrong, I loved Kelvin and still got love for him, but I do not think I could ever trust him again after what he put me through. Five years is a long time to be with someone. Well it was not five years straight; it was on and off. He cheated on me for the first year we were together, then we took a break and here he comes calling my phone talking about he misses me about six months later. I fell for it then; everyone deserves second chances, right?

Our relationship was going smooth for a few months, and then this nigga cheated again. After that, I broke up with him and we were not together two years. He did not have a number at the time so he DM'd me about how sorry he is, and he wanted to make things right. I gave him another chance but was still having some trust issues from the last time we tried things. That is where I fucked up at. He cheated before; he would do it again. One day, some random chick called his phone blabbing on how she was his girlfriend, and at that point I was done with him. I vowed to never give him another chance... ever!

Before Sammy, Kelvin was the only one who could really tear the pussy up. Do not get me wrong, Wade is good in the bedroom, but he is no Sammy, let alone Kelvin. Wade is better with his head game. Still not better than Kelvin or Sammy. I could always cum that way but with Wade's dick, I would have to play with my pussy or use one of my toys just to cum. I could never understand how your dick game wasn't even all that, but you could still cheat on the woman you could barely make cum. Niggas just out here disappointing all these women, thinking they really laying down the pipe. I know them tricks were faking. I faked it half of the time. Do not even know why I stayed with him so long.

I was a little upset on how Sammy walked out on me and still wanted a nut... bad. He had stopped just when I was about to orgasm. I wanted to cum multiple times. Like a dummy I thought to have Kelvin to come over to finish what Sammy started. I had to make a promise to myself that I would not let the dick convince me to take Kelvin back... at least try. Since Kelvin and I had broken up, he did not know where I live, and I wanted to keep it that way. I already have one too many people knowing where I reside, and I do not need no mess jumping off. And just when I thought...

LALA: "... We can meet somewhere..."

KELVIN: "Great. Let me take you out to dinner."

I was in no mood to hang out with him in public. Probably end up seeing someone I know then they will think we are trying to work things out again. Did not too much give a damn what people think, but still do not need folks in my business. Honestly, I just wanted to finish what Sammy started and keep it moving, so basically, do Kelvin how he would do me.

LALA: "Why don't we just get a room?"

KELVIN: "That's cool," I rolled my eyes. "I'll pay," even better. I know Kelvin. At the end of the day, all he just wants is to fuck. We ended the conversation then he sent me a text with the address to the hotel about ten minutes later. He did not waste no time. I was still sitting on the couch ass naked, so I got up and headed to the bathroom to take a shower. Once I got out, I slipped on a maxi dress, my Nike slides, grabbed my keys, and headed for the front door. I checked my phone and saw that Tiffany had texted me saying she would call me later; she was in a meeting. I texted back 'K' then closed my phone and locked my front door. Once I was heading out, I checked my mailbox, which only happens once a week because I do not be expecting any mail. It's usually a bunch of sales papers they could keep and bills. I got to my car and was on my way to Kelvin.

Kelvin kept calling and texting me to see where I was at and if I was still coming. I did not respond to any of them. I will get there when I get there. After a while I was starting to get frustrated with him blowing up my phone and made a pit stop to get something to put in my stomach. Did not want to be fucking then my stomach ends up growling or making some weird noise. After I was done eating, I chewed on me a piece of gum the rest of the drive.

I finally made it to the hotel. I was not expecting the Hilton. I am not a hoe or anything, but I am pretty sure he spent about ninety dollars on this room. The Hilton is not all that cheap unless you have a membership or something. And even then, you have to book a certain amount of rooms just to get a discount. I looked at my phone for the room number and rode the elevator to that specific floor.

Once I made it, he was calling my phone again. I ignored the call and knocked on the door. He opened it and my mouth dropped to the floor. He was looking as good as I remembered, but more handsome. His body shinning like he had slapped a bottle of baby oil on his body. He had the towel wrapped around his waist and I thought I was peeing on myself.

KELVIN: "You had seen me calling you. Bring your ass in here so I can teach you a lesson." I was stuck. My body wanted to move, but my feet were staying still. I had to say a little prayer that I would not fall back into his arms again. "I'm not playing with you La. Bring your ass here."

You know what I did? Brought my ass there. I could feel him walking on my heel, already hard dick touching my back. Something told me to turn my ass around and go back home. The lights were dim. He had toys, rope, lube, and more; some fifty shades of grey shit. I saw candles lit, rose petals, and fruit. Boy, I was scared.

KELVIN: "Take off that dress." I still had not even said a word since I walked in, but I took instructions well. I slide that damn dress off and just looked at him. Nipples erect, waiting for his mouth to slob on them. "When I call you, you answer me. Do you hear?" I did not say shit, but my head nodded. I do not know where he got this from or when he found this side of him out, but I liked it.

He walked towards me and started caressing my titties and then put the right one in his mouth. He has big lips and a fat tongue. My breasts are not that big, so he was able to fit my whole nipple in his mouth. I moaned lightly. He pushed me on the bed gently and opened my legs. I wanted to cum just by him breathing on my pussy. Fat Lucy had to calm down... immediately. He opened my lips with his tongue and went to work. Slow licks, up and down my clit. He had dreads so I grabbed a hold of them as he continued to work his magic. I did not notice when he grabbed some toy and inserted it inside of me. My pussy started creaming. He still knew my body. Exactly what to do, how to do it

KELVIN: "Mmm, just how I remembered. I miss you baby." NOPE! I was not going to fall for it this time. Kelvin knew *exactly* what he was doing. He stood up and dropped the towel on the floor.

I was trying hard to hold my moans in but, that dick just felt so good. He is moaning, I am moaning... loud. He took his penis out of me and started devouring fat Lucy, then put his penis back in. I had at least three orgasms at this point and was ready to stop. He was about to nut by the way he clinched his face, and I pushed him off of me, slipped my dress back on and left. No goodbye; no see you later, no nothing, just like Sammy did me. Could that be the reason he left? It felt too good. Once I got to my car, I sat there, car still off taking a mental break. I had to breathe, get my mind right.

For the first time in a while, I cried. Cried because I felt like what I did was wrong. I vowed to myself I would not have no dealings with Kelvin ever again... just when I thought, I was back where I started. I could not allow myself to get trapped and tied into his bullshit. My phone rang and it was my girl, Tiffany. At that point I really missed my girl Jean and thought of how she was always there for me whenever Kelvin broke my heart or did some hurtful things to me, and I needed her. I needed both my girls Jean and Tiffany before I have a breakdown.

LALA: "I need you." I cried out to Tiffany.

TIFFANY: "What's wrong La? Where are you?"

LALA: "I need you and Jean. I am sorry Tiff. I am sorry for acting like a spoiled brat. I need you both." I placed my head on the steering wheel and let the tears fall.

TIFFANY: "La, where are you? Just tell me where you are, and I'll have Jean come over with me."

LALA: "At a hotel."

TIFFANY: "What the fuck happened? Did someone hurt you? I will kill a motherfucker if they did. Tell me what's up La."

LALA: "Kelvin. Sammy. Wade."

TIFFANY: "Did they run a train on you or something? Did they rape you? Baby tell me what is wrong. Send me your location, I'm coming right now." I ignored the fact that she said, *'running a train.'*

LALA: "I fucked up Tiff."

I cried even harder because this was a lot on me. I had not even given myself time to get over Wade. I just started talking to Sammy because I felt single and wanted to hurt Wade like he hurt me. I felt that Wade abandoned me. Why should I sit around wondering what I did wrong when I have been nothing but loyal to him our entire relationship, but he could not seem to keep his dick in his pants? Why did I fall so fast for Sammy knowing that it was just supposed to be a friend with benefits thing in the beginning? And why did I allow Kelvin to come back into my life? Just why? Why am I attracted to dudes who just walk out on me or hurt me? I need to re-evaluate my life.

TIFFANY: "LaLa?" I had blacked out thinking about my life.

LALA: "Yeah?"

JEAN: "Where are you?"

LALA: "Jean?" I lifted my head and wiped my tears away.

JEAN: "Yeah, are you okay?"

LALA: "I thought you were mad at me..."

JEAN: "Baby that's beside the point. Are you okay?"

LALA: "I just need my girls right now. I made a huge mistake and don't know where to go from here." The tears just kept flowing because I knew I was at a bad place in my life.

TIFFANY: "Tell us where you are La."

LALA: "... At a room with Kelvin..."

JEAN: "How did that happen?"

I felt embarrassed. Both Jean and Tiffany told me to leave him alone, I let my sexual desire get in the way.

LALA: "Y'all know how he does... I break up with him then he hit me up out of nowhere on that '*I miss you*' shit." I rolled my eyes.

TIFFANY: "And you fell for it?"

I already knew this was coming. Both Tiffany and Jean had their own opinions about Kelvin, and he was on their shit list. I let the sex get the best of me because it was so good. Maybe this time he really did change but I was not trying to find out. I wanted to see what was up with Sammy. I felt something there between him and needed answers as to why he walked out. I really thought he was the one for me. Kelvin was just a fantasy for me, Sammy is real love that I want to experience.

At this point I knew I just needed to focus on myself and get me right. I ended up telling my girls to meet me at my house for makeup, drinks and to talk. I cranked up my car, put it in drive and was on my way. As I was driving out of the parking lot, Kelvin texted me, but I ignored it. I was in no mood to talk to him or deal with his bullshit.

Chapter Eighteen

It Was the Homey- Tiffany

JEAN: "So the dick had you screaming that you love him?"

LaLa rolled her eyes and we all burst out laughing. Sammy had her sprung, screaming out shit after just a few weeks. My girls had finally come over and were big chilling in La's crib, having drinks and catching up. Looks to me, La had pulled herself together after the miniature breakdown from leaving Kelvin. She still had not heard from Sammy and Kelvin just keeps on blowing her up. As for Wade, neither of us was too worried about him. He had his chance with my girl and blew it.

LaLa had ordered us all wings and fries. Jean is about the only one who eats the celery sticks on the side. It was just like old times with them, like we had not even had a disagreement and stopped talking. Although we originally came together for La's melt down earlier, La did indeed apologize to Jean and Jean apologized as well. La felt as though and kept going on and on how she did not even need to do so, for the simple fact it was LaLa doing all of the shit talking.

Eventually she will apologize to Ray as well. We all know he adores and loves my girl Jean and would never do anything intentionally to hurt her. Maybe, La was just jealous as to how close they were getting. We don't usually keep secrets between us three and ever since Ray came into the picture; I would admit everyone has been keeping them. La probably felt the most betrayed when she found out I already knew about Jean and Ray.

TIFFANY: "You're thinking about calling Sammy? I thought you two would be good for each other."

JEAN: "And you need as well as deserve a good man at this point." She took a sip of her wine and looked at us both.

LALA: "I don't want to seem so crazy..."

TIFFANY: "But you are..." We all burst out laughing as La rolled her eyes at my comment.

LALA: "Don't get me wrong, I do want to call him and see exactly why he left the way he did. You guys I really liked him, and you know it doesn't take that long for me to give up the pussy."

JEAN: "Yeah, you need to work on that."

LALA: "I did... with Sammy. I usually am giving it up after the first couple days of knowing the brother. Sammy was, *is* different. Like I can really see myself with him for a long ass time."

TIFFANY: "If you really feel that way you would call him. If you do not get an answer, move the hell on. Just know at the end of the day, you got us, and you tried with Sammy." I grabbed her thigh to assure her girls will always be around.

LALA: "I appreciate that."

JEAN: "Have you heard anything about Tony and who shot him?"

I turned to Jean as I was taking a sip of my wine.

TIFFANY: "Not at all. They are supposed to be doing some investigating, video watching and shit to see if they can find out who shot him. It is just a waiting game at this point. I went to go see his mother the other day to see how she was doing. She did not look too good. First Tim and now Tony."

LALA: "Damn. Both of her sons gone within two years. I know she must be going through it."

TIFFANY: "They still hadn't found out who killed Tim, fingers crossed they get it together with Tony."

I think one of the main reasons I stuck around with Tony after the cheating was because I know he was grieving and still not over losing his little brother. Leaving him probably would not have been the best thing for him at the time. He seemed so suicidal. I am not going to justify the cheating for him but losing his younger brother may have been a reason why. His brother Tim was like a little brother to me that I never had but always wanted. I think I was sadder about Tim getting shot than Tony getting shot. I was letting my emotions get the best of me. He had deceived me so much throughout our relationship that I had more hate for him than love. Tim never did anything to hurt me. He was even there to talk and comfort me when Tony wanted to fool around.

Everyone knew Tim was in a gang, selling drugs, so the police just assumed it was a deal gone wrong. After about two or three months they really just gave up and forgot about the case. Tim was a good man and did not deserve to die the way he did. They shot him twice in the chest and once in the neck. The doctors tried to save him, but he lost too much blood. He died three months after his 22nd birthday. At least he made twenty-two, but he should have still been here. His mother needs him the most. Shit, at times, I need him.

She is trying so hard to move on from everything. Tony is still semi alive. He is just still paralyzed from the neck down. Investigators are still around to be there when he wakes up to get information on who shot him. Maybe the person, who shot Tony, shot Tim too, and would probably come back to finish the job. I did not really know Tony was into selling drugs. I knew he was a weed head, getting high multiple times a day, every day. Sometimes I find myself thinking about Tony and missing him. Like what if... what if Tim was never shot and killed. Tony would not have been so vulnerable and hoe'ish. He would be more responsible, being a big role model for his little brother. Growing up and seeing their father cheat on their mother, both Tim and Tony needed different.

I remember having a conversation with Tim just before he was gunned down in broad daylight. He was telling me how he was ready for change and wanted to give up the gang. He told me he wanted to get a real job and go to college to be an engineer. Tim showed me his acceptance letter from Devry University starting in the fall. He was tired of seeing his mother down and out and wanted different for his whole family. Tony and I together were relationship goals for Tim. He even had his eye on some chick he saw at school. I miss his smile. I miss everything about Tim and want him alive. Ever since I found out he was shot; I have not been down to the hospital to see him. I was scared, and too busy dealing with everything that has been going on with my life, my girls, my business and my special friend.

JEAN: "I think you should go see him, Tiff."

TIFFANY: "For what?"

LALA: "If it makes you feel any better, we can go with you."

I did not want to see Tony at this point. I do not know what I would do if I did. I was still hurt by how things ended, and I never even got an apology. I know it is not good or healthy to hold on to that hurt, but it was getting to me how they suggested going see him. At that moment, I thought it would be a good idea. To be able to forgive and forget because I have yet to forgive him. Just been walking around with hurt on my shoulders. Maybe he would wake up and it would make his mother happy to know not both of her sons have passed away. Seeing his mother, the way I did hurt, and it did nothing for my pain that I was suffering. I wish Tim never left us! He was the glue to this whole family, and I would do just about anything to get him back.

I suggested we not go see Tony while tipsy and drunk, and to just wait until tomorrow. LaLa wanted Jean and I to spend the night but I wanted to sleep in my bed and Jean wanted to be under her man.

JEAN: "You should call Sammy."

LALA: "I'm not doing that shit. I'm going to wait until he calls me, and if he doesn't oh damn well."

She walked us both to the front door, a hug a piece and said our goodbyes. I looked at my phone and it was Monika telling me she would meet me at my house. That is another reason I could not really spend the night at La's. I already had plans with another friend and let me not tell La because she would get all defensive and think Monika is replacing her like she did with Ray. I was not up for that. Jean and I literally parked right next to each other which was good because we left La's house pretty late.

TIFFANY: "I love you girl." I hugged my friend and she kissed me on the cheek.

JEAN: "I love you too. Drive safe." And I did. She got in her car and pulled out of the parking lot before I did since I had to text Monika back to let her know I was on my way.

I bet you are wondering about Keyvaune. He got a little crazy on me. The first night we had sex was *great*, and I do mean great. But It was like everywhere I went; he was coincidentally there which drove me insane. I could be at the grocery store, he was there. Getting my car washed, he was there. At the bookstore, he was there. Dude does not even read books, but just so happens to be in the same bookstore as me, something was not right.

It freaked me out to the point where I had to block him from my phone and delete him on every social media. I know I have some good pussy, but he did not have to go out of control the way he did. I appreciated the flowers and chocolates he would get sent to my job but I'm not the one who craves attention, and every time he sent flowers, all the brawds would be hovering over my desk, *'girl he loves you,'* this and that. None of them really even liked me before I started getting lunches and chocolates. Now all of a sudden, it's, *'girl we need to hang out sometime.'* Girl bye and you can have him.

I was about a street away from making it home when I kept noticing a car was following me. It made me a little nervous, so I sped up and did a quick turn. What do you know, the car turned with me. I turned again at the next light, and the car did the same. Berry Street and Psi Lane is well known to me. I know all sorts of back turns, short cuts, and back ways that I could lose a mother fucker in a quick second. I whipped up in the gas station and sat at one of the pumps. The car did the same. I waited until they got out, but they never did. Their windows were tinted but not too much to where I could not see.

TIFFANY: "This nigga got a lot of fucking nerve." I said to myself. I got out of my car and walked to the car that was following me. Bold, huh?

TIFFANY: "If you don't leave me the hell alone, I'm going to get a restraining order and get somebody to beat your ass." I beat on the hood of the car as Keyvaune rolled down his window.

KEYVAUNE: "I don't want any problems, Tiffany. I just wanted to know why you have not been returning my calls. Did I do something wrong?"

TIFFANY: "*Yes*, this exactly what you're doing now. Following me everywhere I go. You need to move on and leave me the fuck alone."

KEYVAUNE: "I thought we had something great going. I would get flowers delivered to your job, anything you could possibly want."

TIFFANY: "This isn't what I want Key. This is too much for me." And it is. He is entirely too clingy. It is one thing to have flowers delivered once a week or a date, but flowers every day of the week, for weeks. Popping up out of nowhere, places he has never been to a day in his life before he met me? And I would know because when I would take him to my special spots, he would tell me he has never been there. That shit is creepy.

KEYVAUNE: "I can tone it down some. Do not do this to me Tiffany. I just lost my best friend some weeks ago. I can't take losing you too." No, this nigga just did not.

TIFFANY: "Don't pull the '*I lost my friend and can't live without you*,' card and FYI, you haven't lost him. He is still alive, just unconscious. You should go see him one day."

Lawd please do not let it be tomorrow when I went. I just could not go through this again like I did with Tony. I mean I understood where Keyvaune was coming from because Tony went through the same thing when he lost

Tim. Keyvaune on the other hand had not lost his cousin,
Tony is still alive, he just hasn't opened his eyes.
I was just about to walk away because I was done for the
night dealing with Keyvaune. He opened his front door and
grabbed for my hand.

KEYVAUNE: "Stop being a bitch… Talk to…"

TIFFANY: "*Stop being a bitch?* You haven't seen a bitch
yet, and if you come around me again, that's your ass." I
snatched my hand away from him and walked away. I
probably should have stayed the night at La's, but I am
pretty sure he was sitting outside her place waiting for me
to leave. Keyvaune is on some real stalker shit and that is
not cute. At this point I was glad my lease was about to be
up in a few weeks, and I have already found a new spot to
live. I just had to do it quickly and silently. If I catch
Keyvaune over by my new place, I will get my nephew to
beat his ass.

   Once I pulled off from the gas station, I kept looking
back to see if Keyvaune was following me, and he was not.
There really was no use in trying to lose him with the back
rounds for the simple fact that he already knows where I
live. Luckily, Monika was staying the night with me and she
is licensed to kill. I have known Monika a little over four
years. She has been a real good friend to me. It has only
been a couple of times that LaLa, Jean her and I have all
hung out together so I would not technically call her their
friend too. Monika is mostly gone for long periods at a
time with business, so I barely get to see her myself. But
when we do link up, it is always *magical*.

Chapter Nineteen

The Next Morning- Tiffany

After Monika had left, I called up Jean and put LaLa on three-way.

TIFFANY: "Y'all want to go see him now or wait?" I fumbled through the channels, looking for something to watch.

LALA: "Damn, good morning to you too honey."

TIFFANY: "My bad you guys." I was a bit scared and nervous to see Tony.

JEAN: "You good Tiff?"

TIFFANY: "I haven't told you guys this because y'all already have a lot going on but Keyvaune... he's been stalking me."

LALA: "What the hell? What do you mean by *stalking*?"

TIFFANY: "Been popping up out of nowhere, wherever I'm at. He was just following me last night and I'm pretty sure he started at your house La."

LALA: "Awe, hell nah. Where this nigga at? He was all sweet and shit at first. I told you... them sweet men are the ones you have to look out for. Give them some pussy, then *boom*. They are crazy over you, doing creepy shit. I know it had to be a minute since he had some too." We all burst out laughing.

JEAN: "You must of have put it *down* on him." I wiped my face from the tears coming down from all the laughing. We had sex only a few times. Do not get me wrong, he has some good penis, but not so good to have me popping up on him and following him around. There is too much penis in this world to go crazy over one.

We were not even dating, just having sex. Maybe he took that a different way. I thought I made myself clear that I was not looking for a relationship. Keyvaune thought he could change my mind but ended up pushing and scaring me away. I kid you not, after the first time we had sex, he was sending flowers and chocolate every day. Before the sex even started, when I did not even notice he liked me, he was only sending flowers, once every other week or so. Now, it was every day.

Shit was annoying. The second time we had sex, that is when he started popping up, delivering the flowers himself. Had people thinking he is my man or my husband. Little did they know, I only really called him when I wanted sex. Most men would love to have someone they could just call for some nookie, a little friend with benefits going on, no strings attached. Keyvaune is a once in a lifetime man that comes in your life that I just was not ready for. If he is the one for me, then fate well let us meet again. How he played the situation out this time would take a while for me to forgive and forget.

I am a business woman and all about my business and making it a success. Maybe once I am where I want to be with my business, then I can think about a relationship, until then, I got to get to this paper. It is nothing for LaLa, she is the make-up artist and has clients out the ass. May not seem like it because she is always down somebody throat, charging them up. Jean has done her part, finding us a popular location, and did the blueprints. It is just me, getting my part of the funds. I want to be successful and make my girls proud, as well as my family. It is just harder than I thought, still having the bills that I do on top of needing the money for our business, and I do not have many clients wanting custom made dresses and sorts. I knew having any type of relationship would hinder me. Did not think it would be too crazy to be having sex every now and again. I mean, women do have needs.

Keyvaune offered a few times to pay my part for the building, but I declined. The building cost eighty thousand and we all need twenty-six thousand a piece. Over the past few years, I have saved up sixteen thousand, so Keyvaune would be loaning me ten thousand. That is a lot of money I just could not take from him. What do I look like having a man pay for what I have dreamed of since I was a little girl? So, he could rub in my face, how if it were not for him, I would not have this building. Nah, I am good. Dealing with men, I have learned that is what they like to do if they help you out with something when you are in a hard place. Throw it right back in your face during an argument.

I am going to get the money and soon. It probably would not be so bad since he declined for me to pay him back. That is just how independent I am. I want to get things for myself, so I will not have people backfire on me. It has been done before. One of my exes, I needed a place to stay and quick. I did not want to be a burden on my girls or family, so he helped me find a place until I was approved for my apartment. I have always been this way and will not change for anyone, after he threw that shit in my face. It is a good feeling to know you made a successful life for yourself on your own.

We finally made it to the hospital to see Tony and so many emotions ran over me. Am I supposed to be mad, hurt, upset, angry, or happy? I did not know. He looked peaceful though. That is what made me want to feel happy for him. The doctor said he was still unconscious but may be waking up fairly soon. His mother had just left right before we came in. She hugged me and her eyes looked cherry red, like she had just got done crying. It hurt me to see her this way because I knew she did not deserve it. After everything she has been through with her boys, she deserved happiness and peace the most. Not hurt and pain. I could see it in her eyes and just wanted to pray for her. Pray for healing and happiness over her life. She told me she had to leave because she just could not sit and see her son in the hospital bed. Also, tried to rekindle relations between Tony and I but I drew the line there.

I sympathized for Tony, but as far as a relationship, I am good on that. Maybe one day we could be friends, but I was not on that either. I just wanted to come and see how he is doing.

LALA: "How you are doing Tiff?" I looked over at her and suddenly became upset. I just wanted justice for both Tim and Tony. Whoever shot them needs to be put away for the rest of their life. At this very moment, I had hoped Tony would wake up. Maybe he could tell us who shot

219

him. Everybody knows he is not a snitch, but this could save his life and bring justice for Tim. I always seem to be an investigator; they need to hire and pay me big bucks.

TIFFANY: "I'm alright." I grabbed a hold of Tony's' hand and briefly stared at him before the tears started flowing. His hand was a bit cold. Both Jean and La walked over towards me to comfort me. I did not know if I was crying because the situation Tony was in or because I still loved him. He is my first true love and we both have grown with each other over the years. I know Tony, and for a fact he has been holding in hurt from his brother being killed. He just tried to find an out and reacted in a way that hurt us both.

Just then, his index finger twitched. It startled me a bit and I stared at him, hoping he would open his eyes. Then...

TONY: "Tiffany? Is that you?" My heart dropped to my stomach, and I ran to hug him. Not too hard because I was not trying to put him in more pain than he already may be in.

TIFFANY: "Oh Tony, you're awake." I stood up to look at him and we made eye contact. "How many fingers am I holding up?" I turned back at La and Jean who both had their hands over their mouth, just as shocked as I am. "Somebody call in the doctor."

TONY: "I am going to kill that bitch." Tony frowned up and balled up his fist.

LALA: "Who?" Jean had already left out of the room to get a doctor.

TONY: "... Pete!"

LALA: "The weird ass nigga who was at Tiff crib, with his feet propped up?" Tony looked pissed and at that moment I knew he was serious about killing Pete. You could tell by the look on both me and La's face that we were confused as to why.

TONY: "I know it was a lot going at the time when I got shot, but I was sober enough to tell that nigga intentionally shot me. And I bet he was the one who shot and killed my brother... I can guarantee I will hunt his ass down and get my revenge."

TIFFANY: "But why?"

TONY: "The fuck you mean why? This nigga shot and tried to kill me. He killed my little brother, Tiffany."

TIFFANY: "You don't know that definitely." But the feeling in my gut told me he knew it was Pete. A part of me even felt like it was Pete who shot Tony and killed Tim. He was just acting too weird for me and suspicious when he was over my house that day.

TONY: "You trying to defend this nigga? What you had something to do with me getting shot?" The doctors stormed in and pushed through La and I.

TIFFANY: "Wha... Tony, no." How could I defend someone I do not even know, let alone vibed with? Pete rubbed me the wrong way when he was at my crib and the thought of Tony thinking I had something to do with him getting shot just did not sit well with me. I backed away from the bed and grabbed ahold of La's hand.

LALA: "Bitch could have said excuse me." La rolled her eyes and Tony just glared at me like he did not even know who I was anymore. Jean was just walking back in huffing and puffing like she had just ran a marathon and the look on her face told me she was not okay. The machine started going crazy speed, letting the doctors know his heart rate was increasing off the charts.

DOCTOR: "I'm going to need for you all to leave the room and once we get him under control, you can come back in." I took one last look at Tony and he still looked as though he hated me. I was simply scared that he was right, scared that Pete actually did shoot him and possibly his little brother Tim. I was beginning to get angry with the situation and wanted to find Pete myself. I decided to call Ms. Musel, Tony and Tim's mother, to let her know that Tony had opened his eyes. She said she was only about ten minutes from the hospital and if I could wait there until she came back.

LALA: "Tiff... what are you planning to do?" I had anger in my eyes and in my walk. Pete had to be found, and I mean *now*! He killed one of the most important people in my life and almost killed another. If Tony did not get to him before I did, he must end! I sat and waited until Ms. Musel got there. Knowing her, she was driving her car like a bat mobile trying to get to her son. Probably running red lights and all. About ten minutes later, she came storming down the hall and embraced me with a hug.

MS.MUSEL: "Thank you so much for being here Tiffany. I know Tony made his share of mistakes but that does not define his character and you were here for him when all those so called heffers are nowhere to be found. I bet he knows now who has his back and who is just using him. You will forever be my favorite and the daughter I never had but always wanted. Thank you so much again." She kissed my cheek as a tear slowly fell down my face and walked up to the front desk to see Tony.

As we were walking out of the hospital, I overheard a policeman looking for Tony. Something told me to go back to his room to make sure everything is okay, but I decided to leave, and make it my duty to find out where the fuck Pete is. I knew nothing about this man but the fact that he killed my little brother Tim, shot my baby Tony and disrespected my home with his bad energy. LaLa and Jean where on my heel trying to figure out what I was planning.

TIFFANY: "He is going down!"

JEAN: "Who?" I did not answer her. Just hoped in my car, cranked it up and waited for them to get in. "Can someone explain to me what is going on here?"

LALA: "Do you remember ol dude who came to Tiffany house after Tony was shot with Keyvaune?"

JEAN: "Dude with the funky feet?" There was a curious look on her face.

LALA: "Yes! Tony says he is the one who shot him, and he may even be the one who killed Tim."

JEAN: "Tiff, whatever you got planned, let me know. That nigga just dirty, knowing he shot and killed folks then come to their loved one's house like he knew nothing."

I did not answer her. Just kept my eyes on the road in silence. No music, no nothing. The drive back home was not too silent since both La and Jean kept asking what I was going to do. I had received a text from Monika saying she missed me and did not even feel like talking to her. I did not feel like talking to anyone, just wanted to fight. I wanted to hurt someone... badly.

Dropping Jean and La off, I said my goodbyes then headed home to plan how Pete is going to get his.

Chapter Twenty

Slim, No Shady- LaLa

Tiffany pretty much kicked us out of her car once we made it back and she dropped us off. I started thinking about Sammy but clearly Sammy was not thinking about me. Before I made it home from running a few errands, I made a quick stop at the corner store to pick me up some street Tacos, and a wine cooler. If I ever wanted some real tacos, *Mehicho* would be the place to go. I ordered me a three piece corn tortilla combo with beans and rice, and extra grilled onions. I would eat the onions by themselves at times, and headed to the fridge to get me a watermelon mimosa Smirnoff Ice. Every time I come in there, the cashier Benjamin, flirts with me and sometimes only makes me pay for the Smirnoff Ice. One day I will give him my number... just not today.

Leaving the store, I saw Slim walk in. Slim is Ray's best friend. There was a time in life when Jean was a little jealous about Slim and Ray being so close. Jean has actually known Ray longer than Slim. That is the part that confused me most. Jean should have been able to relate to me being jealous about her and Ray. She is just not *as* dramatic as I am. I guess her and Ray both sat down and had a conversation how Ray would choose her over Slim any day of the week. That was my fault not letting Jean know how I really felt about the situation. Now that I think about it, Jean and Ray are perfect for each other. They have that once in a lifetime type of love for each other, and I look up to their relationship as goals hoping to find my King. Thought it was Sammy, but I still had not heard from him.

I never knew why he called himself *Slim* because he was not. There is nothing slim about him but his hair line. Slim is a chubby dark skinned brother who is always dressing to the Tea, baby. You would catch him wearing all the finest shoes and clothes. If you ever want some designer clothing for the low, he would be the one to hit up. I believe him and Tiffany are trying to collaborate and him be her vendor for our store we are opening soon. Just waiting on my girl Tiff. Jean and I have offered to help but she is so damn independent that she wants no help from no one. That is one of the main reasons I fuck with Tiffany; she is all about her business, keeping me on my toes. All I knew for sure, is that Slim has a huge ass crush on me, and ever since he first saw me, at my birthday party a few years back, he has been trying to shoot his shot. Do not get me wrong, he is an alright looking brother, and his personality makes him handsome... sometimes. I could just never get myself to really like him or actually agree to go out on a date with him.

SLIM: "Aye, La. Wassup?"

LALA: "Sliiiim, hey." I opened my arms to initiate a hug. He could give some good ass hugs... like a fluffy teddy bear. I bet it is nice cuddling with him in the wintertime, which is around the corner. Folks should call him Teddy and not Slim. He hugged me tight, but I did not think it was too long or anything. I actually wanted him to keep hugging me. With all of this mess going on with Wade, Kelvin and Sammy... a hug from Teddy, I mean Slim, was everything to me. Made me feel wanted again, but a hug from Sammy would make everything better.

SLIM: "Damn girl you're looking good, like always." He looked me up and down.

LALA: "Thank you baby." I smiled from ear to ear.

SLIM: "Hey now. You're going to be calling me baby for real if you don't quit playing."

I rolled my eyes and looked him up and down. He had on this red polo shirt and some dark blue jeans, and black forces. Boy made sure he did not leave the cologne at home. I bet you could smell it a mile away. Did I really just catch myself checking Slim out?

LALA: "Here you go with this shit."

SLIM: "And I am not going to stop until you find you a good man, or I get me a girl." He licked his lips and stared me up and down, while rubbing his hands like Birdman. "Let me take you out. What you got planned for the rest of the day?" I looked at my phone and still no text or call from Sammy. Dammit, no calls or text whatsoever.

LALA: "Nothing major, just binge watch, so why not? Sure."

This nigga eyes opened so damn wide, and his mouth dropped to the ground. I do not want to sound conceited or no shit, but I know I was looking damn good. Like Teddy said, I am always looking good.

SLIM: "Aight bet. Let me get some gas really quick and we can head out. Do you want me to trail you back to your crib and we can ride in my car, or you can just meet me up there?"

Any other time that Slim has asked me out or tried to talk to me, it was like his lines were rehearsed, and was not attractive at all. This time was different. I actually wanted to go out on this date with him and see what he is about.

LALA: "Just trail me back to my house and I'll ride with you." I am always down to save some gas, and free food some real Me'ish right about now.

SLIM: "Bet." He started walking towards the store door. "Oh, did you get some gas? I can pump it for you if you give me a moment to pay for mine." He is just so damn sweet.

LALA: "Nah." I raised the bag of food I had in my hand. "This is all I came in here for."

SLIM: "Okay beautiful. Give me a minute."

He turned and walked into the store, and I made my way to my car. At that moment I really hope he did not take me out for food because I was not about to waste my $3.76, and my free tacos. I saw him walk out from the store and towards the pump where his car was parked. He looked over at me and winked and I smiled back. Slim was really looking good today. I snuck a few bites of my taco in while he was in the store and pumping, damn near eating the whole plate. He drove over to where I was parked and rolled down his window.

SLIM: "You ready?" I had not chewed the rest of the taco that was in my mouth and felt a little embarrassed talking to him with a mouth full.

LALA: "Yeah." I struggled to get out, while covering my mouth.

SLIM: "You got a little something on your chin." I looked in my rear view mirror and saw green sauce dripping down my chin. I ran out of napkins from the food and checked my glove compartment... nothing.

LALA: "You wouldn't happen to have a napkin in your car, would you?" He reached in his glove compartment, got out of his car and walked over to give me a handful of napkins. "Thank you. Now I'm ready."

Slim walked back over to his car and I pulled off, only slightly so I could get in front of him. Continuously checking my rear view mirror to make sure he was still behind me. I had received an incoming call from Kelvin but was not in the mood to talk to him, so I sent the call to voicemail. He left me a message too. I did not want no dealings with Kelvin or Wade. Sammy is about the only man I want to talk to, and that was about to change. I started thinking about what Jean said on how I should call him. What if he did not answer? What if he sent me to voicemail just like I did Kelvin? I really wanted answers from him why he left so suddenly. Like my pussy is not good, or something. I have never gotten any complaints and it was not going to start now.

I was not trying to seem like the crazy girl, popping up at jobs and houses, but Sammy was about to get a taste of my crazy side. It is hard for me to understand why I just could not let go and leave the situation alone. If I called him and he did not answer, the next move would be to pull up on him. I know exactly where he stays, which car he drives, and where he works. I would have known where his mother stays, however I don't remember the apartment number, and the way the complex is set up, you would need the apartment number or building number to know where to go.

We pulled up to my house, but I wanted to change and freshen up a little.

LALA: "I'll be right back."

SLIM: "No rush baby." I just know he was looking at my ass as I walked away. Turned around and there he was... staring hard.

Once I made it into my apartment, I ran to the bathroom to take a quick shower then slipped into a sun dress. It was a little too hot to be wearing them tight ass jeans. I took a look in my bathroom mirror to make sure I was looking good. It is not too hard to impress Slim, but I still wanted to look good; to impress myself or just in case I saw someone I knew. I am trying to have him smell me from a mile away, like he had me, so I sprayed on some Dark Kiss from Bath and Body Works, and some lip shine from Bath and Body Works as well. One last glance in the mirror, I headed out the door.

BENNY: "Damn, you are looking good La."

I rolled my eyes and walked away. I made it to Slim's car and got in.

SLIM: "Damn girl. Did you take you a quick nap or something?" I was not even gone that long, and he decides to exaggerate.

LALA: "No. but I did take a shower."

SLIM: "Well you look and smell good." Slim always knew what to say to put a smile on my face.

We pulled up to this Hookah bar called MetajaZZ. Out of all my years living in Dallas, I've never seen or heard of this place. It looks like it be popping on the daily. I felt like I was dressed for the occasion. He had already booked us a table; I assume it was when I was freshening up. Some tall and fine dude walked up to us, with open arms to dap up Slim.

WORKER: "And who's this fine little thang you got with you? You got any friends that look as good as you?" I blushed. He had these light brown eyes with a little glow in them if he was under the light.

SLIM: "This here is Latonia. She goes by LaLa." He extended his hand out to me to shake. I snapped my neck and glared at Slim for calling me by my government name. "LaLa, this is Dre. He's the assistant manager at this spot for the past two years, but has been my boy for a decade now."

LALA: "First off, please do not ever introduce me by my government name. Secondly, why are you just now inviting me here? This place is amazing." I looked around in awe like I was at a museum or something.

DRE: "I'm glad you like. I did some of the decorations myself. And yeah Slim, why haven't you brought Miss *LaLa* by sooner?"

SLIM: "Because *Miss* LaLa wasn't giving me the time of day." I rolled my eyes and looked at Dre. He was just so damn fine and those eyes, but I came here with Slim and was not about to do that hoe shit to him.

DRE: "Oh *this* is the one who you been trying to get with but always turning you down? Why are you doing my brother like that girl?" He folded his arms across his chest and glared at me. I just wondered what all Slim has been telling Dre about me.

SLIM: "We can save that conversation for another day."

DRE: "Aight! Let me walk you both to your table." He turned and headed toward a crowd of people. "Right this way." Slim let me walk in front of him and I could not help but admire how beautiful and creative the inside of the hookah bar is.

There were purple, blue and a little red over the walls with all types of paintings hanging up. It looked something like an art gallery. Some sections had tables or booths, and other sections allowed you to sit on bean bags and pillows. There was a big ass bar, with damn near every alcoholic beverage you could possibly think of. Some of those bartenders were looking mighty fine too. Male and female. There also was a stage, and signs hanging up on the wall for Open Mic. I know my girl Jean sings so I definitely should tell her about this.

We made it to the booth to sit down and Slim just stared at me with his hands crossed on top of the table.

LALA: "What is it Slim?"

SLIM: "You are beautiful as fuck to me." I blushed a little then looked away. A few moments later, our waiter walked up, and I was baffled. I cannot believe they have this ghetto ass thot working up in this spot. I looked to my right and see Ray's baby mother, Bethanee. She was walking so stank, pregnant and all. It disgusted the hell out of me. After what Ray and Jean told me about her, I was ready to slang her across the ground a few times. I do not even know why Ray was fucking with her in the first place. Jean was definitely an upgrade for him.

LALA: "Can we request a new waitress? I am not feeling this one." Bethanee knew about me. She knew I am one of Jean's best friends and how I was about to beat her ass that night she was popping off at the mouth at Ray's spot.

SLIM: "What is wrong with this one?" I looked back at Slim and mugged a little.

BETHANEE: "What can I get you two today? We do have a lunch special going on and two-dollar margaritas with happy hour."

LALA: "You can get us a new waitress." Slim smacked his lip at me but I did not care. I did not want my food or drinks to be served by someone I knew for a fact did not like me.

SLIM: "What is up with you? Do you even know this chick to be acting so disrespectful?"

I honestly wanted to clown Slim for coming at me like this behind this bitch.

BETHANEE: "Look, do not be coming up in my place of business with your drama little girl. I need my job to provide for my child." She rubbed her belly and I wanted to throw up. "Now what can I get you both?" Besides the fact that her and Jean had their beef, I knew how Bethanee plays around. She knew about Wade and me but decided to try to fool around with him. When I found out, I beat her ass and I would feed these hands to her again, pregnant and all.

LALA: "Ma'am, could you please get us a new waitress? I do not want you serving our food and drinks."

SLIM: "Chill out La. She's pregnant."

LALA: "And you think I care?"

SLIM: "Bruh, are you intimidated by her? Think she is too pretty to bring you food and shit?" The fact that he even made that statement rubbed me the wrong way and that was the last straw.

LALA: "If you want her that is all you have to fucking say. Why is it a problem that I want a new damn waitress?" I stood up from the booth and raised my voice. Not giving a fuck who turned and looked my way. "I do not like this girl and do not trust her bringing me food or drinks!" I could see fear in Slim's eyes.

SLIM: "Okay damn, that is all you had to say. Sit down, you are drawing attention over here."

BETHANEE: "Girl, I will mop the floor with you."

  Everybody knew Bethanee could not fight if her life depended on it, so I did not understand why she was talking like she could. When she was with Ray, he even knew she could not fight. That was one of the main reasons he would try to talk her out of arguments. Bethanee started smirking and I bumped into her.

BETHANEE: "Watch yourself hoe. You can catch charges hitting a pregnant woman." I did not give a fuck either and just mugged her. Next thing I know, Dre comes speeding our way.

DRE: "Slim, why the fuck you bring this loud, ghetto ass chick up in here?"

LALA: "Loud and ghetto? Nigga you got the city hoe working in your spot. She does not even know who the daddy is. I simply asked for a new waitress, and she started popping off. Customers come first, right? Do not go disrespecting me when all you know about me is my name."

DRE: "I know you a hoe who did not even want to give Slim the time of day." I could see Bethanee teasing in the background. "You are coming in *my* place of business attacking my workers. I do not need your service and you can tear your ass." He said nothing but a word. I did withhold myself from slapping the shit out of him and decided to destroy his business. Took one last look at Slim while he just sat there. Bitch made nigga for real. Stepping out of the booth, there were a few flowerpots on counter tops that I knocked on the floor; splattering glass everywhere. A waiter had just come out with a tray of food that I tipped over...

SLIM: "La, chill the fuck out."

LALA: "You shut the fuck up talking to me. You are a bitch and I want nothing else to do with you. You allow this whack ass nigga disrespect me because I requested for a different waitress? Kiss my ass Slim, and you go figure out who is really your baby daddy, bum ass, dick sucking bitch." Heading towards the exit, there was a table with dirty dishes still on it. I pushed them on the floor, and I heard someone gasp.

DRE: "Control your bitch Slim."

SLIM: "You don't even know what's going on, and you called her a bitch bro. That's disrespectful." Just as Dre was about to speak...

LALA: "Control this..." I flipped a table over and knocked pictures right along with everything on the front counter off. "Now tell your hoe ass waitress to clean this mess up... bitch." I do not know if I am more pissed off at Slim for not defending me, or at Bethanee and Dre. All I know is, Slim bet not hit me up ever again. Looking around... somewhere to get away from Slim and this ratchet as business.

Chapter Twenty one

-Back in MetajaZZ - **Slim**

DRE: "You Slim, next time you think about bringing one of your bitches here, don't…"

   Both Dre and I looked around at the mess LaLa had created, while Bethanee was standing back with a smirk on her face. I do not know what I was thinking. I should have stood up for LaLa. All she had wanted was a new waitress. Had I known about the beef between her and Bethanee, I would have never said LaLa was overreacting. Dre calling her a bitch was a little extra.

DRE: "Just making us black folk look bad."

   I knew he was angry, also by the way he kicked the glass across the room.

SLIM: "Chill out D…" He turned to me and snapped his neck

DRE: "Chill out? Your bitch came up in my spot and destroyed it. You been going on and on how you are always asking her ass out and she keeps turning you down. Now all of a sudden, she is just this spectacular ass hoe who can come in my place of business, fucking up shit."

SLIM: "All she wanted was a new waitress." Bethanee just stood there.

DRE: "I have never had a problem with Bethanee waiting tables and she is too pregnant to be getting into any altercations. Your bitch just does not know how to be respectful."

BETHANEE: "And that is for sure. She is just mad that I'm having a baby." She rolled her eyes.

DRE: "You hush up back there and get back to work. This mess is not going to clean itself." I knew of Bethanee and how she treated my boy, Ray. So, how LaLa was acting did not seem too much. If Dre knew the type of person Bethanee is, he probably would have never hired her. "Should have just left the bitch where you found her."

SLIM: "You got one more time to call LaLa out of her name, or you and I are going to have some problems." Dre looked up at me and mugged the shit out of me.

DRE: "So, it's hoes before bros now?"

SLIM: "She is not a hoe. The bitch you got working for you is the hoe." I pointed over at Bethanee and her mouth dropped to the floor. "All that fuck shit she did to Ray, and you have the nerve to call my girl these bitches and hoes?" I bet that refreshed his memory. Dre knew of Ray and hung out with him a few times, and he knows some of the deceiving shit Bethanee has done to him. I left Dre standing and walked towards Bethanee; she was looking quite scared. "And you know damn well that is not Ray's baby, so stop dragging him along with you." I walked out of the restaurant looking for LaLa...

-LALA

A few minutes later I turned around and saw Slim running after me. I was in no mood to ride in the same car as him, so I started walking away about to call Jean to come get me.

SLIM: "La slow down." Once he caught up with me, he grabbed my wrist and pulled me towards him. "What the fuck was that?" Snatching away from him, I walked away again. "You hear me fucking talking to you." I turned back to him, and he looked scared as hell.

LALA: "I don't know who you think you're talking to, but you got the right chick. I fight niggas. You let that bitch stand there and disrespect me. I am supposed to be your date and he steady calling me bitches while you are standing there looking stupid and pitiful.

SLIM: "Aye, you really need to chill the fuck out with your mouth." He pointed his finger in my face and I smacked it away.

LALA: "Fuck you." I turned and began walking.

SLIM: "Nah, fuck you bitch." Something in me snapped. Turning back to Slim, I looked him dead in his eyes...

Smack!

He held his face and glared at me. I did not give a fuck though. He saw how I reacted when his homeboy called me a bitch, then he turns around and calls me one. Just when I thought Slim was this sweet guy, he turns out to be a complete asshole. All I fucking wanted was a different waitress.

LALA: "Don't call me ever again." I turned away and started walking to the Jack in the Box across the street. I was going to sit there until Jean came to get me.

SLIM: "La?" So many cars driving by, and I was just standing there, waiting to cross the street. "La?"

The last car drove by and that was my chance to cross the street. I dialed up Jeans' number, but she did not answer. I started to call Tiffany, but I remember she said she had a meeting to go to, so I figured she would not be able to answer the phone. I scrolled down my call log to see who I could call to come pick me up. My friend list is not that long, so I really had no one else other than Jean and Tiffany. Finally making it to Jack in The Box, I sat in one of the booth's and continued to scroll.

I looked outside and saw that Slim had pulled up in his car. Rolling my eyes, I got to Rays' number. Ray and I had just started being cool and hitting it off so I was a bit skeptical on asking him for a ride but he said if I needed anything to hit him up. Slim walked inside sweating... I have no idea what the fuck he is sweating for, but his forehead was shinny.

SLIM: "La, stop tripping and let me take you home." He sat inside the booth, breathing a bit heavy. I had to remember he is a little heavyset.

LALA: "Nah, I'm good bitch." There was a white family a few tables from where I was sitting and apparently heard

241

me. Who I assumed to be the dad glared at me while the little girl, who looked about twelve, and the son who was probably ten, looked back at me. I did not give a fuck though. Should not have been listening so hard. I smiled at them because they started staring too long for me. The phone just kept on ringing until...

RAY: Wassup La?"

LALA: "Can you please come pick me up? I am at this Hookah bar called *MetajaZZ*. Well really across the street at Jack in the Box. I got you on gas."

SLIM: "La, get off the phone bro."

RAY: "Is that Slim?" I rolled my eyes.

LALA: "That's irrelevant. Can you come pick me up? I have gas money."

RAY: "Ye..." Slim snatched the phone out of my hand and I jumped up, ready to fight his ass.

SLIM: "Aye she is tripping right now... there is no need..."

RAY: "It's me bro... Ray."

SLIM: "Oh wassup? Anyway." He smacked his lips. "She is tripping hard as fuck right now. I will take her home."

LALA: "No the fuck you're not. Ray come get me." I yelled out.

SLIM: "No need for that. La, get your shit. Let's go. Causing a scene, got these white folks staring at me nshit." Slim made his way out of the booth and began walking towards the front entrance.

LALA: "I don't give a fuck." The white daddy looks like he lowkey wanted to fuck me. "Give me my phone Slim." The Jack in the Box worker came over to where I was standing just as I was starting to head to the door.

EMPLOYEE: "I'm going to have to ask you both to leave." She said ever so kindly. She folded her hands in front of her as she looked back and forth between Slim and me.

LALA: "See what you did? Did not nobody tell you to come over here. I was just fine by myself." The volume on my phone is pretty loud. If you were about two or three feet away, you can still hear what the person on the other end of the phone is saying.

RAY: "So do I need to come get her?"

LALA: "YES!" I moved past the employee.

SLIM: "No." The employee was still standing there, staring at us. Ol daddy was still staring at me and by that time the mother had come out of the bathroom.

SLIM: "Let's go La." I was not trying to have the police come just because this nigga did not want to give me my phone. I started walking closer towards the front door but looked back at daddy. He was still staring and so was his girl... I saw no wedding ring. I gave him a little wink and blew a kiss. She *gasped* at me, and daddy eyes got wide like a deer in head lights.

LALA: "Give me my phone dammit." Slim was already outside and I was making my way towards him.

SLIM: "I'll give it to you once you tell Ray you do not need him to pick you up and get your ass in my car so I can take you home." I folded my arms across my chest and glared at him. I wanted to beat his ass at this point.

LALA: "Give me my phone Slim." I said calmly.

SLIM: "Get in the car, La." I could hear Ray yelling through the phone... 'just get in the car La. Stop being dramatic." How could he be on his side though? I mean I understand we had our own beef, and I was giving him hell in the beginning, but we have moved past that. I walked towards Slim's car and pulled on the passenger's door. It was still locked.

LALA: "How you expect me to get in the car and it's locked?" He started walking towards his car and clicked the unlock button on his key. I pulled on the door to open it and just stood there until he got in the car.
LALA" Can I have my phone now?"

SLIM: "We had a deal. Finish it and I'll give it to you."

LALA: "I don't need a ride Ray..." I rolled my eyes. "Now give me my phone." I extended my hand out over the top of the car so he could place my phone in my palm.

SLIM: "Imma hit you back later." Slim ended the call. "You are not going to be on no fuck shit, huh? I give you the phone and you burn off, because I promise I will not chase after you this time. You just on your own." He probably said that because the passenger door was still open, and my leg was hanging out. It was too hot to be doing all this back and forth and I no longer felt like waiting for someone to come get me. I sat inside and closed the door, waiting for him to get inside and place my phone in my hand.

SLIM: "You really do have a bad attitude. You just need the right man to put your ass in check." Slim fixed himself and adjusted his seatbelt.

LALA: "Oh and I guess that will be you?" I rolled my eyes and faced front to buckle my seat.

SLIM: "Just might!" He cranked up his car and drove off towards my house. I looked over at him and the sun was glowing all on his skin. Maybe he could be the one to put my ass in check because Kelvin, Wade and them were just getting their ass beat by me. Slim is different indeed and I kind of liked it.

Once we made it to my apartment, he did not park in one of the parking spots, he pulled up to the curb in front of my building. A part of me wanted him to park and come upstairs with me, but the other part was too prideful to say so. I looked at him while he was looking at me as he turned down the radio. Something in me wanted to kiss him. The way he handled me back at Jack in The Box made me feel like I could see myself with him long term.

Maybe he was right, I just need somebody to put me in my place because I know at times I can get out of hand. Let that had been Kelvin or Wade, we both probably would have been in handcuffs, on our way to get booked in jail for fighting.

SLIM: "It was nice seeing you. Just wish the date went as smooth as I would have liked. Hopefully, we can do this again... minus the drama." Why could I not just get the nerve to tell him to come upstairs? I was starting to feel guilty on how I acted on our date, but Bethanee should have not come for me. I will beat her pregnant ass for Ray.

LALA: "Do you want to come up?"

SLIM: "For what?" He frowned up and I felt ashamed.

LALA: "Oh never mind then, honey." I opened the door and was beginning to step out.

SLIM: "I wasn't trying to be rude or anything. I am simply curious. I did not think you would even want to see me again."

Before you brought your ass to Jack in the Box, I did not want to speak to you or hear from you again; I thought to myself.

LALA: "Park the car... apartment 8012, second floor."

I stepped out of the car and closed the door behind me. As I am walking toward my apartment, I turned back, and he was still parked there. At that point, I did not get my hopes that he would actually come up to my apartment.

Not going to lie, I thought he would be rushing to park, but it hurt a bit to see him still sitting there as I got to the front.

   Once I made it to my door, I walked in and plopped down on the couch. I checked my phone to see if I had any missed calls or messages but none. Henny was calling my name. I walked to the kitchen to fix me a drink and something to snack on. It was about time to go grocery shopping because there was barely shit in there to eat, so I ended up popping me some popcorn, and dashed a little sugar on it. As I was walking back to the couch, I heard a knock at my door. It better had not been Wade, Kelvin, shit not even Sammy. I did miss that dick though. Looking through the peephole...

SLIM: "Can I come in?" I opened the door wider, and I wanted to jump on this man, fuck his brains out and make him call me mommy. As he was walking inside, I was looking him up and down. I have never fucked a big nigga, but I have heard they can fuck good, so I was going to have to give it a try. He sat on the couch, and I made my move.

Chapter Twenty two

Baby, we are Having a Baby- LaLa

Sammy finally hit me back up, but I was not trying to talk to him. He kept going on and on how the pussy was too good to be true and was not trying to fall in love. Oh, so you just get up and dip out on me? I wanted to give him a taste of his own medicine. You do not just go M.I.A on me out of nowhere and think everything will be peachy once we are back talking. Hell no. He had been blowing up my phone, but I was only answering his calls every so often. Kelvin had been calling me too but lawd knows I am not giving him the time of day whatsoever. He would have to catch me in traffic if he wanted to see me. Which I can guarantee, would not happen. As far as Slim and I, we been hitting it off real strong since our little date, and I can say I am starting to catch feelings for him. He definitely isn't on some crazy, stalker shit either. We have just been cooling and vibing, still going out on dates.

Slim pulled up on me and told me to come outside...

SLIM: "How you are doing baby?" I smiled from ear to ear.

LALA: "I'm alright. What about you?" He kissed my forehead, sending chills up my spin.

SLIM: "I'm good now that I get to see you." It had been almost a week since the last time Slim and I had saw each other because I have been too busy trying to hide from

Kelvin. Sammy did come over a few days ago... and we had some great sex. After I nutted, I had my girl Jean call my phone with some fake ass emergency, and rushed Sammy out. He did not even get a chance to nut. I did not care too much neither.

I had been so damn horny since Kelvin and I had sex, which was about a month ago. Around the time my period comes, I get a little hornier and I was trying to do right with Slim and not have sex after a few dates. I wanted to wait a couple months. I let him know ahead of time and he did not too much care. He was simply happy to actually be able to take me out on a date.

SLIM: "I've been missing you." I wasn't going to lie, I missed him too.

LALA: "Same. I've been missing you too, baby." He turned around and walked to the trunk of his car and pulled out a bag.

SLIM: "This is for you, Queen." He handed me this huge black bag that did not feel too light, but it was not heavy either. I smiled from ear to ear, excited to see what was in the bag. I walked to the hood of his car to sit the bag down and have better access to open it.

LALA: "Oh my gosh, thank you baby." I turned back to give him a hug and kiss. There was a Gucci bag and dress, with a perfume and lotion set from Bath and Body Works, as well as a Pandora bracelet.

SLIM: "You like it?" Slim knows I'm crazy over Bath and Body works and was running low on my Cactus Blossom.

LALA: "Like it? Baby I love it. Thank you so much!" I kissed him again but went all out with tongue.

SLIM: "I'm glad you like. Now go put it on so we can go." I was a bit confused because he said that he had to work today, and we had to reschedule our date. I was not going to question him at all. I kissed him one last time and ran up to my apartment to shower and change.

As soon as I got inside, Sammy called me...

LALA: "What is it?" I threw my keys on the couch.

SAMMY: "I miss you... Let me come by." I stopped in the doorway of my bedroom and was silent for a while.

LALA: "For what?"

SAMMY: "I'm confused on why you've been treating me all bad and shit, like I really did something wrong to you. I told you what happened, and you are still mad. Get over yourself." I tossed the bag on the bed and folded my arms.

LALA: "Get over myself? You walked out on me because my pussy too good. I had been calling and texting you and you could not even pick up the phone or a simple text. That was fucked up. *Just when I thought* we had something special, you leave over pussy. You know how stupid that sounds?"

SAMMY: "If it is so stupid, why you still mad? You are being dramatic Latonia. I tried to come back through and talk and make shit right. I know you were calling but I did not think that was a conversation to have over the phone.

Simple as that. Stop being mad and let me make shit right with you." I flopped down on my bed once I looked at the black bag. I thought about Slim and how he was waiting outside, while I'm upstairs on the phone with another man, actually thinking about giving him another chance.

LALA: "We should have just kept things on fucking, friends with benefit terms and we wouldn't be in this situation."

SAMMY: "I agree."

LALA: "What?"

SAMMY: "I agree with you. But I disagree at the same time. If we kept talking how we were, as well as having sex on the side, it was bound that we would want something more. You're the whole package La. Good, strong, smart woman, *and* you got some good, 'I'm thinking about giving you a baby', pussy."

I laughed some but thought about when I told him that I loved him. Did I really, or was it just the dick? Before Sammy, Kelvin was the only man who could do my body right, sexually. Maybe it was the dick that I was telling I love.

SAMMY: "Hello?" I got lost in my thoughts.

LALA: "Yeah?"

SAMMY: "You good La?" Fondling through the bag Slim had given me. I slipped the dress on and glanced in the mirror...

251

LALA: "I'm just confused."

SAMMY: "About what?" I could not really tell him that I was talking to someone else. That is the reason I was confused in the first place. I was catching these feelings for Slim, but never let the ones go I had for Sammy. At the end of the day, at least I knew what it was like to have sex with Sammy, and he would not disappoint me. Slim on the other hand, I did not know. Just my luck his dick is not even big enough. Now that I think about it, I never saw a bulge in his pants like I did Sammy. Every woman deserves to be pleased sexually and I honestly didn't want to take that chance with Slim.

LALA: "Don't even worry about it."

SAMMY: "Can I come see you?"

LALA: "When?"

SAMMY: "Now! I'm outside your door." I bucked my eyes wide like a deer in head lights. This could not be happening to me right now. Slim is still downstairs waiting on me to get dressed for our date, while Sammy is knocking on my door.

Knock. Knock.

LALA: "How do you figure I'm home? You cannot just be popping up like that." I got up from the bed and began walking towards the front door.

SAMMY: "You had no problem last time. What is the issue now?"

LALA: "Last time we were talking on good terms. Right now, we're not." I looked through the peephole.

SAMMY: "Dammit La. I am trying to make things right with you. Stop fighting me." A part of me did want him to make things right but a small part of me wanted him to leave me alone. I saw myself with Sammy for long term and I knew he could make me happy, but Slim... I could not do him like that. These last couple of weeks with him have been great, but deep down inside, Sammy is who I really want. I had to remind myself that Slim is still downstairs waiting on me. What was I supposed to do?

SAMMY: "La? Do you hear me talking to you? Open up the door. I'm not taking *no* for an answer." I wanted to cry so hard. I heard a beep on the other end of my phone, looked down and saw Slim was calling. Lawd do not have this man come knocking on my door while Sammy is still outside.

LALA: "Hold on..." I paced the room.

SAMMY: "No. You open this damn door, or you won't hear from me again. I cannot keep doing this back-and-forth shit with you La. This shit is becoming toxic. Let me go if you don't want to be with me, simple." He is right, but it was hard for me to let him go. I knew if I put him on hold to click over, he would hang up and probably not answer the phone. Slim eventually hung up, and not even thirty seconds later, he was calling again.

LALA: "Sammy, hold on… please." *Click*. "Hello?"

SLIM: "Damn girl, what you doing up there? Do I need to come in to let you finish getting dressed?"

LALA: "NO!" I rushed him. Sammy still had not hung up and started knocking on my door again.

SAMMY: "I know you're in there La. Open the damn door and stop being childish."

SLIM: "Who is that? I'm about to come up…"

LALA: "NO!"

SLIM: "What the fuck is up with you?" The tears started flowing.

LALA: "Nothing…" I could not keep lying to him and I did not want him to come up or I knew for a fact I was fucked.

SAMMY: "Open the door La." *Click*. Sammy hung up the phone, and I began to panic.

SLIM: "Yo, who the hell is that? You're being weird as fuck right now." Tears started to fall down my face.

LALA: "Slim we need to talk…"

SLIM: "About what… are you crying, and who is beating on your door?" My palms became sweaty, and I was nervous as hell to even talk about this with him. If I kept this going, everybody would end up being hurt and I did not want to be the cause of that.

LALA: "I don't know so much about this anymore."

SLIM: "About what, La?"

LALA: "Us!" My voice cracked a little. There was no more knocking from Sammy, and I thought he had left. Until I walked over to the door and looked through the peep hole and he was still standing there, looking down at his phone. I had received a text from Sammy...

'Clearly you no longer want to be with me, and I'm not about to force anything on you. I know you are inside the house and you refuse to open up the door for me. Got me out in the hallway looking stupid. Don't say I didn't try...'

I looked through my peep hole and he was gone. My tears started flowing harder, I could not stop crying, and I was not about to go back on what I was saying to Slim. I honestly felt I could not be with him. Our friendship was the only thing on my mind, that was hindering me from speaking to Slim.

SLIM: "So you wait until I buy you shit to say you can't fuck with me no more?"

LALA: "It ain't even like that Slim, so chill out." I did not mean to rush the conversation, but I had to call Sammy back before he left the parking lot. "Can I call you back?"

SLIM: "Call me back? What the fuck? Girl just delete my number." *Click*. He did not even give me a chance to explain myself. I only had a brief conversation with Slim about Sammy, but he knew what was up. Slim knew I still had feelings for Sammy and that may have been the reason he was going extra hard to fuck with me in the first place. I went back to my call log to Sammy's number and gave him a call.

SAMMY: "What?"

LALA: "Come back." I looked through the peephole to see if Sammy was still there...

SAMMY: "You gone open the door this time?"

LALA: "Yes!"

SAMMY: "Aight." I hung up the phone and waited for him to come knocking on my door again.

About three minutes later... *Knock. Knock.* I walked to my door and looked through the peep hole, it was Slim... My heart dropped to my feet. What the fuck was he doing knocking on my door after what he said and where the hell was Sammy? I opened my door and just as Slim was about to speak, I can see Sammy walking up in my peripheral... I was done for. Slim clearly saw my facial expression and looked over to where I was looking. Sammy walking hard and strong, looking mean as ever.

Chapter Twenty three

As soon as Sammy made it to my door, Slim glared at me.

SLIM: "Is this why you wanted to talk about *'us'*? Got you a new nigga already and you just called it off with me."

SAMMY: "Who is this nigga?"

SLIM: "I *was* her nigga..." Now Slim and I were going heavy with the relationship, but we never made things official, and we just started kissing about a week ago so he should not be calling himself *my nigga*.

SAMMY: "Oh yeah? That is why you were not trying to open the door? Was he in there?" Sammy pointed inside.

LALA: "You need to chill out."

SAMMY: "I don't need to do a damn thing. You called me to come back for this shit?" Slim snapped his neck at me.

SLIM: "Oh yeah? You called him back? This why you were taking forever to come back downstairs? I am in my car waiting on you, and you doing some fuck shit. Then try to call things off. You really were not trying to fuck with me in the first place. You were just playing me because I am this fat nigga, but you really got me fucked up. I am not desperate if that is what you think. I can get another bitch, I just wanted to try my luck with you to see where things could go with us. But would you look at that... you played me. I was just your rebound nigga."

LALA: "It's not even like that... I can... You knew about Sa..." Slim tossed his hand up at me and smacked his lips.

SLIM: "Don't even worry about it La... Y'all be good." Before I could even say anything, he turned and walked away. Sammy was just standing there, looking at me like I was stupid. My eyes started watering up.

LALA: "You can stop." I wiped the first tear that fell.

SAMMY: "Stop what?"

LALA: "Staring at me like that. It's really not what you think."

SAMMY: "Despite how I may feel about you right about now, I'm not about to let your ass go again. Hearing what he was saying to you, had me thinking that I could have really lost you if I did not get my shit together. He didn't give you the chance to explain yourself, but I am."

That is when the tears started falling down my face. I thought Sammy would feel the same way Slim felt, by the way he walked up to my door and saw Slim standing there. Sammy wiped the tears from my face, and grabbed a hold of my chin, looking me deeply into my eyes.

SAMMY: "I can't lie and say that I don't like you, and not really feeling your ass. I'm feeling a little played, but I want the truth."

I knew for a fact I was looking sad as hell. I grabbed a hold of the doorknob and walked backwards into my apartment, Sammy followed and closed the door. My palms became sweaty again, but I knew I had to talk to him about what was up. I just wish Slim did not storm off the way he did, and I could have explained myself to him. At the end of the day, Slim is a cool ass nigga and I hate how things ended between us two. I was not trying to hurt him, just wanted to follow my heart with Sammy.

We made it to the couch at the same time because I was stalling by trying to straighten up the house.

SAMMY: "You want to talk or clean?" I sat the vase back down on the table and sat next to Sammy. My body began to get hot. I just did not know where to begin...

LALA: "Long story short. We bumped into each other one day, he took me on a date, that did not end well. After that, we started going on out more. You and I was not talking, and I did not think we ever would again. I called and texted your phone so many times, and never got a response from you. I am too pretty to be sitting around, moping on why some nigga is not pressed about me. The more Slim and I would go out on dates, the more I caught feelings for him..."

SAMMY: "Slim?"

LALA: "The dude who was standing next to you... that's his name." The way his face turned up let me know he was questioning why a big nigga like Slim, was even being called 'Slim.'

LALA: "I already know what you're thinking. Do not do him like that. He is really sweet and that's what got my attention. It wasn't the fact that he was always taking me out, buying gifts and shit."

SAMMY: "Damn this nigga was doing it big for you. How many dates y'all went on? You fucked him too?" I turned my face up.

LALA: "Okay don't even start that shit because I don't know who you've been sticking your dick in since you went *fucking* M.I.A on me."

SAMMY: "No fucking body. I have been sitting around, thinking about you the whole damn time. I had to call up my boys to see if I was tripping or what the fuck to do. I even called my mother... You know she has never met any of my girlfriends, but one? I mean she has talked on the phone with one. After that first bitch cheated and broke my heart, my mother knew about nobody else. But you, I had to call her about you."

   I just wanted to love this man like I could not love anyone else. Despite me feeling Slim, and all of the time we were spending together, I could never get Sammy off of my mind.

LALA: "You could have at least picked up the phone. I am not trying to make myself look better than you in this situation, but you do not know how that made me feel? I had to move on and get over you." We both turned completely to each other.

SAMMY: "I understand that La, and I do apologize for dodging your phone calls. I hope we can move past this." I rolled my eyes playfully.

LALA: "I guess."

SAMMY: "The fuck you mean you guess. Girl if you don't want to fuck with me no more..."

LALA: "I'm just kidding godamn, calm your ass down." I frowned up.

SAMMY: "Yeah okay. You better be kidding... Bring your ass here." He playfully grabbed me around the back of my neck and pulled me closer to him. "I missed you La."

LALA: "I missed you too Sammy." He looked me deep in my eyes, then came in closer for a kiss. Fat mama got a little too excited. Maybe she missed him more than I did. I pulled away and straddled his waist, still kissing him.

He had on a Polo button down shirt, so I took the honors of unbuttoning it. He was trying to help unbutton it, but I was in charge, and slapped his hands away... still kissing him. When I made it to the last button, he snatched his shirt off, leaning up to have easy access of slipping the shirt off. Still straddled around his waist, he grabbed ahold of my back, and stood up so I was not able to fall off. Walking towards the room, I had him make a quick stop by my dining table where I had my bottle of Henny and picked up the bottle.

LALA: "Shot?"

SAMMY: "Yes ma'am." I popped the bottle open took a shot and passed it to him to take his shot. He ended up taking another. "Give me another."

Oh, okay buddy, I thought to myself. After putting the top back onto the bottle and placing it back on the table, Sammy headed towards the room. He gently laid me down on the bed, and sexed his mouth with mine, while sliding his hand under my dress. I had no panties on, so it was easy for him to get to fat mama. She is freshly waxed too.

SAMMY: "Damn, I missed her." He kissed me passionately.

LALA: "She missed you too." I grabbed ahold of his waist and made my way to his belt buckle to undo his zipper. His dick was already hard, and it made my pussy more wet. Once I pulled his dick out, I jerked it some, and he began to moan. I pulled away from kissing him to lean up and kiss his dick. My mouth was creating more saliva than usual and made sure his dick would know it.

SAMMY: "Damn baby. I love that shit." His moans turned me on more than the Henny was doing. I love the way his dick was filling up my mouth. He does have a big dick and it was sometimes a struggle to deep throat him. But I want to let him know, his dick belongs to me. Going back and forth from sucking the head, to deep throating, to devouring his shaft, Sammy pulled out of my mouth and instructed for me to bend over. I got my ass up so fast and tooted that ass up in the air.

SAMMY: "You say, yes daddy." He slapped my ass just hard enough to make my pussy throb for him. "Now say it!" I did not know what freaky shit he was on, but I loved it.

LALA: "Yes daddy." He slid my dress up... the same dress Slim bought me. He was eating my pussy from the back while I was attempting to pull the dress over my head. The way his mouth felt on my pearl, was so warm and soft. He pulled away from my pearl and slowly and gently inserted his penis. I became weak in my knees.

SAMMY: "Oh my Go... I missed this pussy baby." He filled my pussy with every inch. I felt it all in my stomach. "What's my name?"

LALA: "Daddy!" I moaned out.

SAMMY: "You love daddy dick?"

LALA: "Yes! I love daddy dick."

His strokes sped up, and I was creaming already. That henny was doing its job. Sammy was fucking me like this *is* his pussy and he would never let another man get a feel or taste of it. I had about four orgasms compared to his one nut. He was not complaining one bit.

After we were done, we both stretched out on the bed. He pulled me closer to him to cuddle and that warmed my heart. However, I was in no mood to cuddle since we both were sweating. He was dozing off, but I had to get my ass up to shower. On my way to the bathroom, I checked my phone to see if I had any text or missed calls. A text from Jean- I would call her later to give her and Tiffany the tea on what done happened to me. A few minutes in the shower, Sammy came in with me and we made love there. He had me pinned up against the wall delivering strokes sent from the stroke Gods. I eventually was able to actually take a shower, and so was he.

Sammy's phone rang and it was his mother. He was trying to get me to talk on the phone with her, but I did *not* want to. He just kept going on and on about me to her. I had never even talked on the phone with Wades' and Kelvins' mother. Maybe it was just my nerves. One day I will be ready, and willing to talk to her on the phone. What was I supposed to say? 'Oh girl your son has some good dick?' I knew for a fact that she would be asking me 101 questions about myself and her son, and I was in no mood to play 21 questions. Apparently, she had cooked dinner and wanted him to come over, and even invited me, but I was not ready to meet his mother. Once he got off the phone with her, we had one last round before he left. Yeah Karla, your son has some good dick.

Chapter Twenty four

Two Weeks Later

JEAN: "What is up with you? You always got a damn attitude, more than usual."

LALA: "I don't mean to. I'm just freaking out right now."

TIFFANY: "About what?"

LALA: "My period is a week late." Both Jean and Tiffany bucked their eyes at me, and at the moment, I knew I fucked up. I knew Sammy and I was having sex without a condom, but I did not think he nutted in me. "STOP LOOKING AT ME LIKE THAT!"

TIFFANY: "Okay, you need to calm the fuck down. Have you taken a test?" I panicked in the backseat.

LALA: "No! I'm scared that hoe might say positive."

JEAN: "Maybe if your ass will chill out and keep your legs closed."

I turned and made a straight face at her.

LALA: "Don't start that shit. I've been giving my goods to one man, and that's Sammy."

TIFFANY: "At least you know who the daddy may be. You need to take a test." I turned to Tiffany and rolled my eyes.

LALA: "Don't you think I know this? I just said I'm scared."

JEAN: "Well you need to get over that and take a test. We don't need you walking around, still doing the same shit you been doing..."

LALA: "Like what, Jean? What exactly do I do?"

JEAN: "Smoke, drink... you know, the regular."

I rolled my eyes and gave her the finger, but as bad as I did not want to admit it, she was right. I just had to calm my nerves to take this pregnancy test. So many questions ran through my mind. Like what if Sammy does not even want a baby? Why he did not let me know he nutted in me? What if he does not want me afterwards? It had to be the precum... this nigga probably trying to trap me.

JEAN: "Would it make you feel better if we bought the test and was by you when you take it?" I pouted and poked out my lip, trying to keep myself from crying.

LALA: "Yes!"

We were already in Tiffany's car because we were having our girl's day out, and ever since she has gotten her new car, she be wanting us to ride with her. I swear these are the days I live for. Sammy and I have been hitting it off strong. He makes me happy as I have ever been in my life. Always calls me beautiful, making me feel like the prettiest girl in the world. I thought of Slim the other day and wanted to call to see how he was doing but thought that was not my place. Knowing him, he probably would not have answered. I also did not want any drama between Sammy and I because I called another nigga. If I was pregnant, how am I going to tell Sammy?

We pulled up to the grocery store because I started craving pickles, and to get a pregnancy test. Both my girls walking behind me for support, and I appreciated it. I am so glad that Jean and I made up when we did because life without her in it, just is not it. I have learned a lot ever since then and appreciate our friendship more than ever. Some dude was trying to get at Tiffany, with them short ass shorts she has on. Honey, these past couple of weeks, she has been feeling herself. I am all for it, but who really got her like this? Tiffany was not paying ol dude in the store no type of attention and I think he had gotten a little mad. Neither one of us gave a fuck. We finally made it to the aisle with the pregnancy test after getting my pickles. I wanted the best one to make sure my results are accurate as hell.

JEAN: "These are $6.99 and come with three of them." I snatched the box from her hand and examined them.

SLIM: "La?" I looked up and saw Slim, actually looking a little Slim, or maybe that was the black shirt. You know black makes you look slimmer. I quickly hid the pregnancy box behind my back, like he had not already seen it.

LALA: "Wassup Slim?" I made an attempt to get out nervously.

SLIM: "What's been up with you? You're expecting a child now?" What was I supposed to say? We only stopped talking a few weeks ago, and I then already got knocked up by somebody else. I also did not want him in my business.

JEAN: "It's for me!" I wanted to kiss her feet at this point. I turned around and mouthed the words 'thank you.'

SLIM: "Oh shit, congrats for you and Ray."

I just hoped he did not go running back to Ray, talking about seeing Jean buying a pregnancy test. We all know that would have started up some drama. It was nice seeing Slim though, but he still does not have anything on Sammy. I had my pregnancy test and pickles; it was time to bounce. Checking out at the register, I started grabbing other shit. A KitKat, a Snickers...

TIFFANY: "Put that back!"

LALA: "You are not my mother, and I'm with child. Let me be." I ended up putting the KitKat back.

JEAN: "Okay now you're being dramatic. We do not know if you are pregnant for sure. You're just psyching yourself out, buying all this junk."

I made eye contact with the cashier... She was kind of cute, with a big booty.

CASHIER: "You're having a girl?" I bucked my eyes at her.

LALA: "What do you mean?"

CASHIER: "I had the same craving when I was pregnant with my little girl." She pulled out a picture of a gorgeous baby girl that looked not even a year old. We all smiled in awe, telling the cashier how adorable her baby is. "Thank you!" She took one last glance at the picture and placed it back in her wallet.

LALA: "Add this on there too. The baby insists." Jean and Tiffany both burst out laughing at me, but I did not care too much. The cashier even laughed. My baby was going to get whatever he or she wanted.

Once we made it back to my crib, I was nervous as hell. I started pacing from the front door to the kitchen, and back to the Livingroom. Jean and Tiffany had already sat down, but I could not stop pacing for shit. I checked my phone to see if Sammy had texted or called me and nothing. What if he does not even want this baby? What if he denies my baby? Sammy already accused me once of sexing Slim. He is always the one talking about getting me pregnant then end up not even wanting the baby. I refuse to get an abortion as well. I was raised differently than most folks. Even if you are not ready for a child or want one, God will make you ready. Each child is a blessing in one's life. I am nervous if I happen to be pregnant, but I am going to make sure my responsibility is taken care of... with or without her daddy.

TIFFANY: "Will you sit your ass down, or go to the bathroom to take the pregnancy test? You are making me nervous and it's not even my baby."

She was right though. I needed to go and take the test before I have a heart attack from working myself up.

LALA: "Can you both come with me?" Jean turned towards me...

JEAN: "So you want us to watch you piss?"

LALA: "Not like you haven't before."

TIFFANY: "And you were drunk then..."

LALA: "You know what?" I snatched the test out of Tiffany's hand and headed to the bathroom. They ended up walking in behind me, but I made it to the bathroom before they did, closed it and locked it behind myself.

JEAN: "Open the door La."

They knocked but I did not answer. It was time for me to be a big girl and do something on my own. Luckily, I had to pee, but they say for best result, take the test right when you first wake up in the morning. If it had got some janky results with this test, I would take another in the morning. Those little two minutes you have to wait for results felt like an eternity. I sat on my toilet and sent Sammy a text...

'Hey, when you get a chance, please call me...
We need to talk and it's urgent.'

I looked back over at the test and saw two lines up and down. I barely read over the instructions because I was so eager to find out if I was pregnant or not. Picking up the box out of the trash, I looked over the back of it. My heart sank to my stomach, and I started sweating like crazy. Your girl Latonia is indeed pregnant. My phone was vibrating. Looking down, it was Sammy...

SAMMY: "You bet not be trying to talk to break up with me Latonia Okins." Ever since we got together, he has been calling me his last name like we are married or something.

LALA: "No." Tiffany and Jean began knocking on the door again.

TIFFANY: "It's been more than two minutes La. What the results say? Am I an aunt or not?"

SAMMY: "Who is that? And what is she talking about being an aunt?"

LALA: "Baby... we're having a baby!" I smiled from ear to ear while Sammy was silent.

Chapter Twenty Five

That Baby Ain't Mine - Ray

When I found out that it is LaLa pregnant and not Jean, I was a bit relieved and actually happy for La. We did have our little beef at one point but since then, we have been closer than ever. Not too close though because I do not want, let alone need Jean feeling some type of way or questioning our friendship. As far as Jean and me... this woman has me smiling from ear to ear, every damn day. Just seeing her smile, makes me smile. I have something planned for her appreciation later on today, but she does not know that. I was skeptical at first telling LaLa because she out of all three of them, cannot keep a secret for shit. Prime example, when she found out she was pregnant, she is calling folks the same day. Like damn La, let it marinate first. I am happy for her though, maybe she can start minding her own business.

I met up with my boy Slim too. I know LaLa and him had a little thing going on at one point, before she got with Sammy. He mentioned how he saw her, Jean, and Tiffany in the store buying the pregnancy test. Jean took the blame for them being in there. I am surprised he did not hit me up, asking was Jean pregnant or anything. I guess he just wanted to wait until I called him because he knew I would. Jean and I are trying to wait a little bit longer before trying to make a baby. She wants to wait until her business is up and popping, and I do not blame her. I am trying to do the same as far as barbering. Make sure our kids want for nothing, not too much because we do not want them to become spoiled brats. We want them to learn and at some point, be able to work for their own. I keep telling her with or without her business up and running right about now, our kids are going to want for nothing. Just like I make sure my baby girl Jean is straight, I am the type of man to do the same for my kids. And to be able to have a child by the love of my life, is an incredible feeling. I just wish Bethanee hoe ass were not a part of it.

BETHANEE: "Are you going to meet me at the doctor's appointment? Can you come pick me up so we can ride together?" I rolled my eyes at the sound of her voice.

RAY: "I'll meet you there." I did not even give her a chance to respond before hanging up. I already knew where the doctor's office is and what time to be there. The nerve of her to ask if I could scoop her up though. Jean told me to compromise with her since I did get her pregnant but damn, how much compromising do I have to do? I do not want Bethanee in my life for the next eighteen years, or after.

LaLa told us about what happened at the hookah bar between her and Bethanee. A part of me wanted LaLa to just beat Bethanee ass, but I do not want her to get a charge. I still cannot believe I let myself slip up and get this girl pregnant. She has already broken my heart numerous times, now I am having a baby by her.

BETHANEE: "You did not have to hang up like that. If you want this coparenting to work, you have to communicate with me."

Yeah, I was not about to listen to her bullshit, so I hung up again. 'Communicate with you? Girl, you could not even communicate that you was not feeling me no more before cheating with another dude. Fuck off my phone talking about *communicate*. Better yet, communicate this dick in your mouth.' I said aloud to myself.

I was talking all that shit after I hung up. I should have let her hear what I had to say, then hung up. Either way it goes, I was already over Bethanee and her shit. She called me back again, but I just sent her to voicemail. She sure as hell knows how to ruin a brothers' day. Just one look at my baby Jean and I am alright. I am grateful every day to wake up to her beautiful face. Look at me sounding all sprung and shit, but I am okay with that, and I feel like we are at a good place.

RAY: "Alright baby. I'm about to head out." I walked over to where Jean was sitting and kissed her soft, luscious lips. I kid you not, that is the highlight of my day.

JEAN: "Be safe. If she tries anything let me know."

I chuckled and grabbed my keys from the key rack hanging up by the door. Jean is sweet, but man once you piss her off, it is over for everybody. Sometimes I was scared to make her mad. Yeah, she sexy when she is mad but then she starts talking and throwing punches. We were play fighting one day and I accidently hit her too hard, and she turned into hulk, started beating my ass.

On my way to the hospital, my phone rang, and it was Bethanee calling me. I sent her to voicemail again, then blocked her number. She had to know wassup because then she called me from Facebook. We are not even friends on there, but she still can call me. I do not like that. Sister girl has issues for real. Knowing I am with Jean, she be trying to talk her way into getting back together. Why in my right mind would I get back with her after everything she has done to me?

I finally pulled up to the hospital and was heading to the doctor's room we are assigned to.

BETHANEE: "What took you so long baby? I was getting worried." I stood in the doorway and just stared at Bethanee. It has got to be the baby having her talk like we are in a relationship.

DOCTOR: "You don't need that stress. It's not good for the baby."

And here she goes, high siding the conversation.

RAY: "For one, I'm not your *baby*, so please don't call me that." I looked over at the doctor and she was frowning up. I did not give a fuck though. I am not about to disrespect my woman, allowing this bitch to call me baby. Simple as that, and a fight can come with it.

DOCTOR: "That was unnecessary."

RAY: "And you still making remarks about it is unnecessary. Yet it is not healthy for the baby. We do not need that kind of stress." I said sarcastically.

BETHANEE: "Calm down you both. I don't need this right now." Bethanee held her stomach.

DOCTOR: "Exactly." She looked over at me. "You didn't have to be rude to her."

RAY: "But why are you still talking about something that has nothing to do with you? Matter fact *who* are you? Where is the original doctor cause shorty bugging?"

BETHANEE: "Okay. Okay. Both of you calm down, please."

   Doctor Wilson walked in and I felt a weight lifted off my shoulders.

DOCTOR WILSON: "Ray, Bethanee, how are y'all? Doctor Terry, I got it from here."

   She was trying to be as professional as she could, but you could tell she has some hood in her.

RAY: "Yeah, Doctor Terry."

   She folded her arms and headed out of the room. Doctor Wilson was checking Bethanee vitals and pulse.

DOCTOR WILSON: "How have you been feeling Miss Spears? Any morning sickness, or out of the ordinary stomach pains?"

BETHANEE: "I have been feeling alright. My feet are starting to get swollen, and back pains. Other than that, it is going pretty well."

DOCTOR WILSON: "I do recommend that you incorporate some walking or minor exercise in your daily life. It will help you later down the road when the baby decides to come." He fluffed her pillow up some and checked his notes. "Are you two wanting to know what you are having?"

BETHANEE: "Yes."

RAY: "No."

Bethanee looked over at me and glared. I simply looked away and made eye contact with Wilson.

DOCTOR WILSON: "Well which one is it?" He looked from one to another.

I did not care too much to know the gender of the baby. Half of me, right along with a few other people does not even think the baby is mine. My potna Slim, Baby, and LaLa all told me that I need to get a DNA test before it is too late. It has already been four months dealing with this girl shit. Constantly calling my phone, sometimes even pulling up at my job. I needed to find out before things got worse. All those late night calls need to end from Bethanee.

BETHANEE: "Just whisper to me in my ear."

I was annoyed at this point and wanted to get back home with my baby Jean, so I walked out of the room to have a moment to myself. We had been talking about moving in together... officially since her lease was about to be up. With LaLa being pregnant, I knew just any given moment, Jean would be coming to me about a baby. The way I have been feeling lately, I would sure give her one. Or however many she wants.

I saw that Bethanee was all excited. I assumed she was having a girl because that is what she always wanted. Just to be able to do her hair. I am not feeling Bethanee whatsoever, but I will not doubt or stunt that she cannot do some bomb ass hair. She braided up my hair a few times. I looked through the door window and saw that she was getting dressed and packing up her stuff. As Dr. Wilson was walking out of the room, I pulled him to the side.

DOCTOR WILSON: "Let me guess, you want to know what you guys are having?" He smiled and placed the clipboard under his right arm.

RAY: "I don't want to sound like an asshole, but no and I could care less. I pulled you over here to see if you could do me favor?" He made a questionable look on his face, letting me know he was a bit worried.

DOCTOR WILSON: "What's that?"

RAY: "If you knew *half* of the shit Bethanee has put me through *while* we were together, you would understand why I could care less about the baby. She played me, cheated on me, and so much more. I do not even think that is my baby, and I do not want to stick around, steady coming to doctor's appointments if it is not my baby. Do not get me wrong, if that child she is carrying *is* indeed mine, you have no doubt I will be here. Bethanee is stressing me the fuck out, and I have a woman at home. I do not want to bring this drama into my girls' life. At some point, we *are* going to try to start our own family. Doc, is there any way you can tell if that's my baby or not?"

I felt like I was pushing it, but it would not hurt to ask. I had to know, before I started going all out, buying diapers and shit for a child that is not mine. I mean no harm to the baby because she is not at fault. It is her mothers', and I know how her mother can be. I do not want any dealings of her hoe'ish ass.

DOCTOR WILSON: "I could tell there was some tension between you two, and some doubts in you as well. She's far enough in her pregnancy where I could do a DNA test. Since you are the potential father, I do not really need her consent to do so. Give me a moment."

I felt so relieved and wanted to hug him but felt that was really pushing it. Looking through the door window, Bethanee was still getting dressed. She was probably taking this long because she is too busy on the phone, telling folks what she is having. All you could hear was her yelling.

BETHANEE: "Oh girl my baby hair finna be tight." Yeah, that is if she actually grows hair. Bethanee knows she is baldhead. That is really why she started doing hair and wearing all that weave in the first place. She barely has edges. That is not my business though.

Doctor Wilson headed back in the room while I waited outside of the room. I checked my phone and saw that I had a text from Jean. I ended up dropping my phone unexpectedly. She had sent me a picture of this red lingerie she ordered online a few weeks ago for her homegirl party coming up. At that moment, I knew it was *definitely* time to go home. She was about to be in one of these rooms, finding out if she is having a boy or girl. I could not even respond to the text, I had to call her.

Chapter Twenty six

JEAN: "Hey baby."

RAY: "You gone do me like *that*?" She laughed but I was serious.

JEAN: "What you mean?"

   I took another look at the picture she had sent. Jean is fine and I do mean fine. She is like a size sixteen, thick in all of the right places, with a nice set of pillows that I enjoy lying on, both front and back.

RAY: "You send me this sexy ass picture and then want to leave. I will run red light to get to you." I thought of that song by *KeKe Palmer, "Yellow Lights,"* and I was just about to risk it all for Jean.

JEAN: "I just wanted you to see what it looks like on me. You can take it off another day." I poked out my bottom lip and whined like a little kid.

RAY: "But I want to take it off today!" Doctor Wilson made his way back to me, so I hurried and fixed my face.

DOCTOR WILSON: "Okay Mr. Ray, I need a sample of your saliva and I can have the results within three to four days." I let him do what he needed, and he put the swab in a container. After walking away, I looked back at the phone and Jean had her little perky titty out, rubbing all over her nipple.

RAY: "Oh I see now you want to play with me... damn baby you are looking good. Just imagine what it's like being in front of you with that on." She still giggling and shit. "Wait until I get there. You gone be in one of these rooms."

JEAN: "Boy hush. I'm about to take it off and head to meet with LaLa and Tiffany." She put her erected breast away and sat the phone down on what seem to be the television stand.

RAY: "They can wait!"

JEAN: "Would you make Slim wait?"

RAY: "Hell yea I would. You cannot do me like that baby. You send this sexy ass picture; I want to take it off with my mouth." I growled at her.

JEAN: "Okay, you nasty!"

RAY: You been known that, and you like it."

JEAN: "I'm about to leave." I accidentally hung the phone up. If only she could see the face I was making. I ended up calling her back on FaceTime so she could see. Baby still had that lingerie on. "I'm going to talk to you later."

RAY: "What do you mean? You really going to do me like that?"

JEAN: "Stop exaggerating and spend some time with your baby mother." I almost hung up in her face for real this time. She knows I hate when she gets to talking about Bethanee and I. She thinks that shit is funny, but it is not.

RAY: "Aight. Imma fuck with you later."

JEAN: "I love you baby." She is giggling and shit like it is really funny.

RAY: "Yeah!"

JEAN: "You're that mad that you can't tell me that you love me?"

RAY: "Have fun with your girls."

She ended up hanging up in my face and I felt bad. She always teasing me, she should at least feel bad about that. I saw Bethanee finally coming out of the room as I was walking towards the elevator. I hurried up and got on before she could see me and start to call my name. She actually did but I just closed the door on her. I checked my phone to see if I had any text or calls from Jean and I did not. Once I made it to my car, I called her phone, but she sent me straight to voicemail.

I decided to stop by the local flower shop and get her one of her favorite flowers: sunflower. She is really not a big fan of roses, unless they are spread across her bed, floor or in her bathwater. She prefers daisies and even succulents, so I got her a few of both. There was a beer and wine store up the street from the flower shop, so I stopped by there to get her favorite wine and some chocolate. Bethanee called my phone, and I immediately became irritated, ended up blocking her calls. I just do not understand why she continues to call me. Majority of the time she is trying to make her way back in my life, talking about 'let us work things out.' Girl if you do not work this dick in your mouth and leave me the hell alone.

I am not on this lease, but I have been living with Jean since we made things official. It just felt weird to me to be committed with her and not live in the same house. For other folks it was cool, but I am not like 'other folks.' I rather be around my woman than ripping and running the streets. Once her lease is up, we plan to move together, this time doing it the right way. We have been looking at a few apartments of her choice, I do not too much care where we live, long as I get to wake up every morning to that beautiful face. I will be the one paying all the bills too. That is just the way I was raised. I do not want my woman paying for anything but maybe her food, car note, or anything she choose to get without me knowing. Even when I just moved in at her current apartment, Jean has not paid one bill. Except for the time she snuck and paid rent.

I walked in and a candle was still lit on the living room table.

RAY: "Damn baby, could have burnt the house down nshit." I said aloud.

JEAN: "But I didn't so hush." She came strolling out of the bedroom, and my mouth dropped to the floor, right along with the flowers I had bought.

JEAN: "Damn, I hope those weren't for me."

RAY: "Shit!"

I attempted to bend down to pick up the flowers, but it was a bit hard because I could *not* keep my eyes off of her. She still had that red lace lingerie on, looking like my lunch *and* dinner. "Damn baby!" At that moment, I said fuck them flowers. I started walking towards her, but she put her hand up stopping me. Oh my, she turned around and that beautiful peach ass cheeks was sitting perfectly in them panties. My man became hard, and I was ready to eat.

JEAN: "Do not be rude. Pick my flowers up off the floor." It was not even demanding because she asked so politely and sexy. So, you know what I did? Walked my horny ass back over to them flowers and picked them up like baby said. "Thank you!"

RAY: "You're more than welcome my Queen." I could not even move now. I was stuck.

JEAN: "You are staying over there or going to meet me in the bedroom?"

RAY: "Yes ma'am!" She turned around and bent over, moving her ass from side to side. My man became harder, but my legs would not move. She began walking towards the bedroom while I was still standing there, man hard, almost touching the bookshelf on the other side of the Livingroom. I had to get it together. I did not know she lied about going out with her girls whatsoever, I am upset that she did not tell me because now I feel like I am about to bust with one damn stroke.

JEAN: "Come on Christi!" She peeped from around the corner. That is my middle name, Christi... When I turned eighteen, I wanted to change it to Christifer, but decided not to because I knew it would make my mother happy. Three years before I was born, my mother lost my big sister... Christi. She had her almost ten weeks early, and she did not make it. They could not control her breathing and she could not breathe on her own. That is where my middle name come in at. I never mind when Jean or my mother calls me Christi. They are about the only other people to know, not even Slim knows.

RAY: "Yes ma'am." As I was walking to the bedroom, felt like a rock was stuck in my throat. As many times as I have seen her completely naked, or we have had sex, I have never been this nervous. As soon as I walked into the room, her legs gapped open with a little of her lip sticking out from the lingerie. We made eye contact and I just stood there. That is how I knew she is the one for me. I have never felt like this about any woman.

She slid the lingerie to the side, exposing her entire goody sack. Opened the lips and began to explore herself while staring me deep in the eyes. Doctor Wilson? You about to deliver another baby. She began to moan, and that shit sounded so sexy. Pulling her fingers out, she sucked on them, just like I wanted her to suck on my man. Baby was a freak fasho and I love every bit of it. She had just got a fresh waxing, so that kitty was looking might scrumptious. Jean is on the curvy side, so she has a little stomach to grip on, and thighs that *always* saved my life.

My man began to pulse, I assumed I was taking too long to taste baby.

JEAN: "Come here sexy." She called me over with her index finger.

RAY: "Yes ma'am." I felt like I was a virgin again as slow as I was going. Jean was back to exploring herself with both her ring and middle finger. I moved her hand to the side and teased her with my tongue. Her moans sent chills up my spin. "You like that baby?"

JEAN: "Yes!" I went in ever so gently with my tongue on her pearl, sucking so softly, like I was kissing her lips. She moaned even louder, and that shit made me feel like I was about to bust. She pulled my face from between her legs and moved on top of me. She pulled my man out from my pants and made him moist with her mouth. Today was the day I bust fast as fuck. I had to pull her head up because one more lick and it was over for me and would need at least thirty minutes to get myself together. I wanted to give her a few strokes before it was over with.

Jean moved towards my face and kissed me with those soft lips of hers. I was glad she took a break from snatching my soul, to regain myself. She moved her hips in circular motion while kissing me. Let me go ahead and put a baby in her real quick. I could feel her lips on my man while she was grinding her hips. She stood up on the bed, squatted and inserted my man. It felt so warm and moist. Moving up and down my shaft, I moaned, she would gasp. A few strokes in, she turned to where her back was facing me and all I saw was ass bouncing on my chest. What a beautiful sight. I was holding on longer than I thought I would. She stopped riding my man and began to devour him. Those soft lips wrapped around my shaft felt like clouds. A few licks and slurps later, she was back riding. Once she came, she did not stop. I was right behind her!

RAY: "Shit! I'm about to bust!" She would usually get off then... but she did not. I was trying to hold it but damn, that pussy was feeling too good. Dr. Wilson, here we come.

She fooled the fuck out of me. I was just about to bust when she hopped off and began jerking my man. One more ass bounce, and my kids were about to start swimming to find me a little girl or boy. I am not going to lie; I was a little disappointed that she hopped off. We had been talking about having kids a lot lately, assumed today we would start making one. Just when I thought... She flopped down, right next to me, and I just looked at her.

JEAN: "What is it?"

RAY: "You kept riding my dick even after I said I was about to bust. I'm thinking we are about to have a baby." She rolled out of bed and headed towards the bathroom.

JEAN: "Not now Ray." She slammed the bathroom door and I just laid there naked, wondering what the fuck happened. Just two days ago, she wanted to have a baby.

RAY: "What's up with you? You were just trying to get pregnant the other day, now it is 'not now Ray.'"

JEAN: "It's too soon." She turned on the bath water and hopped in the shower. I hopped up from the bed and made my way to the bathroom. She did not lock the door, so I was able to walk in.

RAY: "What do you mean? If not now, then when?"

JEAN: "When you put a ring on my finger. When you find out if that baby is really yours or not. I have better things to do than to worry about if I am going to have to share you as a father to somebody else kid. Let her shine. I can wait."

I was baffled at this point and hurt. I really wanted a baby by her, but I have to accept the fact that she is not ready. I headed back to the room to get a pair of boxers so I could hop in the shower with Jean.

A few minutes later she got out and was laying back down... naked. I was Letting the water run down my spine once she got out. A nigga was really feeling down.

Chapter Twenty seven

Four Days Later...

Bethanee still had been blowing my phone up, trying to get back with me. I do not know if it is the baby, or if the bitch really crazy. Even though I blocked her number, here she come calling me from somebody else's phone. I will be glad when Doctor Wilson calls me. He said three or four days, and I am on day four, losing patience. After Jean had told me she was not ready for a baby, I had been a little distant from her. Instead of sleeping at her crib, I was at my potna Slims', sleeping on his couch. I needed to catch up with him anyway. When Jean calls, questioning me on why I was not home, I just tell her I am chilling with the homie right now. I know we are about to move in together, so I cannot be doing this shit. I just choose to distant myself to get over the hurt. I was really hoping for a baby with Jean.

Jean had called me while I was sleeping.

RAY: "Hello."

JEAN: "Why haven't you been home? And do not lie, talking about you '*chilling*,' I know when something is up with you, Ray. Did you forget we were friends seven years before being in a relationship? Did you forget I know where Slim stays? I got to hear on the streets that you have been there. Now get your ass up and come open this door."

I still had the crust in my eyes when sitting up on the couch.

JEAN: "Hello!"

RAY: "I'm getting up, damn."

JEAN: "Don't *'damn'* me. You need to hurry up." It was eight in the morning and she over here beating on the door. Here comes Slim, running from his bedroom, damn near scared for his life.

SLIM: "Who the fuck is that beating on my damn door this early in the morning?"

RAY: "Jean!" Slim and I was up till about four in the morning turning up, drinking and smoking, so this alarmed him with Jean doing here, and it was not putting a smile on his face.

JEAN: "Open the door, Ray!"

Boom. Boom.

RAY: "I'm coming!" I had to whisper, damn. She was still on the phone, so she heard me.

JEAN: "You must have some bitches in there, trying to hide them? I will fuck you, Slim and whoever else the fuck up."

At this point, I was scared to open the door. I looked back at Slim, and this nigga was standing there about as scared as I was.

SLIM: "Open the door before she beat it down." He whispered.

JEAN: "Ray Cristi Jones, if you do not open this damn door, we're going to have some problems." I had to say a little prayer.

I opened the door, Slim ran in the room, Jean bust in with Tiffany, and La behind her. I kid you not, first time in my life, that I have known La, and she stayed quiet during some drama. Shout out to the man above for giving her this baby. Jean slapped me back to reality and stood over me. Her eyes were red like she had been crying and my heart sank to my stomach. I looked over to La, and she looked pissed; arms folded with a glare in her eyes. I looked over to tiffany, she looked about as pissed as La. Looking back at Jean, her eyes were just so red, then began to fill up with tears.

JEAN: "So wassup? Where the bitches at?"

RAY: "In the back." All three of them gasp, next thing I know, I am getting another slap to the face. "I was talking about Slim. He the bitch."

SLIM: "What!" Here he comes from around the corner. "Look Jean, I know you're pissed at Ray, but there are no bitches up in my crib. My girl does not play that shit, just like you. For the past couple of days, it has just been Ray and me. No extra. I promise you."

LALA: "Yo *girl*?"

SLIM: "Oh so because you dogged me, I can't have a woman?"

LALA: "Ain't nobody..."

SLIM: "Anyway..." Slim cut LaLa completely off, and she just stood there, mouth touching the floor.

TIFFANY: "Oop!"

SLIM: "There are no bitches in here."

Jean turned to me and I instantly felt my heart sank again. I really hurt my woman, not even intentionally trying to. I was just hurt that she all of a sudden did not want to have a baby, so I distanced myself. Had I known it would make her feel this way, I would have never done it. I should have thought of the times I went M.I.A whenever Bethanee hurt me. That is my fault for not thinking straight. If she were hurt then and we were only best friends, what made me think she wouldn't be hurt now? We sleep in the same bed every night and I just up and leave instead of sitting down with her and communicating. Whenever I am hurt, I just shut down. If I am going to be committed to Jean, that is something I must work on. I am trying to have a kid, yet I cannot even communicate to my woman that I am hurt.

RAY: "Look, I know how mad you may be but it's not what you think. I just needed some time to myself."

JEAN: "Time for what? I did nothing to you, and you distance yourself from me for days." The wells of her eyes began to fill with tears, and I sat up to comfort her. "Please do not touch me. I want answers as to why you decided to be distant from your woman. But you are talking about marriage and having kids when you up and leave for three, four days."

My phone rang and it was some unknown number. I assumed it was Bethanee, so I forward the call. Whoever it was left a voicemail, and Bethanee does not usually do that.

JEAN: "Okay so, Bethanee hurt's you and you think it's okay to hurt me?" All eyes were on me and I felt even more guilty.

RAY: "Jean it's not even like that." I tried to grab her, but she backed away.

JEAN: "Then what is it?"

RAY: "What you said to me…"

JEAN: "The fuck are you talking about?" My phone rang again. The same number who called earlier was calling again. "And who the fuck keeps calling you?"

RAY: "Man I don't know." She snatched the phone from my hand and answered it for me.

JEAN: "Who is it?"

DOCTOR WILSON: "It's Doctor Wilson. May I speak to Ray?" Jean looked over at me, with curiosity written all over her face.

JEAN: "You got something?"

RAY: "The fuck are you talking about?"

DOCTOR WILSON: "I'm just calling to give him some results."

JEAN: "What type of results?" I snatched the phone from her and held it to my ear.

RAY: "This is Ray!"

DOCTOR WILSON: "How you doing today? I just wanted to call and let you know of the results from the DNA test." I walked away towards Slim bedroom so I could have a peace of mind. "After several blood tests, I found out that you are ninety-nine-point ninety nine percent... *not* the father." I dropped down to my knees in a sign of relief and began to cry. Jean and Slim ran over to me to make sure I was okay.

JEAN: "Hello, Doctor? This is Jean, Rays' wife. Is everything okay? He just fainted."

DOCTOR WILSON: "Give him some water and fan him some. He may just be overwhelmed. I hope you are as happy as he is to know that Bethanee's child she is carrying, is *not* Ray's child."

JEAN: "Are you serious?" Jean fanned while mouthing to Tiffany to bring me a glass of water.

DOCTOR WILSON: "Yes ma'am. You both go be happy without the stress of another woman's issues."

RAY: "Thank you so much, Doctor. You do not know how much I appreciate this." I managed to yell out. I took a few sips of the water and a deep breath.

DOCTOR WILSON: "My pleasure. I assume you will not be at any other doctor appointments with Bethanee?"

JEAN: "Hell No!" Doctor Wilson chuckled some.

DOCTOR WILSON: "Ha, well it was nice knowing ya my brother. Maybe I will see you again when you get your wife pregnant."

RAY: "Oh for sure, Doc. Thank you again."

DOCTOR WILSON: "You're welcome. You all have a great rest of your day."

JEAN: "You as well. Thank you." Jean hung up the phone and stood over me, with her arms folded.

JEAN: "I'll meet you at the house." She bent down and kissed me on the forehead. I did not know if I should be scared or relieved. I knew for a fact I would take my ass home.

... Just when I thought I was about to deal with Bethanee for another eighteen years, that baby is not mine!

Chapter Twenty eight

Locked Up – Bethanee

It had been about a week since I last heard from Ray. How could he abandon me like that? We have a whole child together. He keeps on playing with me, I will end up putting his ass on child support. He lays up with me to make this child, and then leave me to take care of it by myself, hell no! I started seeing this fine light skinned brother, by the name of Pete, so I am not tripping too much that Ray does not want to be with me no more. When I finally drop, I want my round from ol girl Jean. My phone rang and it was my baby Pete.

PETE: "What you got going slim thick?"

BETHANEE: "Trying to see why my baby daddy not answering my phone calls. He ran out before I could tell him when our next appointment is." I gently sat down on the couch and picked up the remote.

PETE: "I can go handle that like I did ol boy. You know I don't play about you, baby."

BETHANEE: "No, that's not necessary. I'll just end up putting him on child support." Although I was not feeling Ray, I thought my baby girl Calie, need both of her parents in her life.

PETE: "Well do what you do baby, just know I can take care of that for you."

Ever since Pete told me what happened with Tony, he has been acting different lately and sometimes it turned me off.

BETHANEE: "Yeah, I know."

PETE: "Imma hit you back up later. I got to go run a few errands."

BETHANEE: "Aiight! Be safe."

PETE: "Fasho."

We both hung up the call and I tried Ray one last time... and nothing. The thought of getting Pete to solve and end my biggest problem, sounded good right about now. I was already feeling bad about ol boy. I knew it would hurt Jean to see Ray gone and hurting her put a smile on my face. Coming into his life and stole him away from me. From day one, I knew Jean would try to take Ray away from me. It was always clear in her actions. My man does not need to run to some female to cry on her shoulder because I cheated. I know I made my share of mistakes, but I was young and dumb. I tried to make things right between Ray and me, but Jean filled his head up with bullshit; 'if she loved you, she would not cheat on you'. Girl shut the hell up and stop trying to throw your pussy at him. Ray was my first love and I would do just about anything for him; I let my so-called friends influence me to cheat on him.

I remember that day like it was just yesterday. I was blowing Ray phone up... just like I am today, but he was not answering. So much anger came over me! Like if you are busy, at least call me and let me know *and* I let him use my car that day because his was still in the shop. I had errands to run just before I went out with my girls. Ray would just not pick up my calls or answer my text. It was about time for me to start getting ready, and I still had not heard from Ray. Here comes my homegirl Riley, 'girl what if he is cheating on you with his so-called best friend Jean?' Then I got to really thinking he was with her. Both Jean and Ray were really close to only be friends, they had to be fucking too.

Riley had to end up coming to get me because Ray still had not come back to the house in my car, nor answered my calls. We made it to the club and there were countless fine brothers, looking like they were ready for a fine sister like myself. We had not been in the club even ten minutes and this tall, buff, chocolate brother stepped up to me when Riley and I were trying to get drinks. He was fine, with some full soft looking lips. I had to check him out and I do mean *check* him out. Boy had a bulge in his pants that I could not keep my eyes off of. He is looking at me, licking his lips, while I am staring between his eyes and his already erected dick.

That night I had on this skintight black dress, with lace in the boob area. There was a slight slit in the side that exposed partial of my tight. I was slim thick then, and had glazed myself in some shea butter, so that little thigh was serving Mr. Man who walked up on me. I never even got his name... Shawn or something like that. My hair was down with weave because I had just got done finishing it

299

before Riley pulled up. The day before, Riley and I had gotten a pedicure, so my toes were fresh and all white in them tall ass heels. He just kept staring at me.

MR.MAN: "How are you doing tonight?" He rubbed his hands together and licked his lips.

BETHANEE: "I am alright and you?"

RILEY: "She is single."

I looked over at her and she took a sip of her drink and then turned away to the dance floor. She knew damn well I was with Ray and blurted out that I was single. I mean I did feel I was single. I had not heard from Ray all day while he was using my car and he knew about me going out that night. Mr. Man asked me to dance and I took him up on his offer, and I took my drink with me.

We made it to the dance floor and *LSG, My Body* came on. Oh, I was giving it to him. Grinding all up on that bulge I saw in his pants. Then he started kissing and licking on my neck, sending chills up my spin. Boy did I want him and bad, but I was in a relationship with Ray. Before the night ended and Mr. Man and I stopped dancing, he asked for my number. Right then and there should have been the moment I told him I was in a relationship, but something came over me and I kept that small thing to myself. He was trying to go back to his room to get to know me more. Where is the harm in that? If Ray can have a close female friend, why could I not have a close male friend?

Eventually I would tell Mr. Man I was in a relationship, or so I thought.

Riley kept edging me on to go with him, but I was not one hundred percent sure. I checked my phone and Ray *still* had not called. I ended up going to his room and we did start off talking; about how he wanted to be in a committed relationship and shit. He was going on and on about his life growing up. I am not going to lie, I was not all that interested in his life, I was worried about that bulge that kept jumping out at me. I mean he sounded like he had a good life and was even questioning me about my life growing up. That was around the time my mother and I had a big fight and she had kicked me out. It was hard to talk about, but Mr. Man made it easier.

Next thing I know, he leans in to kiss me and I did not stop him. It just felt so right, and I did not want it to end. He then started fondling with my dress, trying to hike it up. I did help him out a bit and finally made his way to my golden pot. Remember I said I was checking him out? That is what I did, nails and all, and they looked freshly done. So, I was not too worried about bacteria under his fingernails. I gapped my legs open a little more so he could insert his finger.

They were pretty fat so one was enough for me. I moaned mid kissing and he pulled away to lick on my neck. That fore-play shit was nice, but I wanted the dick. I straddled him, not trying to be too aggressive, I decided to continue to kiss him. He reached in his pocket to pull out his wallet and my first impression was, "I am no escort." He was just getting a condom... I got off and helped him unbuckle his pants because he was starting to take too long for me. He whipped out this *big* monster. Dick had veins in it and it was just thick. Ray has a big dick too, but I have never seen any veins in it. Placing the condom on, I pushed him back and straddled on top of him. It hurt at first trying to get it in, but after a few bounces, that shit started feeling good as fuck.

He began moaning and frowning up. Grabbing my ass to help me bounce more because the feeling in my thighs was beginning to go out. Mr. Man caressed my breast and helped me pull my dress over my head to expose them both. He wrapped his arm around my waist and grabbed me from the back, placing my left breast in his mouth. Next thing I know, his finger was in my ass. That gave a spin for my pearls. A breast in his mouth, a finger in my ass and that monster in my pot. I was screaming so damn loud and did not give one fuck who heard me. We switched positions and he was on top. Good thing the air was blasting because I was beginning to sweat, and I did not want any of his sweat droppings to drip in my mouth... because it was open.

I looked down and saw my pot beginning to cream and there he goes with that finger in my ass again. We were both moaning and a few pumps later, we both came. This one nasty motherfucker; he did not stop there. Started eating my pussy like it was his last meal. I had squirted so hard it scared me. He laid down next to me and all I could do was stare at the ceiling, *"what the fuck did I just do?"* I just laid there for at least ten, fifteen minutes and ended up calling Riley to come get me. Mr. Man hopped up and walked to the bathroom to freshen up, while I was laying on the bed, cuddling a pillow. Pussy just throbbing for more of him. Once Riley texted and said she was outside, I grabbed my purse and headed out. Mr. Man ran after me to get my number and asked if we could do it again sometime... my dumb ass gave him the number and said yeah. I made it to Riley, and she was cheesing ear to ear while I was looking like I had lost my best friend, better yet, like someone had just died.

Ray's friend Slim ended up telling him that he saw me at the club grinding on him that night. Turns out, Ray's phone had died that day and he ran over a nail and was stranded on the side of the road with a flat tire. I did not have a car charger at the time. I just felt so guilty once Mr. Man started texting and calling me. Turns out his name is Keyvaune. Once Ray found out about me grinding on Keyvaune, I came clean about it and how I was upset with him because I thought he was with Jean. He forgave me... probably because I did not tell him about me going to Keyvaune's room. Me dancing on him was nothing really major to Ray and I was glad he did not flip out. I thought I had pulled the greatest scheme of all time. One day while I was out waiting on Ray for our date, Keyvaune saw me and when he came in for a hug, he grabbed my ass. Ray had just come around the corner and saw that. Just when I thought I was on a role and in good with Ray, here comes Keyvaune wanting to feel up on me. A big fight broke out and Ray and I separated for like a month.

I was pissed at Riley because she basically pushed me to dance with Keyvaune and go to his room. Me and her had stopped talking for a while and she finally apologized to me. During the entire time Ray and I were separated, I was texting and talking to Keyvaune. That probably was not the best thing to do, knowing how I really wanted to be with Ray and was texting him to make things right again. Keyvaune just has some good dick, and that finger in my ass was something new to me that I was too afraid to ask Ray to start doing.

I just assumed he would think I got it from my one-night stand with Keyvaune. Little did Ray know, Keyvaune and I had sex multiple times. I guess you could say it was all my fault why Ray and I did not work out. I do not think I would go back and change a thing other than stopping after that one time with Keyvaune, because it was a great experience. I regret breaking Ray's heart!

Chapter Twenty nine

Snapping back to reality-

I paced back and forth in my apartment, but my feet began to hurt so I took a little break and tried calling Ray again...nothing. This nigga is really ignoring me. Is this how he wants to start this co-parenting thing? I will make his life a living hell fooling with me. Now I know I did my share of wrong, but he does not have to take it out on our child. Our innocent little baby. I am going to call him again later, and after that, if he does not answer, I am going to let Pete handle him for me. I have been through too much with him to allow him to turn his back on my child and me.

Pete sent me a text, saying he was pulling up and I have not seen my man in a few days. He is this known drug dealer in the streets, and people know not to mess with him whatsoever. That is really how ol boy Tony got shot, messing with the wrong nigga out here. I heard he had woken up in the hospital though. My baby needs to go ahead and finish that up before he gets back out on the streets snitching and shit.

I freshen up some and tidied up the house. A few moments later, Pete knocked on my door. I hurried to open it, arms wide open and lips puckered for a hug and kiss, but he pushed past me, pacing.

PETE: "This nigga isn't even dead." He began to pace, angrily, and when he does that, it makes me nervous. Pete is crazy! There are no loops around it at all. He is just loony

305

in the head. The way he was raised had a lot to do with it; Seeing his mother sniff crack right in front of him, while riding a new nigga dick every day. She was even sniffing crack when she was pregnant with him, up until about the sixth or seventh month. He was actually a preemie baby, born at seven months. The doctor did not even think he would make it but look at him now... just crazy!

BETHANEE: "What in the fuck are you talking about?" I was still standing in the doorway with it wide open. Dropped my arms to the side a little disappointed.

PETE: "That nigga Tony. He is not even dead."

I had already known that, but Pete being the nigga he is, I assumed he knew too. The streets talk and Pete's always running in them. He should have been the first to know but looks like he is the last. He started rubbing his head with his hands, making me more nervous than I was before with the pacing. I finally closed and locked my door. Walking towards him...

BETHANEE: "Can't you just finish the job?"

PETE: "How Bethanee? Think! Use that huge noggin that you have covered in fake ass hair."

BETHANEE: "Okay, look bitch!" He glared over at me and walked towards me like he wanted to hit me.

PETE: "I told you about that bitch shit. I am not a bitch, and you know how I feel about that word." Whenever he did not do what his mother told him, she would call him a bitch. I did not really give a fuck. He is in *my* house, so I will say what I please. If I felt like he was making a bitch move, then he is a bitch. He thinks it is okay for him to talk to me the way he does, with the big head jokes, or my body weight, but it is a problem when I do it to him. Be having the nerve to call me a hoe because I have male friends. As Harry Truman says, *'If you can't stand the heat, get out of the kitchen.'*

BETHANEE: "You know Pete, I can care less about what you are saying right now. I salute you for stepping up and trying to take care of myself and my child, but you are not going to keep talking and disrespecting me and think I am not going to say anything to you. Your dick's not that good to be dealing with it either. So, you either respect me, or get the fuck out!" His dick was average, and I have had way better. My pot became full thinking about **Keyvaune**. The way Pete looked at me let me know he actually cares about me. His eyes soften up.

PETE: "Look, I apologize for talking to you like that. I know we do this a lot, but I really care about you. Like I never want to lose you." I was honestly over Pete and wanted to stop fucking with him.

BETHANEE: "Respect me then. That's all I ask of you." Knowing damn well I wanted the money too. Being pregnant is hard, and my feet be hurting waiting them tables. A little help never hurts, or does it?

PETE: "I got you baby girl." I looked him in his eyes but did not believe one word that was coming out of his mouth. All I know is, the next time he disrespects me, he is getting his ass handed to him.

BETHANEE: "What you plan on doing about Tony? You going to finish that?" I wobbled and made my way to the couch.

PETE: "I will have to. I cannot allow that nigga to keep roaming the streets like he did not steal nothing from me. Nigga hit me for fifty K, then took my kush and Crystal."

I bucked my eyes wide. I knew this Tony dude stole from Pete; I just did not know what exactly. Crystal was Pete's girlfriend, until she had gotten a taste of Tony. I also heard Tony is the ex of Jean's friend, Tiffany. I do not know her too well so I could care less about her nigga getting shot. Jean's nigga Ray, is next fucking around with me and my baby.

PETE: "Aye, I'm about to head out. I got some shit to handle."

While rubbing my belly, I turned and looked at Pete.

BETHANEE: "You can't sit a little longer?" I gave him puppy dog eyes, and that usually works... not so much this time.

PETE: "I'll come back later." We both knew that was a lie, but I had too much going on to pursue the issue at hand.

BETHANEE: "Mhmm." He walked over and kissed me one last time and headed out the door. After struggling to get off the couch and locking up, I headed to my room and turned on my stereo. Pandora began to play Erykah Badu, *'Didn't cha know,'* one of my favorite songs by her.

I grooved to the music and relaxed in my bed. Reaching for my phone, I decided to call Ray again. This time it went straight to voicemail, so I left a message for him to call. After that, it was over for him.

At Tiffany's

My phone rang but I did not notice the number calling, so I forward the call to voicemail. They ended up calling again.

TIFFANY: "Who is it?" I answered angrily.

TONY: "Is that how you really answer the phone for your man?" I rolled my eyes at the sound of his voice.

TIFFANY: "Tony what the hell do you want? You are not my man and haven't been for a while."

TONY: "Damn I thought we were better than that."

Do not get me wrong I did feel sorry for Tony, but I was done trying to work things out with him because I felt pity towards his situation.

TIFFANY: "I did too but then I find out you have been busy with other bitches behind my back while I have been faithful to you. Bringing that shit into my home. You are foul and full of shit. Crystal... Bethanee, wow." I thought of that Crystal chick he was fucking in my bed. I did not know much about her, but she left her wallet at my house when I kicked her ass out with the butcher knife in my hand, right along with Tony. The nerve of this nigga to have some random chick where we lay both our heads at night. The bitch luck I did not cut her because I was close. I did snatch her up a bit, ass naked being dragged on the floor. I still cannot believe he was fooling with Bethanee.

TONY: "Now wait a minute, Tiffany..."

TIFFANY: "Nah you wait a minute hoe. Why is you calling me like I really fuck with you?"

TONY: "Hoe?" I rolled my eyes at the thought of him thinking he was anything more than a hoe.

TIFFANY: "That's exactly what I said... hoe."

TONY: "I get shot and end up in the hospital. I called to say thank you for showing up and being there when I opened my eyes. And I was wondering if..." There he goes with that pity shit. He did the same thing when his brother Tim got shot. I wanted us to be friends, but he wanted to work things out because he lost his little brother. This time in age, I was not about to fall for that shit.

TIFFANY: "Yeah, you're welcome. Now you have a great rest of your day."

I hung up my phone before hearing what he had to say and blocked his number. I was fed up with Tony's shenanigans and wanted no parts of it. I remember him say how he knew who shot him and I did not want that drama in my life whatsoever. I was ready to go to war behind Tony but the fact that he called my phone with that *'baby'* shit was it for me. I am at a place where I am happy who I am with, happy where I am at in life and going to keep busting my ass to get where I want to be in life. Business will be booming!

Bethanee's

About twenty minutes later I got a knock on my door. I was not expecting any company, so I was a bit confused as to who was knocking on my door. They began to knock again as I was walking towards the door. I am far long in my pregnancy, and it takes me a little minute to get to place or I might pee on myself.

BETHANEE: "Who is it?" I yelled about just in case I could not get to the door in time.

DETECTIVE RICHIE: "It's detective Richie! I'm looking for a Bethanee Spears."

I bucked my eyes wide open, like what the hell have I done for a detective to be knocking on my door. Looking through the peep hole, it was this tall, chocolate fine brother standing outside of my door in a suit. I turned the locks and opened my front door in awe.

BETHANEE: "How can I help you?

DETECTIVE RICHIE: "Are you Bethanee Spears?"

I frowned up.

BETHANEE: "Yes I am. What is going on? Is someone hurt?" He placed his hands behind his back.

DETECTIVE RICHIE: "Someone was hurt, and I believe you had something to do with it, right along with a Pete Anderson. I am going to need you to come down to the station with me ma'am!"

What have I done? I should have never fucked with Pete and just minded my own business.

BETHANEE: "Excuse me? I am pregnant." I rubbed my belly.

DETECTIVE RICHIE: "Congratulations. Now, let us go." He grabbed a hold of my arm and began to pull me.

BETHANEE: "Let go of me!" I tried to yank away.

DETECTIVE RICHIE: "If you continue to resist, I will have to put you in handcuffs, and you will be charged.

BETHANEE: "What is going on? I did nothing." Still trying to get away.

DETECTIVE RICHIE: "Ma'am, I'm trying to give you the benefit of the doubt because you are pregnant. Now you need to stop resisting and come on." I began to cry. I have never been in a situation like this. Not even a lousy speeding ticket. NO type of confrontation with the police and here I am about to go to jail, while pregnant. I am too pretty for jail and do not want to raise my child in prison.

BETHANEE: "Can I at least grab my phone?"

DETECTIVE RICHIE: "You won't be needing that." He pulled me some, backing away from my front door.

BETHANEE: "Can I at least lock up?" Finding every reason and excuse I could think of to keep from going down to the police station.

DETECTIVE RICHIE: "Go right ahead." He unhanded me and I walked into my apartment to grab my keys. Walked back to the front door, I took one last look inside of my place and closed the door. Rubbing my belly, I prayed I did not end up in prison with my baby. I hid my face because I did not want anyone knowing I was being taken into custody for questioning. Everyone and their mama was outside their apartment being nosey.

Chapter Thirty

Finally making it to the station, I assumed my baby did not like where we were at because she started to kick and move around too much. Richie walked me into an interrogation room and sat me down. He offered me coffee or water, and a cigarette.

DETECTIVE RICHIE: "I forgot you're pregnant. Excuse me." He left the room and I was in there alone for what felt like an hour. Once he came back, he had himself a cup of coffee and a vanilla folder that he threw on the table. I jumped a little, rubbing my belly because she started kicking again.

DETECTIVE RICHIE: "Ms. Spears, do you know a Pete Anderson?" I looked at him like he had stupid written on his damn forehead, but I did not want to catch an attitude with him. End up staying in here way longer than expected. I was getting hungry and angry; hangry.

BETHANEE: "Yes I do, he's my boyfriend. Is there any way I could get something to snack on? My baby is starting to move around a little too much for me."

DETECTIVE RICHIE: "I can get you a sausage, apple sauce or Jell-O, and when was the last time you saw your boyfriend?"

BETHANEE: "I don't remember." I lied. "Can I get apple sauce and Jell-O, with two, maybe three pieces of sausage?"

He looked at me for a moment and I just smiled. A few seconds later, Richie had gotten up and walked out of the room. Coming back with a plate that had about four pieces of sausage, and both Jell-O and apple sauce. He placed the plate in front of me as he sat down, and I did not waste any time to eat.

DETECTIVE RICHIE: "Now that you have your sausage, back to business. He's your boyfriend but you don't remember the last time you saw him?" He began writing stuff down and I was getting nervous. I know exactly why I was here in this room, being questioned.

BETHANEE: "Is that a problem?" I managed to get out with a mouth full of apple sauce. "It's not like we live together." I shrugged my shoulders. "I don't remember the last time I saw him." He leaned forward, crossing his hands with one another.

DETECTIVE RICHIE: "Look, you look like you're about four, maybe five months pregnant, and I know for a fact you don't want to spend the rest of your pregnancy in prison, nor lose the rights of your child, having him or her be put in the system right after birth. Not even getting a real chance to hold your child." I stopped eating for a moment to listen to Richie. "I am trying to help you as much as a can, but that is going to be hard if you do not work with me and tell me what I need to know about Tony Sheen getting shot. I know you two have a record of being together, so I know for a fact you know him."

He opened his folder and had text, pictures, call logs and more of Tony's and I conversations. "I also know that you two got into it bad after the breakup and those harsh words you last said to him, brings me to the conclusion that you were the one to set Tony up and Pete, the boyfriend you don't seem to remember the last time you saw, shot him."

At that moment, I knew I was fucked unless I talked. Pete kept going on and on how it would not catch up to me and no one would know. That was around the time I found out I was pregnant. I was just so upset because Tony was talking about going back to his girlfriend Tiffany. Kept screaming how I wanted him dead and more. Now I regret saying those things. I regret fucking around with him. I regret lying to Ray. I regret cheating on him. I regret not wearing protection when I was fucking Tony. He knew I was pregnant with his baby... but still decided to leave me. I just decided to pawn it on Ray because I knew he would step up and now he is not answering my calls. Pete just wanted to do something because he knew he shot my child's real father... Tony!

BETHANEE: "What's the deal for me? Do I get to go home and live my life in peace with my child? Just erase all of this?" The proof was in the pudding so no need of me lying about it.

DETECTIVE RICHIE: "Get to talking." He pulled out his tape recorder to get my confession. I had my doubts on telling him anything.

BETHANEE: "I set him up!"

DETECTIVE RICHIE: "Who is him?"

BETHANEE: "Tony, I set Tony up. I knew he was doing some fuck shit... excuse my language. I knew what he was doing, and I was hurt by it. He had told me he was done messing around with this chick who is friends with my ex, but he lied. They were still fooling around with each other; in fact, they were living together. After that, I started finding out about other chicks he was fooling with. Turns out, he was sleeping with Pete's girlfriend, Crystal at the time. I was hurt because he knows this is his baby, and just because I have a record of sleeping with men, he does not believe this is his child. When I started fucking with Tony, I cut everybody else off. I can even take a DNA test to prove this is his baby. Pete was trying to get with me at the time, but I was not really feeling him. He knew I was vulnerable and decided he could fix everything by killing Tony. He suggested to end all my problems and he would help take care of my baby, even the idea to pin the baby on my ex-boyfriend Ray. Pete is crazy."

I paused and took a sip of my water, while twirling my index finger around my temple.

BETHANEE: "I was trying to make things right with Ray so I thought it was a good idea but that backfired on me because now he's not even answering my calls, knowing I'm pregnant." I broke down crying. "First Tony denies our child, then Ray." The tears flowed down my face, onto the table. "I can't go through this pregnancy alone! I am having problems with my mother; I do not know who my daddy is. I have no one! I am probably better off in prison. I just do not want to lose my baby. The only thing really worth living for at this point. I'm just so scared to do it alone!"

Maybe I do not need to be someone's mother right now. I am not ready for that responsibility... and to do it all on my own.

DETECTIVE RICHIE: "Let me tell you what I can do for you. Give me where Pete is now, and I can get you a deal with only three months in prison." I looked up to him, with tears in the wells of my eyes.

BETHANEE: "What! Three months? What happened to going home? Forgetting this ever happened?"

DETECTIVE RICHIE: "You set someone up to get shot. He could have died, and you probably would not even see outside again, and your child would for sure end up in the system. You would have been an accessory to murder Ms. Spears... murder. Luckily for you, Tony woke up. Now you can either take the deal and tell me where Pete is, or go to prison just like him, for the rest of your life." He sat back in the chair and folded his arm. "This is up to you."

BETHANEE: "And how do I know you're not just setting me up again? Telling me you'll give me three months if I tell where Pete is but really going to throw me in jail forever."

DETECTIVE RICHIE: "Unlike you, I don't want you to have your child in prison. I grew up in a broken home as well. Mother was a crack head, daddy nowhere to be found. I decided to be different and do different. I'm just trying to help you out."

BETHANEE: "Can I get this in writing?" He stood up and walked out of the room. I finished the rest of my sausage and apple sauce and about ten minutes later, he came back with some paperwork.

DETECTIVE RICHIE: "Read over this and if you agree..." Handing me a pen, "sign."

Just when I thought I was about to get away free, I was about to spend the next three months of my pregnancy in prison. AT least by the time I get out, she would just be born. My baby girl was the only thing on my mind. She could not be away from her mother and I was not going to let that happen. I signed the paperwork and wrote down the address where I knew Pete would be, Next thing I know, two officers walked in, handcuffed me and walked me to get booked.

Pete too

Boom. Boom. Boom.

"Pete Anderson, open up!" I was just finishing rolling my blunt, about to light that hoe up when some niggas started beating on my door, calling my government name at that.

PETE: "Who is it?"

Boom!

DETECTIVE RICHIE: "Pete Anderson, you have the right to remain silent. Anything you say or do can be used against you in the court of law..." He right along with about three other officers bust into my crib. The detective pulled out his handcuffs and cuffed my ass before I could even get a taste of my blunt. Just when I thought I was going to get away later tonight...

PETE: "That bitch set me up!"

I walked my ass to the back of the cop car and was on my way to spend the rest of my life in prison. Tony lucky I did not get to finish the job, let alone Ray for putting my baby Bethanee through this mess. Nobody knew where I was at but Bethanee, so I know she had to be the one to snitch on me. I love that bitch, but she has to die. Her and that fatherless child.

Chapter Thirty one

LeZ' Be Honest- Tiffany

It has been a few weeks since I last saw my girls LaLa and Jean. I mean I talk to them faithfully every day, I just had not seen them. With LaLa being newly pregnant, I feel like I have been a bad friend. She keeps throwing in my face how she has been reading this book that constantly telling her that her close friends and loved ones should be around her the most. Not saying that LaLa is not important to me, but I have other stuff going on right now.

MONIKA: "How are you doing, baby?" I looked up from the stove, scrambling eggs and saw my baby Monika. She walked over to me and grabbed me from the back. Yeah, I said it, *she*. Monika and I have known each other for about three years now. One Night we were a little too drunk when she came in town to visit, and one thing led to another. Now we have been dating for four months now and no one knows but us two, and of course the man above. Setting the spoon down, I turned around to her and wrapped my arms around her neck.

TIFFANY: "I'm alright and you? How did you sleep?"

MONIKA: "Great! Last night was great too." She smirked and kissed my lips; chills ran up my spin.

Monika is great. She works in real estate. Jean and LaLa have met her maybe once before, but she is always going out of town, so they never really got to go out with her, let alone the chance to get to know her. Monika is more like me. She is gorgeous, smart, smooth chocolate skin, long, soft, silky hair and a body that even I cannot resist. I never thought I would be attracted to another woman. Do not get Me wrong, there are many women that I think are beautiful, but seeing myself sleeping with them was out of the question, until that one drunken night with Monika and me.

I remember it like it was yesterday. She had come down from Miami to visit me. She was staying with me because I thought it was dumb of her to get a room when I have plenty of space at my condo. I wanted to go out and have drinks and she was down to have a good time on her vacation away from work. One drink led to another, then we were on our way in a Lyft to my place.

Even when we got to my house, we were still drinking. Shots after shots. I ended up popping a frozen pizza in the oven right along with some fries. That was around the time Keyvaune called himself trying to get with me. The flowers and chocolate were nice and all but, I was single and wanted to live a single life. We were watching a movie that night and Lamman Rucker was looking extra fine in *'Why Did I Get Married.'* However, the dress Monika had on made her titties pop out, distracting me from the movie. Next thing I know, my pussy ends up in her mouth and I am having the best orgasm I have ever had in my life. I wanted to marry that woman right then and there. When she left to go back home, we basically became a couple that following day and kept it to ourselves.

MONIKA: "What do you have planned for today?"

TIFFANY: "I was thinking we just chilled in the house." I began to smell the eggs, so I hurried to turn the stove down some. Monika just stood there with her arms folded, mad. She always looks sexy when she is mad. That would be the best time to have a little taste of her cookie.

MONIKA: "You don't want to get out? Maybe go shopping or something?"

TIFFANY: "No, do you want to?" Scrambling eggs, hoping she would say no.

MONIKA: "No offense but I'm tired of just sitting in the house. I want to go somewhere fun. Let us get cute and go somewhere, bae." She playfully grabbed ahold of my waist.

Everyone that knows Monika, or anyone that is cool with her, knows she is a lesbian. Me on the other hand, people know me for taking dick. I know for a fact Monika is going to be trying to hold hands, kiss all up on me, take pictures and shit. I am not ready for the world, let alone my friends know I decided to swing the other way and eat a little pussy. Had it been a few years ago, I would have slapped someone for asking if I would ever bump coochies. Now look at me... bumping coochies. It is just something about Monika that makes me want to risk it all but not the fact of people knowing I like women.

MONIKA: "You're still in that embarrassing stage of your sexuality, huh? You are still keeping me a secret." She pulled away from me and leaned up against the countertop. "I do not know how much more of this I am going to allow Tiffany. It has been four months of dating and the only time you want to be seen in public with me is if we're going to the club with some skank ass dresses on or probably to go get something to eat, that we would order... for pickup! This is ridiculous at this point."

She walked away and headed to the bedroom. I knew she was right. A part of me was embarrassed to be seen in public with Monika. I love and adore her entirely; I just was not ready for folks to know that side of me.

Sitting the spatula down on the counter, I turned the eggs off and made my way to the bedroom. She was laid out on the bed, watching a show called, 'Here's My Story.' That is how I knew she was pissed off at me. We binge watch that show together and she happens to decide to watch it alone. Last time I did that, and she had a whole fit.

TIFFANY: "So you're that mad at me to watch *our* show by yourself?" Monika sat up on the bed and looked me dead in the eye.

MONIKA: "Tiffany, do you know how that makes me feel that I think I'm falling in love with someone who is too ashamed to walk out in public holding hands with me? Like crap. I have known you all of these years and you weren't shy then with your sexuality. You knew I was into girls but that did not stop you from slapping my ass in the clubs. Now that we have made things official, you're *embarrassed*."

She rolled her eyes and turned her back on me. She is in love with me!

MONIKA: "I cannot be with someone like you." Back still facing my way.

TIFFANY: "Someone like *me*?" I pointed to my chest and walked in front of the television, so I knew I had her full attention.

MONIKA: "If you weren't ready for all of that, that is all you had to say instead of pulling me into this whack ass relationship. Your closest friends La and Jean does not even know about us. You all tell each other everything but you choose to keep me this big ass secret." Bouncing up off of the bed, "I could have stayed my ass in Miami." Monika walked over to the closet and began to pack her bags.

TIFFANY: "Where are you going? Your flight doesn't leave until another two days."

MONIKA: "I know! Until then I will be in a hotel."

TIFFANY: "Now you're just being ignorant." I snatched the bag from her hand and threw it down.

MONIKA: "You touch my stuff again; I will have to beat your ass." I did not give one, two let alone any other fucks. She started packing again.

TIFFANY: "You're not going anywhere." I unpacked the clothes she had put in her bag and she walked up on me. Folding my arms across my chest, I waited for her to swing. "I don't give a fuck how mad you are. You are going to put this shit away, I am going to finish cooking breakfast, we are both going to eat it while finishing up, *'Here's My Story,'* probably end up fuck...

MONIKA: "Tiffany, I love you, but I can't."

    I sighed, wondering what else to say to make her change her mind. My heart ached and that is when I knew I was falling in love with her as well. I could not keep hurting my baby. I had to be open about this. Monika is the best thing that has ever happened to me and I could not lose her. I just stood there while she continued to pack.

TIFFANY: "Monika, I love you!" The wells of my eyes began to fill with tears. "I don't want you to leave. Just give me time to open up."

MONIKA: "How much more time, Tiff? It has already been four months. You want another four months?"

TIFFANY: "If that's not too much to ask for." I smirked a little and wiped the tears away but by the face she made, it was her 'bitch you really got me fucked up,' face. "I'm just kidding, baby." I knew I had to give her something or I was about to lose her.

    My phone rang and it was Jean calling. Monika looked at my phone then back at me. I was stuck! I wanted to go run for the phone, telling my girl Jean that I am in love with my girlfriend Monika. Next thing I know, Monika grabs my phone and answers it.

MONIKA: "Hey Jean, this is Monika!"

JEAN: "MONIKA! Hey girl. It has been a minute. How have you been?"

MONIKA: "Great! Think I found the love of my life." She looked me right in the eyes when she said that, and my heart fell to my feet. I have got to make things right with this woman. It was time for me to open up and love her both in private and public. She deserves that and more.

JEAN: "Awe shit, me too girl. You remember Ray? You may have met him like once or twice."

MONIKA: "Oh yeah. Was he not your best friend? That's your little boo?" I am not sure if Monika was trying to throw shade or if she was honestly questioning their relationship.

JEAN: "Girl yeah. We started off as best friends but decided to make things official. How long you going to be out here? Ray and I are having this get together Friday and I would love for you to come through."

   While Monika was catching up on the phone with Jean, I snuck off to the kitchen to finish breakfast; hopefully, she decided to stay. Today was the day I had to tell Jean and La about Monika and me. A few minutes later, Monika came walking out of the bedroom; no bags in hand. I assumed she was staying as I began cheesing from ear to ear.

MONIKA: "We're going to Jean and Ray's get together Friday." Plopping down on the couch, "breakfast ready?" She sounded so ugh.

TIFFANY: "Where is my phone?"

MONIKA: "Left it in the room, on the bed." The bacon was just about done. I turned the eggs off to let them cool and popped a few pieces of bread in the toaster. Walking to my bedroom, I looked over at Monika as she was hunched down on the couch. Although she is upset with me, baby still looks fine. I picked my phone up off of the bed and three wayed LaLa and Jean. They both picked up around the same time.

TIFFANY: "Come over now!"

LALA: "Oh now you want to talk."

TIFFANY: "Don't start that emotional shit. I have food!" Walking back to the kitchen, I fixed both Monika and I plate.

LALA: "I'll be on my way. Better have some apple juice too." I laughed to myself because she knows I keep apple juice just for her.

TIFFANY: "And you Jean?"

JEAN: "I'll be on the way too. LaLa I got you something for the baby."

About an hour later, both LaLa and Jean was knocking on the door. I had got up so fast from that couch that it scared Monika. The pizza had just got to my place not even five minutes before they were here so I knew LaLa would be happy to have fresh food.

JEAN: "Ahhh." I felt like I had not seen my girls in so long. Hugging them both, LaLa looked over my shoulder and saw Monika sitting on the couch.

LALA: "Monika. How have you been?" LaLa has no filter whatsoever, especially with her being pregnant. "You look like a whole dude right about now. You're still cute though and your ass looking fat in them shorts." Monika had gotten up from the couch and made her way to hug both LaLa and Jean. It was funny but cute to see LaLa wobble her way inside.

TIFFANY: "Okay, not too much now." She rolled her eyes at me and continued to feel up on Monika. Just when I thought I was not ready to let the world know that I love Monika, LaLa had about two seconds to ply her fingers up off of my woman. I was getting jealous, and I never get jealous. Walking over to Monika, I pulled her away from LaLa. Jean had to end up closing the door.

LALA: "Damn Tiff. Is she your woman or something?" LaLa turned and frowned up at me.

TIFFANY: "No, but at least give her some space." What the fuck was I thinking, why did I not just come clean and say 'yea?' I knew I hurt Monika by the way she looked at me.

LALA: "Oh pizza... and it's still hot!" Monika pulled me to the bedroom. Or should I say yanked me.

MONIKA: "I'm leaving! We legit just had a whole argument about how this shit makes me feel and you stood there and lied."

TIFFANY: "Lower your voice!"

MONIKA: "Don't tell me what the fuck to do. I *am* your girlfriend and you are over here trying to play Miss innocent, steady lying to folks. I am done with this relationship, and don't call my fucking phone ever again."

Tears fell down her face. I fucked up, I really fucked up. LaLa nosy ass was already ear hustling in the doorway. I could not hide it no more. Turning towards both LaLa and Jean, Monika and I stood there in silence; her eyes red and filled with tears and my heart ached.

TIFFANY: "Jean, La... Monika and I have been dating for the past four months now. She is actually one of the reasons you guys haven't been seeing or hearing from me much." Monika stood there with her arms folded, eyes still wet from her tears. "I love this woman, from the top of her head to the bottom of her feet. Matter of fact, I am in *love* with this woman." As hard as it was to finally tell them, it felt good and a weight lifted from my shoulders that I would not have to hide in the closet about our relationship. The world should know who is helping me keep this smile on my face.

JEAN: "Is this who you were talking about when you said you found the love of your life, Monika?" Monika wiped the tears from her eyes and shook her head yes. "Why have you been keeping your relationship a secret, Tiff? You two look happy together." I looked over at Monika and she was still wiping tears away. Grabbing her hand, I pulled her closer to me.

TIFFANY: "Because I was ashamed to tell folks. Monika is all out in the open with her sexuality, me on the other hand, I was still in the closet." I grabbed a hold of Monika's hand and made eye contact with her, "but not anymore. Monika Wilson, I love you so much and I will shout it out to the world if that will make you happy and stay." She wiped her cheeks and embraced me with a kiss.

MONIKA: "You do that shit again, and it is fuck you. I do not care how good you eat my pussy; I will leave your ass in a quick second." Never did I know I would enjoy eating her golden kitty but I would do it as much as she wanted.

LALA: "Oh I'm getting so emotional. I am happy for you guys and my bad for feeling up on her. You really looked like you wanted to beat my ass."

TIFFANY: "I did!" We all burst out laughing and made our way back to the living room, while LaLa brought the entire box of pizza with her. I ended up fixing only margaritas for Monika, Jean and I, and brought LaLa her cup of apple juice. Just when I thought I was about to lose my woman...

Friday Is Here

RAY: "Wassup everyone and thank you all for coming out. There is plenty of food and drinks for everyone so eat up and turn up."

I looked around and saw a room full of people that I love and adore so much, even my parents. My girl Tiffany and Monika was here, looking ever so happily. LaLa and her boo Sammy, Slim even had some chick there. She is cute. I wonder how La is feeling about that. I and everyone else in there were having a good time, vibing and everything. With everything going on, this get together was well needed.

Ray talking...

SLIM: "You good man?" He placed his hand on my shoulder, trying to calm me down.

RAY: "Just a little nervous is all." My hands became sweaty.

SLIM: "Calm down, my boy. Here, takes a shot of this. It might help you out." He handed me a shot of henny that I threw back like it was juice. "What does it look like?" I pulled out a pick box wrapped in gold ribbon.

JEAN Talking...

My baby Ray is looking so fine tonight. He has met my parents before, so I did not have to really introduce them again. He was over there talking to my pops like they were the best of friends, thought that was cute. I was trying to keep LaLa company since she is the only one here that is pregnant and around all this liquor. My girl doing good and I am so excited to meet my niece or nephew. She wants to keep the gender a secret until she gives birth, but Tiffany and I keep trying to have Sammy talk her into a gender reveal... it's really not working, but we're going to keep trying so we can plan a big party.

RAY: "May I have everyone's attention please?" Ray tapping spoons against wine glasses nshit, trying to be formal. "Baby, can you come here please?" He held his hand out and I walked over to him, smiling ear to ear. "For all of you who do not know, this woman right here used to be my best friend. For the past seven years, almost eight, she has been there for me when no one else was. Our friendship did not start off so peachy since she had me waiting for a phone call, but that first moment I laid eyes on that beautiful face, I knew she would be in my life for a while. And if I had not craved seafood that day, I do not know if I would have gotten the chance to actually get to know her." I looked over at La and Tiff. We all knew exactly what day that he is talking about. "Since that day, I have cherished every other day of our friendship; being there through my heartbreak, my downfalls. Your parents taking me in and loving me like their own, even your friends. We all know La was the toughest to get through, but she a real nigga." We all laughed. "All of those late-night rides we used to do... talking and vibing with each other."

EVERYONE: "Oooo."

RAY: "Not like that, just really talking, getting to know one another you guys. Those used to be the best conversations I have ever had, and I would not mind having them for the rest of my life. I guess what I'm really trying to say is..." He went in his pocket and pulled out a box. Getting down on one knee... "Jean Michelle Robinson... will you give me the honor of making me the happiest man and marry me?"

I wanted to faint...

JEAN: "Yes... Yes, I will marry you!" Ray got up and kissed me.

Just when I thought it was going to be another two years before he asked... You can now call me, Ms. Jean Michelle Washington!

To Be Continued...

Will Bethanee have her baby in prison, and must give up her rights? How will Jean and Ray turn out or even LaLa and Sammy? Tiffany is open to her sexuality now, but will she stay that way? Pete did not seem so happy finding out his love turned him in... *"Who Would Have Known*, coming to you soon. In the meantime, stay tuned for, *"Dear Uncle," "Here's My Story*, and *"Finding My Peace,"* as well as other books.

ABOUT THE AUTHOR

 My name is Jaquella Loyd, some call me Jay; but my Author's name is Jae Loy! I was born and raised in Dallas, TX and can count on one hand how many times I have left the state. I graduated top 25% of my class 2013, from North Mesquite High School, and went to Texas Women's University, graduating within three years. I have always been the artsy type, whether it was theatre, singing, drawing, you name it. I was more in the scenes during high school, but due to me being a theatre major, I was more behind scenes during college. I have so many poems and songs written and just started writing books about a year ago. But it was my grandmother who pursued me more to write.

I also have a small business called, So Fine Treatz, located in the DFW, selling both vegan and non-vegan treats such as cookies, cakes, brownies, cupcakes, and more. One bite will have you feeling oh, So Fine! With some busy schedules, it gets hard cooking every night and takeout isn't always the best, so 'Jay preppin' is in business as well. I can customize meals to meet one's diet, including up to three different meals for the week. (Vegan, Keto, Pescatarian, Weight watchers, Mediterranean, Raw food, and Alkaline.) I love working out, trying to stay fit and motivated so those prepped meals come in clutch. I dib and dab in the candle business, as well as body/lip scrubs that will leave you feeling soft, smooth, and relaxed.

To learn more about Author Jae Loy and her upcoming books, visit the publishing website at: www.Ajbpublishing,com